Remains To Be Seen

A Novel by Christopher Knopf

Published in the USA by:
BearManor Fiction
PO Box 1129
Duncan, Oklahoma 73534-1129
www.bearmanormedia.com

ISBN 978-1-59393-747-8

Printed in the United States of America.
Book design by Brian Pearce | Red Jacket Press.

*Dedicated to my loving and always supportive grandchildren,
Alexandra, Amanda, Daniel, Jennifer, Lauren, Michael, Michelle, Shane,
and Shannon.*

Oh, to be Machiavellian,

Oh, to be unscrupulous, oh to be glib!

Oh, to be ever prepared with a plausible fib!

OGDEN NASH

One

He wasn't breathing. At least he felt he wasn't. He was looking out the window, through a narrow slit between the curtain and the window frame at the black Mercedes parked in the early morning rain across the street. The two men in the front seat were speaking quietly, neither animated nor smoking, as they looked toward the hotel. Just looking, watching. He didn't have to hear to know what they were talking about.

He pulled back from the window into the darkened room, sank to the edge of the bed, looked about at the veneered and marquetized furnishings, table, cabinet, commode, chipped and worn. *Petit, mais agréable,* the Michelin Guide had assured him, one of Beaune's *de bon confort,* crowning the hotel with *une symbole rouge.* Well, try the plumbing! Try the damn elevator at two in the morning when the electricity's turned off! For 200 euros a *night?* You *bought* your way into the Guide! He'd *bet* on it!

He tried to think. How in God's name had he allowed himself to get into this mess? None of which he'd truly bothered to understand, nor had cared to know, nor had taken the time to learn, though he'd been warned. On the bed beside him lay the International Herald Tribune. He didn't have to turn to the obituaries to imagine what the next day's notice could read. "The remains of David 'Scott' Fitzgerald, American, age twenty-eight..."

He checked his pulse. Christ! 110. He'd shaved, toweled off his face, but it was wet with perspiration. His clothes clung to him like he'd been papered. One thought went through his mind. He had to get out of there. Get to his car. But how? It was parked on the street, his rented Ferrari F430 Scuderia, in full view of the Mercedes. There was the back entrance to the hotel, and one he assumed through the kitchen. But both he was sure were being watched. He slipped on his travel vest, verifying room key, wallet, passport, keys to his car, took a shuddering breath and slipped from the room.

The ground floor lobby, as he eased off the stairs, was deserted, six-thirty by the wall clock, still no one on duty. He looked through the glass topped entrance door for the Mercedes, but its view was blocked by a white minivan trailing a plastic covered utility trailer drawn up before the hotel. The gnawing in his stomach was more than fear. He was hungry, hadn't eaten since yesterday morning, his senses aroused by the smell of fresh baked bread. Bread. The one damn thing the French got right!

The dining room, empty for the most part at such an early hour, was off the lobby as Scott sat huddled in a secluded corner over the usual Continental breakfast of croissant, baguette, butter, jam, and coffee thick enough to paint walls. Ten minutes ago he'd asked for a pot of warm milk to thin the coffee. Was it coming? Of course not. This was France. You wanted something done? Get in line and hope it wasn't August. Anyway, the waitress seemed far more involved with the three at the table across the room, its only other occupants.

Two were a couple, Americans, early twenties. Newlyweds on their honeymoon? He couldn't tell. Tennessee, Alabama, from the bits of conversation he could make out. The third was older, in his thirties. English good, French accent heavy, he wore a black mountaineering hat, and a red leather coat over a white turtle neck shirt. There were some papers on the table between them, topped by a pen, along with coffee. Whatever their conversation, the Frenchman seemed to be trying to convince the young couple of something one of them, at least, the young man, seemed reluctant to do.

The kitchen door opened and an *aide-serveur* arrived with his milk in a Quimper ceramic teapot, the traditional milkmaid, in her blue and burnt orange dress and white apron emblazoned on it. He reached for it, yanked his fingers away. It was hot! He'd asked for it *chaud!* Warm, Goddamnit! Didn't the French understand their own *language?* He caught himself. *Assez* chaud, he remembered. *That* was warm. So, one for them. Slathering jam on his baguette, he raised it to his mouth, stopped cold, the baguette poised midair, mouth open, frozen. One word from the table of three had caught his ear. He listened for more, could hear nothing more, only muttering. But he'd heard that word. He was certain.

Looking about the room, he saw it was clear. No one was noticing him. Picking up his plate and coffee, he eased his way toward the three, took up residence at a table within earshot. The Frenchman was talking.

"It is just a cell coming through. Perhaps an hour."

"What if it isn't?"

"It's jus' a cell, Billy Joe, what he said," the girl pleaded.

"What if it isn't?"

She released her hold on Billy Joe's arm, turned to the Frenchman, with an imploring look. "Menser Oobert?" Her accent was terrible.

"Monsieur," he corrected. "Hubert."

She was small, tight round ass from what Scott could see, perfectly molded inside white jeans, a face of peaches and cream. Clearly the adventurous one of the two, Scott saw her eyes throw daggers at her husband, if that's what he was.

"Y'all said we could go balloonin'."

Ballooning! Scott *had* heard the word! *Ballooning!*

"Mary Lou…"

A distant peel of thunder did nothing to melt her resolve.

"It's what y'all *said*, Billy Joe! Y'all promised!"

He was slight, with a thin scattered moustache, a devotee of the road less taken.

"Here is my suggestion," Hubert confided, calming things down. "It is a forty-minute drive to the lift-off area. I will phone ahead to the chase car, tell them to meet us. If it still rains, I bring you back here to Beaune, no charge. If it stops and is clear you will have the most beautiful experience. We leave in ten minutes, yes?"

"Yes! Yes!"

Scott could see that Billy Joe could do nothing more than swallow his doubts as Mary Lou quickly signed the release form, absolving Buddy Bombard Balloon Adventures of all responsibility in the event of maiming or death. Billy Joe, under her penetrating glare, did the same, quickly followed her as she headed from the room.

"How could y'all even *think* about it?" she scolded. "Honestly. I should have listened to my father!"

Hubert, who had encountered worse, began to gather his papers, started to rise, when:

"I was wondering…"

Hubert's head came up. Scott stood before him.

"…could you take one more?"

There was a croak in Scott's voice. A small one, but a croak. One corner of his mouth appeared to have a slight tremor. His face glistened with sweat, Hubert noticed.

"170 euros."

"Credit card?"

"Of course."

Scott produced his Visa.

"And passport."

Also produced, hand shaking, as he slid onto a chair.

"Too much wine last night. But hell, when in Burgundy…" Scott offered, forcing a grin.

"Chaptalisation."

"What?"

"The sugar."

"Right."

Hubert nodded in shared understanding, opened the passport as Scott hurriedly signed the form without reading. There, on the opening page, was Scott's picture and name, David S. Fitzgerald, date and place of issuing authority, New York City, date and place of birth, San Francisco. Two pages in, Hubert found a solitary entry, Paris de Gaulle, France, September 12, Scott's date and place of arrival into the country seven days ago — fifteen days after the passport's issuance. Flipping through the last of the passport's pages, Hubert prepared to return it, when he was brought up short. A single page half way through the passport noted a departure from Paris five days later, to Chisinau, Moldova, and the same day a return. Moldova? A small landlocked state between Romania and the Ukraine, he knew of it as the poorest country in Europe, but never knew anyone who'd gone there. He glanced across the table at Scott, studying him really for the first time, saw a medium height, undeniably handsome sort, tousled brown hair, a disconcerting mixture, Hubert thought, of faux sincerity and winning charm. Closing the passport, Hubert ran off the credit card on a handheld VeriPhone, returned both passport and credit card to Scott with a smile.

"Ten minutes."

His room was as Scott left it, too early for maid service. Curtains still drawn, lights off, he verified the Mercedes was still there in the rain, a veritable watch dog with full view of the hotel. Except the entrance. The minivan blocked that. Sudden pressure in his bowels took him to the toilet. He tried in the dark, gave up in frustration, returned to the bedroom, grabbed his plaid-lined Eddie Bauer raincoat from the back of a chair. It was half length, with an attached hood. He looked about the room. What else? His Tumi two suiter was on the couch, packed and ready for travel. No way could he take it. Why would he? He was going for a morning's ride in a balloon, would be brought back to the hotel when it was over. Oh, really? By the time the Mercedes found out, he'd be across three *departments* and gone. As for abandoning his rented Ferrari? So, sue him!

Returning to the lobby, Scott found Mary Lou and Billy Joe waiting, both in raincoats, Billy Joe's a blue Lands End nylon with hood, Mary Lou's with a clear plastic hood over her head. Six feet separated the pair. Neither was talking to the other. Hubert appeared in a rain slicker, a fountain of cheer.

"We go!"

Leading the way, Hubert stepped into the rain, opened the minivan's rear sliding curbside door. Mary Lou entered, ignoring Billy Joe's offered hand. Billy Joe followed. Pulling the hood over his head, Scott started to enter after the two, pulled back as the sliding door closed in his face. Hubert was opening the front seat passenger side door. Scott stared. The *front!* In full view through the windshield of the Mercedes! Hubert stood patiently in the rain, half smile on his face as Scott wavered. No recourse, Scott entered, sat hunched low, hood drawn down, half hiding his face. Thankfully the rain pounding the windshield obscured all view, inside or out, as Hubert closed the door, circled the front of the van, slid, dripping wet, onto the driver's side, pulling the door closed after him, started the engine, activating the windshield wipers, which immediately cleared the glass, offering, Scott saw to his horror, full view of the Mercedes, and worse, full view of him!

Go! Scott's pleading was silent, but a scream in his head!

Hubert didn't go. He was on the cell phone.

"Trois passagers, juste le départ."

Go, go!!

"Essayons Forêt de Chaux."

Please, God! Go, go, go!!!

· Scott's hands were clasped in front of his face, head down, teeth clamping on his thumbs nails.

"Quarante minutes, voir-vous là."

Closing the cell phone, Hubert slipped it into his pocket and secured his seat belt. With a jerk the van and trailer pulled away from the curb. Hunching low in his seat, Scott closed his eyes. His breath was labored, his mind projecting fantasies of his end. Eyes narrowed to slits he half-saw passing street signs. Avenue de la Republique. Rue Thiers. And the ever-present infuriating, confounding, repetitive designation, the curse of every city and tourist in France, "Toutes Directions."

Teeth chattering from the jolting cobble-stone street, Scott squeezed his eyes fully shut, anticipating the inevitable. The Mercedes would come alongside the passenger side of the van, raking it with a hail of bullets. Or the driver's side, ramming the van into a Total gasoline station pump where it would explode in engulfing flames. Or would force the van to the curb where strong hands would haul Scott into the Mercedes, never to be seen nor heard from again.

Five minutes. Seven. Scott's eyes pinched open, saw they were passing beneath the Ramparts that virtually circled the city, onto Rue de Seurre. A stop light! A motorcycle drew beside them, the driver rasping, re-rasping its engine, then snarling away with the change of the light.

Jesus, *go! Just go!!!*

They were moving again as he realized that he was swearing, the words dropping from his mouth in a steady inaudible stream of muffled obscenities. He should have gone to the police. He could *still* go to the police. But even if he could get to them, try to make them understand, he had no proof it was true.

"Nobody is going to murder you, Monsieur," they'd say, regarding him as some form of delusional absurdity. "This is Burgundy. Nobody is murdered in Burgundy. People live so long they die of boredom."

He shivered and began to swear again, when suddenly the road bed was smoothing out and the van was accelerating. A sign flashed by telling him they were on D973. D973! They were out of the city, heading east! With all the courage he could muster, he stole a look back over his shoulder through the van's rear window. Splattered with rain he could not see much. But he could see enough. Ain't nobody following!

With a bark of laughter Scott muscled his body half upright in his seat. He'd done it! He'd beaten the sons of bitches! *Christ*, what a ride! He hadn't buckled up and now he did. He hadn't taken a breath forever it seemed, now did. Deep luxurious breaths, unaware he was gasping. As for having to go, all urges gone. He gave his leg a victorious slap of his hand, which drew Hubert's questioning gaze, when just as suddenly Scott's sense of euphoria was history. What if the rain didn't stop? What if there was no ballooning? He didn't dare go back to that hotel. They were headed for a *foret* — a forest. He'd heard it. What was he to do if there was no going up, take off in some goddamn woods? At least in a field he'd be near a house, a town. There were wild boar in those woods, and gypsies. When his body exploded against the restraining seat strap as a hand came down on his shoulder.

"Y'all got a match?"

Mary Lou. Seat belt loosened, she was leaning forward, her face inches from Scott's, one hand holding an unlit cigarette, the other lingering on his arm.

"Pas de fume," Hubert answered.

"What'd he say?"

"No smoking."

"Oh."

She flopped back against the seat in a display of petulance. But that lingering hand. Had Scott read it correctly? Whatever fears he'd been contemplating, his fantasies overrode. The rain would abort the balloon trip. On the trip back their eyes would meet, his and Mary Lou's, low-lidded, sensuous, inviting. They'd return to the hotel. Billy Joe would be exhausted. She'd encourage him to take a nap. A long one. She'd come down the hall. Scott's door would be open, Scott waiting. It would not be slow and teasing. Clothes would be ripped off and discarded, the two of them collapsing naked on the bed, entwined, her low-throated ecstatic moans...

When suddenly an unaccustomed quiet overwhelmed his delusions. He looked at the windshield. The wipers were off. It had stopped raining!

Thirty-five minutes out of Beaune, the van entered the Foret de Chaux, for centuries a vital resource for the factories at its edge: saltworks and glassworks, the last thing Scott knew about or cared to know. Climbing past beech and conifer trees lining the forest road, they broke finally into a nearly empty car park. The chase car, a replica of the van, Scott saw, was there and waiting, along with two men who, under Hubert's direction, immediately pulled the plastic cover from the utility trailer.

Bounding out of the van, Mary Lou hurried to Hubert, and was gently eased out of the way, as first from the trailer came the wicker gondola, which was hauled to the center of the parking lot and laid on its side.

"Her time o' the month. Damn thang for a honeymoon, right?" Billy Joe offered with a wan little laugh in effort to explain away his wife's mood and behavior as he waited for some understanding acknowledgment from Scott, who gave no indication he'd heard nor cared. No choice left to him, Billy Joe exited the van.

Alone, his mind in a swirl, Scott tried to review. By the time the men in the Mercedes discovered he was gone it would be too late to do anything about it. Unless. Supposing they *had* noticed. His blood ran cold at the thought. But no, the Mercedes had not been following. The only thing now was to pray they had not discovered his absence too soon. It was out of the question for him to show trepidation. That could raise questions. Already he sensed Hubert was suspicious of something. He would have to look as unsuspecting as he could, and yet take care.

He looked through the windshield. A liquid propane burner, the size of a large suitcase, had been attached to a gimbal on the wicker gondola. Fuel tanks were mounted outside the basket. The collapsed nylon balloon, hauled from the trailer, had been unfurled and was being stretched like a gigantic ribbon along the pavement — seventy feet, from what Scott guessed — its fire-resistant throat rapidly hooked to the gondola, its gaping opening facing the burner.

Ignited by a built-in electric spark, the burner's blast valve began to spew roaring flame into the throat of the balloon. Fascinated, Scott watched his means of salvation rapidly begin to fill with hot air, the balloon beginning to lift its top from the pavement. He was minutes from freedom, free of pursuit. His mind swirled with the thought as the minutes went by. In a day he'd be home and out of reach. *Christ*, what a story he'd have to tell, how he'd made his would-be executioners look like fools. That one was worth a half dozen interviews at least. Not to mention women. Wait'll *they* heard. When suddenly, he felt the blood leaving his face. Out of nowhere: people! Hikers, bicyclists. Jesus! Where had they come from? None, he quickly saw, with a sense of tentative relief, seemed to have the slightest interest in anything other than the balloon. Gawkers come to watch, he was sure, looking them over, when a tap on the window brought him face to face with Hubert. He was gesturing. The multi-colored balloon Scott saw, held down with ropes by the two men from the chase car, was filled and upright. So was the basket, Mary Lou and Billy Joe already in. It was time!

Scampering from the van, Scott hurried to the gondola, boarded it ahead of Hubert who followed and took up his pilot's position at one end. The spring-loaded blast valve on the overhead burner was closed and waiting.

"Le vent de la nord," Hubert called out to the two holding the ropes. "Je vais prendre a deux cents mètres et l'appeler."

One of the two answered, something Scott couldn't understand.

A center bar ran through the basket. Mary Lou and Billy Joe had already taken hold. Scott did so as well. The ropes were released and drawn aboard, Hubert activating the blast valve on the burner. A roaring flame was fired into the mouth of the balloon, and up it rose, ten feet, thirty, sixty, Hubert shutting down the burner leaving nothing but silence as it climbed, out of the clearing, above the trees, the landscape of Southern Burgundy spreading out before them. Châteaux, streams, a scattering of vineyards now, Scott saw the gently undulating countryside dotted with farms and grazing charolais cattle.

A blast from the burner brought Scott up short. Hubert was looking for a southerly breeze, and now he'd caught it. The burner shut down. Six hundred feet above ground the balloon was gliding silently south as Hubert steered by alternatively infusing and releasing hot air to find the layer of wanted wind.

Scott drank in the air, and more than that the euphoria of accomplishment. Unable to calm the drumming of his heart, he ignored it and began plotting his moves. On landing in some village — it was always a village, he'd read — he'd rent a car. No car rental agency? He'd take a train or bus to the nearest town that had one. No going to the airports in Paris, De Gaulle, or Orly, they'd be looking for that. He'd cut across to Nantes in Brittany, get a puddle jumper flight to London, then home to New York.

"Mary Lou an' Billy Joe Alpers." Heavily Southern, the voice brought him back to reality. She was on the opposite side of the basket, facing him, her hand held out. "We're from Anniston. Albama?"

Scott took the hand, which lingered in his, soft and inviting. He knew inviting when it was offered. Then on to Billy Joe's, manly and firm, but not naturally so, Scott was certain.

"Scott Fitzgerald," Scott offered in return.

"*Scott* Fitzgerald?" Mary Lou queried, her eyes suddenly widening. "Not *the* Scott Fitzgerald?"

"Twenty-four hours a day, I'm afraid." His name, in fact, was David. But long ago he'd appropriated Scott. Not out of any respect for the legendary author; Scott had little respect for anyone other than himself. Thus the name. It was a grabber.

"Billy Joe! D'y'all know who this *is*?"

If Billy Joe heard her he gave no indication of it. He was staring down at the ground six hundred feet below. His face was green as they saw the chase car along with the van with its trailer catching up to, slowing, running with the balloon over dirt roads then asphalt, Hubert in occasional conversation with the lead car as to speed and direction.

"Hon, this is Scott *Fitzgerald*. The famous *writer!*"

Billy Joe gave no acknowledgment, turning greener, shade by shade. Mary Lou's face flashed anger, which she quickly camouflaged, turning back to Scott with an alteration of mood so swift it almost seemed manufactured.

"Oh, I know it! That'un! I've read it," she said. "For Whom the Bell Tolls! How'd y'all *do* it?"

"Well, I've…"

"All that stuff 'bout the Mexican revolution!"

"You had to be there."

"Y'all were *there?*"

"Two ways to write about it."

"Wow!"

"Get it out of National Geographic or go to the source."

"I mean, like *wow!*"

She was wet. He was sure of it. Anniston, Alabama. He'd never set foot in Alabama in his life, never had a desire to go there. But that could change.

He glanced quickly down at the trailing vans, when a shot went through him. It wasn't a bullet, but the effect was the same. Trailing the two, a quarter mile behind, was the black Mercedes.

Two

It would be difficult to pinpoint when and how it all began, but, if one were forced, it would have to go back two months to the arrival of a delivery truck.

With "Signature Collections" on its panel, the truck angled through mid-town Manhattan traffic, cut off a taxi, braked before a Fifth Avenue monolith, and pulled into a clearly marked "No Parking" zone. Ignoring the cabbie who'd screeched to a stop, backing up traffic, and who's gotten out of his cab, shouting obscenities in Russian over angry horns, the Delivery Driver opened the rear of his truck, took out first a dolly, and then a luxury suitcase, wrapped in clear cellophane, topped with a bow.

Entering the entrance foyer, suitcase on his dolly, the Delivery Driver crossed through early morning bedlam to the gold-lettered information board, found "*New York In Review* Publications," thirty-second, thirty-third floors, a sub-column of offices below each. Administration, Editorial, Advertising, Operations, Circulation. Finding the one he was looking for, the Delivery Driver crossed to the elevators.

One could argue, actually, it was already in motion at nine o'clock the night before as a cleaning woman pushed a vacuum cleaner along a dimly-lit, deserted thirty-second floor corridor separating secretarial bays from offices. Glass framed awards won by the Publication over the years were secured to walls. From somewhere, a fax was accepting an inbound communication. On desks, occasional red lights blinked on phones from unanswered calls.

Coming to a woman's shoe, the vacuum cleaner skirted it. Another shoe. A blouse and pants. The cleaning woman, the good domestic that she was, noticed nothing, moved on, past a closed office door. Lettering on its glass top read, "D. "S." Fitzgerald."

Inside the office, illuminated solely by the light of a screen saver on the desk computer beside her, Scott's secretary, Wendy, a round-faced little fire plug, lay flat on her back, on the desk, stripped to her bra, Scott atop her.

"I want that tailor here at ten," he exhorted between thrusts.

"One time...you should know this..." she gasped.

"Eight hundred bucks for a baby shit-blue Hilfiger luxury collection tux and they can't even get the *sleeves* right?"

"...I'd been here two years, two and a half years..." she panted.

"And the final on my acceptance speech, proofed and typed, on my desk by three..."

"It was Franklin — he promised me my own office — he was just trying to get into my pants. I got a closet..."

"And reconfirm my limo," he said, driving into her, "six forty-five, not some kid driver who's working his way..."

"So when you get that corner suite..." she was reaching climax.

"And on the button if he wants a tip..."

"It's got that assistant's office looking out on Trump...oh, *God..!*"

Wendy wasn't the first to land atop Scott's desk. Lured by promises of their own secretarial office when his time came due for a corner suite, Scott had gone through half the secretarial pool. One had taken umbrage when it became clear she'd been deceived. Going up and down the corridors howling "Sexual harassment!" her accusations were treated with traditional corporate response. She was fired.

So it was Scott who sailed through life unfettered by consequences, albeit with one fatal flaw: the inability to recognize the signs, all of which were embodied in that gift-wrapped suitcase hauled along on its dolly through the thirty-second floor corridor that following morning.

Reaffirming its destination on an electronic dispatch, the delivery driver came to an office designated "T. Garner, Articles Editor."

On a cellular phone, desk piled with manuscripts, Tally Garner rose at the knock on her door. At twenty-seven, dressed in business suit and Timex watch, the first thing one would notice about her, those green eyes dancing, would be the speed of her smile, a centered, bright young woman, trim athletic body, totally lacking in artifice. At the moment though, little of that shone through. She was incensed.

"Dan, this is bullshit!" she said, phone to ear as she crossed to answer the door. "It's the worst idea I ever heard, there's got to be a better way. At least give me a shot at him first."

Reaching the door, she opened it, and saw the suitcase on the dolly.

"Oh, great, real subtle," she said into the phone at the sight of it. "Give me ten minutes with him — *ten minutes*, Dan, I'll be up!"

She snapped off the phone as her gray-suited assistant, Warren, rose from his bay. Older than Tally by half, Warren's face, unlike Tally's, wore an eager anticipation as she signed for the delivery.

"Tell him I want to see him," she told Warren. "My office."

Six doors down, surrounded by congratulatory baskets of chocolates, fruit and champagne, whacked-out art on his walls, Scott stood mid-room in his office, on a high, in a tuxedo. A tailor was pinning final sleeve adjustments as Scott, wearing an ear-clip phone, ogled a leggy Swedish model ratcheting her hips out of their sockets as she pranced before Lexus' newest on his four foot plasma TV.

"Gordon," he said, speaking into the ear phone as he lamped the model, "she's your client. I need her. I want her. It's my big night!"

At Scott's desk, Barry Costigan, down from the thirty-third floor editorial department, as close to a friend as Scott had in this world, was typing on a laptop. Rolled up sleeves, tie, early-thirties, a soothing counterpart to Scott's brashness, Barry spoke as he wrote, as all the while co-workers passed by Scott's open door with thumbs up, "Crazy! Cool!"

"It has always been my intention," Barry was reading aloud off the laptop, "to see the homeless as real, each a separate and unique…"

"Barry, this is the *Ellies!*" Scott interrupted. "*Size* man!" Then improvising, "In accepting this award, my second, little did I realize when I went into the streets, living among these desperate blah, blah, blah…!"

When Wendy appeared in the doorway.

"She wants you. Her office."

Hanging up his phone, Warren rose from his bay, crossed the hallway to Tally's office, stuck his head inside without knocking.

"You're on the list."

Tally's chin came up. She stared at the man seated on the couch across her office. Dressed in green shirt, blue pants, formless sweater, he was forty, listless, paunchy, hunched forward, hands clutched before him, rocking, rocking as Warren awaited her reply.

In Scott's office, everything, as usual, was going his way. The tailor was making adjustments. Barry was doing the same. Scott was pressing his no fail agenda on the phone.

"Tell her? I don't know what to tell her, Gordon. Tell her I want to have her babies," when Wendy reappeared in the open doorway.

"She's on her way up to the thirty-third floor. But she'll wait for you."

The smirk on Warren's face as he hung up once again was uncontrollable. Crossing once more to Tally's door, he stuck his head in.

"He says go on, he'll catch you later."

Anger flashed in Tally's eyes.

In his office, Scott, still on the ear phone, was growing hostile.

"Gordon, you're either on the bus or off it!"

"Kay," Barry interrupted, "So when you say, 'Back in the days of the depression, the homeless…'"

"Barry! Barry! This is about *me! My* journey!" Then back to the ear phone, "*Threatening* you? Gordon, of course I'm threatening you..!"

Scott stopped as Tally appeared in his doorway, Warren behind her, bearing the gift wrapped luggage. Scott's eyes lit up at the sight of it.

"Tumi?"

"Better," said Tally. "Steuben," which went right over his head despite Warren's uncontrollable snicker.

"Love it, *love* it!" Then with sudden insight, "Aw, Tally…"

"Scott, I'm not really good at this stuff…"

"You think I'm leaving."

"I think you better come down to my office. Someone I want you to meet."

"Tally, Tally," Scott's arms wrapped around her. "You think I'm going to bail on you? For Christ's sake, have you got a better friend?"

She shrugged loose from his grasp. The last thing in the world she wanted was any part of him near her.

"Scott, I've got five minutes before I have to be in Dan's office. You're not going to want me to go up there before you come down to mine."

"Know what?" Scott replied, "I'm pitching you to run the new monthly, 'Spinster Of The Month.' It could use your insight." When the ear phone grabbed his attention. "Gordon, great! What are best friends for? And I want her in the limo when they pick me up." He started to rip off the ear clip, verbally lunged back onto the phone. "Hey! What's her name?"

The night of the National Magazine Awards. The Ellies. A banner above the dais in the Waldorf Astoria's Ballroom said so. Numbered tables with sconces of fresh-cut flowers filled the room, along with Manhattan's tuxedo and evening gown-attired top journalistic people, pre-dinner, milling about with drinks and hors d'oeuvres and agendas, all doing the first name thing.

"I'm seeing Tom this weekend in the Hamptons."

"Have you read Jason's new piece?"

"Laura's throwing a do. I thought you were on her list."

The radiant model of the Lexus commercial towering over him on his arm, Scott luxuriated in a tight little knot of A-list publishers: *Harpers*, *Atlantic Monthly*, *Vanity Fair*, the three of them captivated by what little there was of the supermodel's gown as they venerated Scott.

"Your thing on the homeless…" *Harpers* intoned.

"Simply stellar," *Vanity Fair* chimed in.

"You obliterated the disparity between your subject and your readers," *Atlantic Monthly* gushed.

"Hardly comparable to our great Utopian thinkers," Scott demurred with winning modesty. By every measure in his element, he'd scoped the room, quickly concluded he had the most beautiful girl in the place. Every eye was on her. The top people were in his orbit.

"You didn't find it threatening?" asked *Harpers*. "Living among that sort of people?"

"To expose a national shame?" Scott answered, taking two glasses of champagne off a passing tray, handing one to the model, already negotiating in his mind how the night was going to play out with her as he heard himself saying, "Once you've slept on subway grates with the abandoned, shared their suffering…"

"And this ravishing young woman is?" asked Atlantic Monthly, eyeballing the model.

"Oh…uh…"

Scott's struggle to remember the name, totally forgotten, was rescued by the arrival of the city's Mayor, late fifties, balding, but a sprawl of elegant composure, his wife on his arm.

"Mr. Mayor."

"I just wanted to say," as he pumped Scott's hand, "I read that work of yours, your second award, I'm told. It's people like you that give this city its dignity."

"Thank you."

"No, we thank you."

"Sir, that's…"

"Enjoy the night. We look forward to your speech."

The Mayor moved off with his wife, leaving Scott to the group. *Harpers* couldn't wait to pull out a business card.

"My office," he said, handing it to Scott. "Thursday. Eleven. Some editors I want you to meet."

Vanity Fair shouldered in, slipping *his* card inside Scott's pocket.

"Aquavit. One o'clock. Lunch. Tomorrow."

An hour and twenty minutes later, over a dessert of strawberries Romanoff and a premier cru sauterne, Robert Klein, at the dais, waited out subsiding laughter from the assemblage.

"The next morning he walks into the editor's office," Klein resumed. "Looks like hell, unshaven. Hasn't slept. 'Joe,' he says, trembling voice,

'Joe, I know I promised you the article today, I know I said. You don't know what I've gone through. My wife — my *wife*, Joe — ran off with her chiropractor? My little girl — my *baby* — she's pregnant? And, Joe... my *house*? I lost it in a poker game?' The editor sits back in his chair, lips pursed. 'I kind of like the one about the knocked up kid. Write that.'"

At Scott's table, everyone's burst into laughter along with the rest of the room. But not at Klein. Seated with the supermodel, Barry and Tally, along with Warren and several of Tally's staff, Scott had his own narrative going. Only Tally held back, unreadable.

"So I said to him," Scott was continuing, "'Excuse me, sir' — that 'sir' really got to him — 'but I'm not moving for you or anyone else. These cardboard boxes are mine. My condo.' Well, the guy's black, six-six, two-eighty. His eyes narrow to f-16. And now we got a crowd. I mean an army. Half the city's derelict, down-and-out, god-forsaken, tree-of-life homeless. And this guy's coming on. The Incredible Hulk. So I jump up into this crouch like an ape. He falls back, right into the stew pot."

The table broke up, Scott included, all but Tally. When Barry's hand was on Scott's arm, directing his attention to the dais.

"To introduce our next award winner," Klein was announcing, "for Feature Writing, Tally Garner, Articles Editor, *New York In Review* Publications."

Polite applause as Tally rose, made her way to the dais, Barry driving a congratulatory punch into Scott's arm.

"Fucking great, man," he whispered.

Settling back, Scott took a final sip of his Chateau Climens, pulled his speech from his inner coat pocket, watched Tally take her place before the microphone. An evening-gowned young woman emerged from the wings, handed an Ellie statuette to Tally.

"Ladies and gentlemen," Tally began, "award winners, nominees, Mr. and Mrs. Mayor, good evening." She set the Ellie on the dais. "This category recognizes excellence in feature writing."

At his table, Scott sat back, arms crossed, beaming in anticipation as Tally went on.

"It honors content, authenticity, originality and style with which the author treats his or her subject. The winner of the year's Feature Writing goes to the author of "Cardboard Condo," a remarkable, inspiring, personal account of how the abandoned survive the streets of this city." She looked out at the crowd. "And if journalists follow the example set by David 'Scott' Fitzgerald — whose name one reads beneath the essay's title — it should be a record year for plagiarism."

A titter of laughter spread through the room at the apparent joke. At Scott's table Barry wasn't laughing. He was frowning, confused, glanced at Scott who sat immutable, staring up at Tally as she continued.

"If plagiarism is defined as an unusual display of intellectual or academic squalor, David 'Scott' Fitzgerald hands down wins that award. Because David 'Scott' Fitzgerald did not write the 'Cardboard Condo.'"

Maybe one or two in the room were giggling, still not caught up in what was happening. Others were staring.

"Nor did David 'Scott' Fitzgerald set foot among the homeless. Nor did David 'Scott' Fitzgerald write this record of their lives. That was done by a penniless, homeless person himself, whose work David 'Scott' Fitzgerald stole, utterly, wholly, without omission, permission or compensation."

Now the entire room was in shock.

"Therefore," Tally picked up the Ellie. "It is with utmost respect and honor I present this year's National Magazine Award for Feature Writing to its proper author, Stuart Johnston Davies."

Too stunned to know how to respond, heads turned to see him rise from a back of the room table. Dressed in thrift shop ill-fitting corduroy jacket, pants and jogging shoes he made his way toward the dais. The man seen earlier in Tally's office.

At the dais, Tally looked toward Scott. He was gone.

Three

The following morning, the thirty-second floor was business as usual as Scott exited the elevator, strode through reception, into the hallway, past Tally's closed office door, past secretarial bays, assistants crisscrossing his path, noses buried in work, no greetings, placid masks that said we don't know you, never heard of you. None of which Scott appeared to notice. He was smiling. A smile that said time to graduate to something else as he skirted a stack of packing boxes, arrived at his door, opened it, and his smile was history.

The inside of his office was totally bare. Pictures, plaques, plasma TV, all his possessions gone. Turning, Scott stared in shock at the packing boxes in the corridor by his door, topped, he saw, by the Tumi suitcase still in its cellophane wrap. Beside it all, bulging forearms across his chest, stood a company guard.

In her office, on a speaker phone, Tally had been giving dictation to Warren when the call from the thirty-third floor came in.

"Dan, you made me humiliate him in front of 2,000 people," Tally was boiling, "which you and corporate should have handled privately. Now you're telling me to…This is gutless."

"Tally," Dan's voice came through the speaker, and it was cautioning, "you're on a conference call. Jack's on line. So is Morgan…"

When Scott burst in, slammed the flat of his hands on Tally's desk.

"Just what do you think?" he thundered.

"*I* think?"

"Ten days with the homeless, living in shit..!"

"You never even *encountered* the homeless, Scott. You were in Bermuda those ten days," as she shoved a document toward him. "Your cell phone bill."

Warren rose to step from the room. Tally waved him back to his seat.

"This won't take thirty seconds." Then turning, "Goodbye, Scott."

The veins in Scott's neck looked like they were ready to explode.

"You can't do this, read my contract!"

"Read the morals clause."

"I'm going to corporate!"

"This *came* from corporate."

"What's this guy going to do with fame?" Scott tried to infuse his anger with logic. "Two days later he's back in the sewer eating road kill."

"That's what's always hit me about you," Tally shook her head in genuine disbelief. "You're a psychiatrist's wet dream."

"What about my first Ellie? Who do you think wrote *that?*"

"I don't know," she answered. "Who did?"

"'A smashing achievement!' they said! '"Powerful, courageous...!'"

"Call it a sudden wave of reasonable doubt," she said.

"There isn't anybody in town who won't go after me!" He was almost yelling as he produced the business cards he'd received the night before. "*Atlantic Monthly, Harpers..!*"

"Then you're off and running."

"...lunch with *Vanity Fair!*" he overrode her. "At Aquavit!"

"I recommend the Sjosmanshiff," Tally suggested. "They do it over wood."

"That's what's always bothered you!" Scott's rage was increasing as he pocketed the cards. "That my wood's bigger than yours!"

"No," Tally answered, and there was no mirth, no word play in what she had to say. "What's bothered me is that you care for nothing. You've replaced the expedition of truth with the rapture of celebrity. A squatter on legitimate writers' intellectual landscapes. You want the result, not the process. Too lazy, lifeless to do the journalistic grunt work by the sweat of your own brow and not someone else's." Then adding, "In case you asked."

Bent over, hands on her desk, it was a moment before Scott answered.

"And I was going to take you to the *New Yorker* with me."

Turning, he was out the door and gone. Through the speaker phone, still on, Tally heard congratulatory voices.

"Well, *okay!* Great girl! Thelma, send two dozen roses..."

The voices went dead as Tally disconnected the phone. She lingered a moment, turned to Warren.

"Where was I?"

"This will put you on notice," Warren referred to his notes, "effective one month from today I will be resigning my position..."

"Make that immediate," she interrupted.

The Aquavit Restaurant on East Fifty-Fifth, the New Face Of Sweden, if you believed the puffery, with its waterfall, high ceiling and minimalist décor, was packed with New York's top publishing world, come for lunch.

Scott, dressed in casual sophistication, open collar, slacks and coat, sat at a table, waiting for his host to arrive, nibbling on a knackbrod from a basket of knackbrods. Turning the card given him by *Vanity Fair* over in his hand, he glanced at his watch, again toward the reception desk. His host was late.

An hour and a half later, the knackbrod basket was empty. So was the restaurant, staff resetting the room for dinner. Only Scott remained, alone at his table. He rose, angrily strode from the place.

Two days later. Thursday. *Harpers* Publishing House. 3:15 by the mahogany encased GPS wireless clock above reception, Scott holding on it, watching the second hand tick away. In muted grey business suit and tie, he sat as he had sat for hours, nodding a forced self-confident smile at passersby too engaged in their own agenda to notice.

When two men emerged from the elevator, approached in conversation. One was the *Harpers* executive from the Ellies Awards who'd extended the invitation. A relieved smile breaking across his face, Scott started to rise, to offer his hand. The pair moved past him without acknowledgment, disappeared through large oak doors, leaving Scott holding his half stand, hand outstretched, like a skier going downhill, smile frozen.

Turning off Fifth Avenue into Soho — a short form for the neighborhood's geographic location, South of Houston — past high-end restaurants, galleries, spas, the taxi pulled to a stop before a converted warehouse, one of dozens in the area now zoned for luxury artists' studios and lofts.

Paying the fare, Barry emerged, looked at the van backed up to the building's entrance. "Della Robia Rental Furnishings" on its panel, Iranian handlers were on-loading a bed, the truck already filled with upscale furniture. A couch, Barry saw, arm chair, dining table and accompanying chairs awaited boarding on the sidewalk.

Emerging from the key-operated elevator, currently open to the handlers, Barry entered the top floor loft, side-stepped two transporting a 50-inch plasma TV into the lift. With a sinking feeling, he looked about.

An open laptop computer and printer sat atop a poker table, a legal pad, dark with illegible scribbling beside it. The Tumi suitcase, clothes bulging at the seams, stood upright before the table. Balled up papers were strewn about the floor. There were still a couple of potted plants. Otherwise the apartment was bare.

On a countertop separating the kitchen from the living room-dining area, Barry saw a half dozen envelopes, Scott's personalized stationery variously addressed and sent by registered mail to *Esquire, The New Yorker,*

People magazines. The stamps were cancelled, envelopes unopened, all branded "Return To Sender."

Barry crossed to the computer. It was on, to Monster.com. 'Build A Better Career,' announced the screen. 'The Get Work Network.' Above the table Barry saw a wall corkboard. It was filled with printouts, the Monster.com logo on the top of each. Job Requests. Red X's angrily crisscrossed each.

Another handler was exiting the bedroom, curtains tossed over his shoulder.

"Where…" Barry started to ask when there was a primal scream from an overhead open skylight. A permanent ladder-like stairway led up.

Stumbling out onto the roof atop Scott's loft, Barry stared in shock. A three foot wall surrounded the roof. All that could be seen of Scott were one hand and a shoe, both clutching the side of the wall, all that appeared to keep him from falling to the street twelve stories below.

"Scott, don't do it!" Barry shouted, running to the wall, grabbing Scott's foot and hand. "For God's sake, buddy! That's not the big finish you want!"

Pulling Scott back over, the two of them collapsed to the floor of the roof, Barry instantly recognizing suicide was not what Scott had in mind. Dressed in vintage Ben Hogan plus four knickerbockers, cap, bow tie and golf shoes, Scott held a golf ball just retrieved from a rain gutter. Color him in delirium.

"That's a Mulligan, goddammit," Scott cried, scrambling to his feet, eyes ablaze. "House rules, Mulligan! I'm a Water Street man!"

He quickly set the ball on a rubber tee. A bag of clubs, Barry saw, stood erect in a wheel cart. Scott pulled out a wood.

"Slice around the Fish Market to Abercrombie and Fitch," Scott said sizing up a shot as Barry watched incredulous, "you and your preppy bullshit, smoke *that* with a three wood." He swung. "Forrre!"

There was the splintering of glass as it hit a window across the street.

"Duck hook! Shit!" Then shouting after, "Yeah? Well, try and get a tee time! Go fuck yourself, fella!"

Reaching out, Barry's arms were around him.

"I should have used a brassie." Scott was almost in tears.

"It's okay, s'okay," Barry whispered.

"Piece of work, that bitch," Scott cried. "I'll take *care* of it, I told her, I mean fucking *deal*! What was it? Parallel parking, or something? Tell me when she's hit by a fucking truck!"

"Why didn't you call me?" Barry asked, genuine pain in his voice as he slowly released his hold on Scott.

"I got a credit card that's at the max, a lap top I walked out with. Twenty bucks in my pants, I'm down to canned hash."

"I'm not leaving you here alone," Barry told him.

"My Panasonic TH-50PX plasma widescreen's gone, the Beamer, too, if those fucks ever find it."

He headed for the wall.

"Scott!" Barry dove after him, grabbed him again.

"Lemme go, lemme go! I'm done, I'm finished!"

Barry let him go.

"Jesus, watch it," said Scott, recoiling. "A guy could go over!"

"When's the last time you ate?" asked Barry.

"An hour ago. Four Pepto Bismol."

"You're moving in with me."

"Moving *in?*" A life line!

"I'll call you after work tomorrow," Barry promised. "You still got your cell phone?"

"Listen, just a couple of weeks. I'll bring my house plants. Women go nuts for guys with house plants."

"It's not the last chapter," Barry encouraged.

"You're going to wake up tomorrow find I'm knocking one out of the park. Get me on the Apprentice. The Donald. Can you call him?"

"*American Idol. The X-Factor,*" Barry promised. "One door slams, another opens."

"Most people don't even know best friends," Scott was building to a high. "It's twenty-four hours, we never close…"

When suddenly from below, a voice, from Scott's computer:

"You've got mail."

Scott froze, stared at Barry, headed like a shot for the ladder stairway, slid on chattering heels down the ladder, bolted toward his computer, dropped onto the upturned suitcase, clicked on the single e-mail, gawked excitedly, and pulled back at what he saw on the screen.

'Tonight. 11:30. South walkway. Brooklyn Bridge.' Below it a single word flashed in a one-by-two-inch box. 'RESPOND!'

Four

From the time he was old enough to remember, Scott had had a recurring dream. A huge pin cushion, devoid of pins, would be bearing down upon him, smothering him in his sleep, waking him with a start. As a young adult he'd taken himself to a psychiatrist.

"Does your mother have large breasts?" she'd asked.

It was a one-time session; he never went back. But now, as he sat on the floor of his loft, in the dark, back against the wall, legs drawn up in a near fetal position, staring, staring at his computer, at the one flashing word, 'RESPOND! RESPOND!' he felt the smothering suffocation of that dream.

The digital clock on the lower right hand corner of his computer jumped from 10:26 p.m. to 10:27 p.m.

Stomach in knots, pulse racing, Scott crabbed, on all fours, across the room to the computer, found the mouse, ran the arrow to the blinking square. With no knowledge his life would ever again be the same, he punched in the command. Two boxes came up on the screen: 'ACCEPT' and 'NOT ACCEPT.' With that giant pin cushion metaphorically pressing down on his chest he stared at his options.

The cross-town bus had dropped Scott off on Centre Street at the Manhattan mouth of the Brooklyn Bridge. He hadn't changed clothes, hadn't shaved, looked out at the bridge with its dramatic buttressed gothic towers as cars from both directions passed by. He glanced at his watch, his twenty-four hundred dollar, Swiss-made Paul Pico, soon to be pawned. 11:17. Scott didn't know much of the bridge's history, but he knew enough. People had *died* on that bridge, not just here and there, but dozens, from the early days of its construction, to stampedes, shootings, suicides. For one brief moment the wiser course impelled him to retreat, forget about this, hightail it away. It wasn't courage or curiosity that decided it for him. It was alternative. There was none. Unsteadily he moved onto the south side walkway and entered the bridge.

It was a mild night. Lights reflected off the black waters of the East River below as he climbed, higher than he realized he would have to. Jesus, the damn thing was long, more than five times the length of a football field it seemed. Midway across, out of breath, he stopped. Other than the traffic with its streaming headlights, Scott was alone — no one else on the walkway — when:

A solitary figure emerged out of the night. Clearly homeless, garments filthy, pushing a loaded market cart, it was approaching from the east along the walkway. Closer and closer it came. Scott started to back away. He turned, stopped short. Another was approaching from the west, an apparition, satanic, a bulging thirty gallon baggie over its shoulder.

Scott was boxed in, petrified, nowhere to go as the figures converged. In a panic, he grabbed a stanchion, pulled himself up onto the railing, his lips drawn back in terror as they reached him, crossed before him, and moved off in opposite directions.

Scott collapsed back onto the walkway, turned to the railing on trembling legs, gripped it, chest heaving, pulse racing. This was bullshit! *Bullshit!* A bar! Any bar anywhere! A triple 190 proof Everclear grain alcohol, that's all he wanted. He pushed off the railing, threw a finger after one of the departing bums, and found he'd flipped it right in the face of a black behemoth. In dark glasses and matching suit, white shirt and tie, it was standing before him, holding wide the door to a limousine drawn up curbside. It was clear. Scott was to get into the car.

Seated in the rear between the behemoth and what looked for all the world like his double, a matching third one behind the wheel, Scott craned his neck. They'd crossed the bridge to the Brooklyn side, had doubled back to Manhattan, taken Pearl Street to Fulton, now were traveling south on Broadway, past silhouettes of monstrous high rises. It had taken Scott that long to find his voice, and now he tried.

"The finger. That's what this is all about?"

He looked from one to the other, got no confirmation, desperately called upon the only wild card in his deck. His mouth.

"Well, Jeez, I mean, the hell, for Christ's, that's just New York, a hey, how are you, you're walking, he flips, you flip, a little social..."

He looked again from one to the other. Nothing.

"Tell you, listen," he shifted gears, "Theater tickets, I'm your man. Any play you want, tenth row center..."

When suddenly, the limousine was turning off the street into the cavernous entrance to an underground garage, totally empty, isolated at this time of night. The limo braked to a stop before an elevator. The vehicle's rear doors opened. The two men emerged, turned to Scott. He was to follow. Punched in numbers on an electronic key pad brought the elevator to the garage. Its door slid open. Scott, offered no option, was escorted inside.

The elevator, Scott recognized, was private. Only one up button. Activated, the elevator began a rapid ascent. Looking about Scott quickly saw it was not usual. The walls were padded in an elegant gold brocade. The floor was marble. Further there was a camera eye peering down on its occupants.

Scott's mind raced. What did they want with him, what could this be about? He'd been fired, what more could *they* want? Was it *Harpers* or *Vanity Fair*? He'd embarrassed them. Were they pissed? That couldn't be it. They'd had their pound of flesh. When — holy shit — it came to him! That thing he'd told at his table at the Ellies, about the homeless black falling into the stew pot! *That's* what this was with these two black guys. It'd been a joke, a joke, for Christ's..!

The stop was smooth, no awareness of it. The door parted, his two escorts leading Scott into an immense rotunda-like foyer. Corridors moved off left and right. A huge gold-plated cuneiform "M" occupied the wall above the unattended crescent-shaped reception desk. Crossing to a pair of large cathedral doors, one of the men opened them, stood aside for Scott to enter. For a moment he stood frozen, every instinct telling him not to do so, to bolt, take off down a corridor to a stairway. There *had* to be a stairway. Down it to the lobby, out into the street! The presence of his escorts ended that option. On uncertain legs, Scott moved toward the door.

Entering a palatial office, Scott flinched at the sound of the doors closing behind him. He was alone. He looked about. Dimly illuminated solely by a lit fireplace, the room was vast, L-shaped into three separate conference areas. There was a bar. Among the superbly crafted furnishings were ash trays, made, Scott realized, from elephant's feet. Exotic animal heads adorned imported wood paneling. Scott moved to one — an African kudu — and he momentarily saw his own head in the animal's place, when his fantasy was trashed by a booming voice.

"In the book of Exodus, God appeared to Moses from a bush that was aflame, but which was not consumed by fire."

Scott spun about, looked wildly for the Voice, found a pair of eyes in a darkened recess staring back at him, scrutinizing, assessing.

"God said to Moses," the Voice went on, "'Come up to Me, to the mountain, and I will deliver unto thee stone tablets, the Commandments that I have written.'"

The eyes rose, and with them a solitary figure. Scott's mouth parted in recognition of the man as he emerged from the thousand pictures Scott had seen of him. Hugo Medlock, sixty, 6'2", dominating, flamboyant, an executive rebel of epic proportions who counted his holdings in billions. He was dressed in pajamas, alligator slippers and monogrammed silk robe. Christ. The man *lived* here. As Scott sank to the edge of a couch:

"Moses," Medlock was going on as he approached, "ordained by God to carry the Word of the Voice. Nothing higher to aspire to than God, am I right?"

Scott nodded, a quick little nod of agreement.

"Bullshit! With that kind of thinking I'd still be wallowing around in my father's debts." He moved behind the bar. "God's a moralist, declaring His love for man, and yelling His head off in agony as millions put all they've got into 'Gonna fuck my ho!' Depressing. We never seem to get any further, do we?"

Scott shook his head, no.

"Bullshit! You're driving me round the bend, Fitzgerald! Maybe I've picked the wrong man."

A loud explosion sent Scott half out of his seat. Medlock had popped open a bottle of champagne. He poured a glass for himself, offered Scott none.

"Picked?" Scott asked.

"I thought I'd seen promise in you. A conniving wonder without a morsel of conscience or conviction."

"I do, I am," Scott answered, charged.

"I thought in you there was the limitless future of a Thenardier, Valjean, the Artful Dodger."

"I'm a simple guy, with a simple dream — the Artful Dodger?"

"Do you have their aberrant fire in your loins for thievery, Fitzgerald, or at heart do you fear deviation, the predatory? Or do you have the passion of a python, the moral decay of a Hessian, a bought and sold mercenary? Do you admit the pleasures of that?"

Scott nodded, a vigorous assent. For his part Medlock stared at Scott, trying to determine the depth of his sincerity. Opening a bottle of antacid, Medlock dropped a pill into his champagne.

"If you've a passport, Fitzgerald, see it's in order. If not, get on it, call my office, they'll run it through. How's your French?

"My what?"

"Votre Français."

"Took it in college, four years."

"You took it two."

"Got As."

"You got C pluses. Do you know your Continental history?"

"I minored in history."

"You minored in debauchery and connivery. That's good. Connivery's quantum physics. It's like a glacier. It takes on a life of its own and determines its own finish. There is no temple-robber pillaging among sacred things so accomplished as that glacier. Do you understand what I'm saying?"

Scott hadn't a *clue* what he was saying, but answered.

"Yes…"

He broke off as he saw Medlock push a piece of paper across the bar. Scott stared at the paper, then at Medlock. Flickering light from the fireplace was playing across Medlock's face. Scott rose, clearly invited to do so, crossed to the bar, picked it up, stared in shock. It was a bank check, made out to David S. Fitzgerald, for $50,000!

Scott's knees began to buckle. He dropped his elbows to the surface of the bar, propping himself from collapsing to the floor.

"Wha…?"

"When I was a boy, and my father was dragged down to his last sixty million, he took me aside. 'It's not what you know,' he told me, 'it's what you own. Possession is power, ultimate possession ultimate power, never to be denied. A denial, no matter how trivial, can start a fissure that can widen exponentially to a flood.' Are you following?"

Scott's head bobbed in agreement even as his eyes remained glued to the check. Picking up his champagne, Medlock ambled out from behind the bar, moved into the room.

"I was seven. I took that advice from that day on. Possession was nine tenths of the law? It *was* the law! And I determined that day forward I would never be denied whatever I coveted. For forty years I followed that principle. Hostile takeovers, malignant pursuits. A shipping line. Two oil companies. Airlines, banks. Mergers and acquisitions, AERs and PEPs, to explain it in simplified language, and always, HDR's enhanced by vertical integration."

His voice took on a hard, bitter timbre. His mouth turned down and his face was dark now as both fists were clenched in front of him.

"What did I do when they sought time and again to bring the full force of anti-trust regulators down upon me?"

He made a movement with his two fists as though snapping something in two, spilling champagne onto his carpet.

"I broke them! And this time will again!"

"*This* time?"

Medlock appeared not to hear, rather stood in stygian reflection, slowly came out of it, looked at Scott with malignant force.

"Are you prepared for the ultimate calumny, Fitzgerald? Deprecation, obloquy?"

Scott wasn't sure of the words, but found himself nodding, yes, yes, fully aware the check was speaking for him.

"There is a quest. A procurement, imprudently denied me." Medlock seemed to be trembling inwardly with rage at the thought. "Obtain it. And that…," he nodded at the check, "is beyond your imagination of what you'll receive."

Five

"We were in Paree, walkin' along the San......"

"Seine," Hubert corrected, lowering the balloon to catch a restorative breeze.

"San. I said!" Mary Lou went on. "All those rabbits an' birds an' seeds an' people paintin', an' there was this un, I mean, God, y'all know, it was a tree, I'm just hung up on trees, that's just the way I feel about it, I mean most of it's not for me, but this un, *God!* I mean just think, every day, those rabbits an' birds, they're with that paintin'!"

She was talking to a blank wall, though Scott stood staring at her, no more than three feet away clinging to the center bar running through the basket below the balloon, the pounding of her voice no match for the throbbing in his head.

"Isn't that right, Menser Oobert?"

"Monsieur."

"I *said!*"

Mary Lou thrust out a petulant lip and fell silent as the balloon sailed soundlessly over newly shorn fields dotted with round bales of wheat. Scott craned his neck. The chase cars were half a mile off, but keeping pace, the Mercedes was trailing at a distance. Turning back with a drawn out expulsion of air, his legs were trembling. His hands, he saw, clutching the center bar, were bare knuckle white. A wave of nausea engulfed him. He was three hundred feet above ground in a fucking wicker basket that sooner or later had to come down, with two guys he'd never met, two faces he'd never seen, waiting to eradicate him from the face of the earth. The *absurdity* of it, like so many other absurdities since that Goddamn lunch!

Aquavit. Eighteen days after his encounter with Medlock, he'd gotten the call. When he'd heard that that was the place he was being summoned to meet, he'd thrilled at the thought. In newly purchased business attire, he'd entered, crossed to the reception desk.

"Scott Fitzgerald," he announced, adding in a strong, clear voice, "Mr. Medlock's table."

"Of course, Mr. Fitzgerald, you're the first to arrive," the girl at the desk had replied. "This way, sir."

Into the power room, the powerful, always absorbed in who was networking with their equivalents, glanced at Scott as he followed the Hostess, suddenly veered off at the sight of a pair of seated Suits — the two who had snubbed him: *Harpers* and *Vanity Fair.* He approached them beaming, hand extended. *Harpers* tentatively lifted his hand to accept the greeting. It wasn't for him. Passing the two, Scott came to the adjacent table where Tom Wolfe and Donald Trump were in the middle of lunch. Scott grabbed Wolfe's hand as it was reaching for his wine.

"Loved your last one, Tom," Scott offered with buoyant cheerfulness. "Good comeback." Then to The Donald as he threw his arms around each man, "Next time go for governor first."

He moved on with a grin, Trump and Wolfe sharing a look, "Who the fuck?" But the effect was accomplished, the room abuzz with who was the newest entry to their club, especially as they saw Scott ushered past the fringes to *the* table, the dominant, ascendant center room table.

"Accepting no calls," he told the Hostess with a wave of his hand in a voice clear enough to be heard by surrounding diners as he slid onto a chair. The Hostess smiled an acknowledging nod, "Of course, Mr. Fitzgerald," and moved off.

Fully aware of the buzz he'd created, Scott feigned ignorance of it, busied himself with the menu. There was Steamed Gooseberry Cod. Braised Short Ribs 'Kalops.' Scandinavian Bouillabaisse.

"Not ready to order, but the Sjosmanshiff," he said as the basket of knackbrod was placed before him along with cheese balls rolled in crushed nuts. "You do it over wood, of course," his eyes rising to the Puerto Rican busboy who had no idea what he was talking about.

Impervious to his error, Scott reviewed.

"Do you have a place?" Medlock had asked.

"Soho. A loft."

"Sleeping on the floor?"

Christ, the man probably knew what *toilet paper* he used.

"I've a condo available. Park Avenue. Yours till."

To Scott's amazed delight, the condo was Bruce Sconzo radical chic, with more amenities than he'd ever imagined. This, he quickly decided, was what he was born to, and wasted no time making the best of it. Three nights after moving in, two young Air France stewardesses were throwing their bodies, barefoot, twisting, jerking about Scott's potted plants, to Lady Gaga's Paper Gangsta blaring from a high tech console.

On the porch, through sliding glass doors, backed by the lights of the city, Scott and the Supermodel of the Ellies wallowed naked in a sunken Jacuzzi, Scott on his cell phone to Barry.

"I'm a fan of the rule," he lectured, the Supermodel running her toes up and down his chest. "You know me, Barry! I'm not going to sacrifice my integrity! But they reap what they sow! You know, you try to bring a little shine, a little renown to that shit-faced company, do them a favor, give yourself up, throw your body in front of the bus, and what does she do? Cuts me off at the knees before two thousand people? Ripped my heart with that fucking smear. Loyalty means *nothing* in this town! I'd like to leave the door open. They have no idea what they're losing me to!"

Out of his reverie Scott sat back in his power chair at his power table, chomping on a knackbrod. If they only knew. Every goddamn one of them! But he'd been warned to silence.

"I tell you this for your salvation," Medlock had warned him. "Many legends have been woven around what you're being asked to pirate, commencing with a brutal murder in the court of Isabella in 1327, first documented by monkish scholars."

Medlock had paused. To continue with the whole of it or not. He'd determined to go on.

"It was not to be an isolated event as others dared similar misadventures throughout Gallic history, only to meet an equivalent end."

Firelight across his face had given Medlock a Mephistophelian hue.

"Some had their tongues ripped out. Others their eyes, burned from their sockets. Still more could be found, their separated limbs hanging from forest trees. I tell you this to advise you of consequences beyond your imagination should you blunder."

Whatever Medlock had been referring to, Scott had only half listened, his eyes locked on the check. *$50,000!*

"Mister Fitzgerald?" Scott looked up. The Hostess was standing before him. "Your party has arrived, sir."

He half rose to welcome Medlock as the hostess withdrew, and he found himself facing no Medlock at all, but a slight, trim-suited man, in his late forties, the sort who might pass by unnoticed, pencil in hand, hurrying from one hurry to another.

"Mr. Fitzgerald?"

"Yeah?" Scott answered, dropping back onto his chair in confusion.

"Elihu Sykes." He offered no hand as he lowered himself to a chair, placed a narrow brief case on the table.

"Where's Medlock? *Mister* Medlock," Scott corrected himself, looking past Sykes for his expected luncheon companion.

"Mister Medlock is elsewhere. You understand."

"I was asked to meet him here."

"No," Sykes answered, "you were asked to *be* here." His voice was toneless and he spoke with a slight lisp.

Scott sat back slowly. The room, he saw, seemed to have given up its curiosity, everyone going back to their lunch. He gave Sykes a hostile stare.

"I don't understand."

Sykes exhibited no indication of acknowledging Scott's acrimony, opened the brief case, removed the first of several items.

"Airline ticket."

He handed it to Scott who looked it over. Air France, flight 1011, economy class — *economy* class? — departure 11:45 p.m., Kennedy, Friday evening, Saturday 1:00 p.m. arrival, Paris, de Gaulle. Return flight open.

Sykes handed him another document, a voucher.

"Paris accommodation."

Scott perused that, too. Hotel Galileo — never heard of it — Fifty-four rue Galilée, Eighth Arrondissement.

There followed several innocuous offerings. A map of Paris. A Guide Michelin of France. 500 euros in cash for transportation to the hotel and incidentals until he'd established bank credit, as a suggestion. A booklet of tickets to the Paris Metro.

"Faster than taxis, and," Sykes concluded, handing Scott a small sealed envelope, "a key to a bank safety deposit box, Crédit Lyonnais, 17 rue de Bassano, in the Sixteenth. It's three blocks off the Champs Élysées, toward the river, close by your hotel. The box is in your name when you sign in."

Sykes wrote the address down on a cocktail napkin.

"Memorize it, then burn it. There'll be a packet. Everything you've been told repeated. Plus whatever more you'll need to know. Under no circumstances are you to contact Mr. Medlock nor mention his name. Under no circumstances are you to talk to *anyone* regarding this assignment. You understand. Under no circumstances are you to entertain personal contacts. Are we clear?"

Are we *clear?* Who the fuck did this pissant son of a bitch…?

"Clear," Scott answered.

Sykes closed his brief case, glanced at Scott. It was a lingering glance that Scott couldn't read.

"Be advised, Mr. Fitzgerald, if anything should go wrong, we don't know who you are. You understand."

Without a parting handshake of farewell, Sykes rose and departed, briefcase in hand.

For several moments Scott sat, his mind wandering into an uneasy zone, unaware of the waiter, speaking, standing before him.

"Hunh?" Scott said finally, looking up.

"The specials, sir."

"The Sjosmanshiff."

"Very good choice, sir."

"You do it over wood, of course."

"Of course."

"If anything should go wrong..?"

Back in the condominium following a trip to his bank where he'd deposited $500 of the $50,000 into his personal account, the rest to his Visa, Scott sat stiffly on the Jeffrey Cohlmia Collection couch, and he looked around. The Lexus model of the Ellies had been invited back for the night. Ten o'clock, he'd made it, so he wouldn't have to bother with dinner. There was champagne on ice, and caviar. He'd set the temperature in the Jacuzzi at eighty-five degrees, just cool enough that she'd want to seek body heat...

"If anything should go *wrong?*"

His initial unease at what he'd been told was tempered now by the three Absolut Vodkas he'd downed in quick succession at the restaurant. Still, *"If anything should go wrong?"*

Christ, they made it sound like he was being sent to steal the Mona Lisa! That's what happened when you ended up with billions. Delusion, paranoia. They'd handed him a ridiculously overpaid assignment, not that he didn't deserve it — he was made for it. But what they saw as perilous was, in fact, an elementary challenge, and little of that. Wasn't it? This wasn't about climbing through some window in the middle of night, or robbing a bank or train with a Marushim N4 assault gun. His weapons were youth, connivance, charm, which is why the old bastard had hired him. If he blew it, the worst that could befall him was ridicule. Wasn't it? Wasn't it? So why *"If anything should go wrong?"* As for all that talk about eviscerated tongues and eyes and limbs? Ghost stories.

Aware he'd been needlessly daunted, he brushed it off, heaved himself from the couch, crossed to the desk. The items given him by Sykes laid out before him, he took stock. The envelope with its key to the safe deposit box, the euros, passport, the Guide Michelin, the map, those were for later. The airline ticket and hotel voucher were now.

He picked up the desk phone, found the Air France 800-number on the face of his ticket, put in a call to the airlines. *Economy* class? Bull*shit!* Ten minutes later he'd upgraded — hell, it wasn't *his* money — to first class. That done, he turned to the hotel voucher, opened the Guide to the Paris insert, page thirty-nine, the eighth arrondissement, Champs-Élysées, St-Lazare, Madeleine. The search for the Galileo took him to page forty-one. He counted, starting with the highest rated hotel on down. The Galileo was the forty-eighth listed in the district — *forty-eighth?* — small, boutique, twenty-seven rooms, no bar, no restaurant. The leading *grand luxe* in the eighth, he saw, was the Plaza-Athénée, phone listed. He dialed the overseas number. An operator answered on the second ring.

"Plaza-Athénée, bon soir."

"Reservations," Scott answered in his best French accent.

"One moment, sir."

He'd spoken perfect French, goddammit, what was this English crap?

"Reservations, bon soir."

"Bon soir," Scott answered, perfecting his pronunciation. "Je voudrais faire des réservations, s'il vous plait."

"If we can accommodate you, sir. What nights would that be?"

Shit! He swallowed his pride, which was never an easy dispatch.

"J'arriverai ce samedi. Je voudrais une réservation ouverte."

"I'm terribly sorry, sir." Again the fucking English. "The hotel is full. The air show, I'm afraid."

"I'll pay full rate," he said in English, giving up on the French.

"This is the Plaza-Athénée, sir. Everyone pays full rate."

"Look! Il faut que you've got une chambre dans une hotel with 210 rooms, God's sake!" he said, unaware he'd fallen into mixing French with English.

"If I could make a recommendation, sir," she answered with disciplined patience. "The Galileo, close by, has vacancies."

He hung up, glowering, tried to take his mind off the failure of his call. His passport had arrived. Its quick delivery, following delivery of appropriate photos, enhanced by Medlock's office as promised, was in order. With his Visa fully replenished, no need to go to a Paris bank to establish an account. There were clothes to pick up at the cleaners. A limo to order to take him to the airport...

No room? He couldn't get his mind off it. The Plaza-Athénée had *no room?* Well, he'd just see about that.

Six

"Wheeee!" Mary Lou's exhilaration was like finger nails on a blackboard to Scott.

They'd been up for an hour. The balloon had been carrying its basket low across a pasture toward a looming row of beech trees. Firing the burner, Hubert had brought the balloon up over them, the bottom of the basket scraping their tops, eliciting Mary Lou's gleeful response. Crossing a knoll, the ground dropped away, revealing a near-distant village.

Hubert picked up his cell phone.

"Il y a un village deux kilomètres en raison du sud," he said into the phone. "Voyons si nous pouvais faire du terrain de soccer." There was a confirming squawk on the cell phone, then silence.

Scott hadn't understood it all, but he'd understood enough. That village ahead. They were going for a soccer field just now coming into view at the near end of the town. He craned his neck. They were flying too low to see the surfaced road approaching the village. But if the chase cars knew where they were, so did the Mercedes.

He surveyed the terrain. It was low-lying open land now, cattle and crops, with minimal cover. If he tried to run for it when they landed, where could he go? A hedge row now and then, what good was that? They hadn't tried to take him from the van or at the launch area for the balloon, where they could have easily. Maybe there was safety in numbers. Maybe that was it. Maybe they were waiting to take him when alone.

A convulsing shudder wracked his body. Was the ancient legend of ripped out tongues and eyes no ghost story after all? He *had* been told, well warned! Why hadn't he taken it seriously, *gone* to the police when he could? Even if he had, if they'd listened to him, his accusation would have carried no weight. It might well be suggested it was but a ruse to conceal his own mendacity. So now he was caught, a trapped rat! There's a way out of this, he told himself. There's *got* to be! Think, Goddamnit, *think!*

"Don' y'all just love the trees?"

He glanced across at Mary Lou. She was clutching the center bar, talking to him, sparkling eyes, abandoning Billy Joe who was as green as the pasture below, apprehension across his face as though he were going to be sick.

"Only God can make 'em, that poem, you know. How do y'all writers *do* that?" she added, bending her body over the pole for emphasis with tinkling laughter, exposing more than the top of her breasts "Where do y'all get your *ideas* from, Scott Fitzgerald?"

For once, Scott had other things on his mind. But he wasn't dead. Not yet, as he stared down the opening of her blouse. It took no special insight to know things were cool between the two newlyweds, and Mary Lou was doing her best to let Billy Joe know it.

"I'm jus' not gonna let you get away without tellin'," she added to Scott.

"We are going for the soccer field," Hubert interrupted with a short blast from the burner, lifting the balloon to catch a slight cross breeze, narrowing it in on the village.

The soccer field came into clearer view, its center scuffed bare from too many cleated boots. The two chase cars, Scott could suddenly see, were turning off the D route leading into the village, onto a packed dirt parking area. The two drivers got out of their vans and hurried onto the field.

"Hold onto the cross bar," Hubert advised, tossing the grab ropes over the side, the balloon lowering as he released hot air. "The basket could tip over. If it does, it will do so slowly, no harm."

"Wheee!" Mary Lou delighted as they lowered over a farmhouse rooftop.

Scott clutched the center pole, his hands bracketing Mary Lou's, the little finger of her right hand locking with his thumb, he noticed. His body was tingling as though standing on exposed live wires, but not from Mary Lou's touch. He didn't have to look to know the Mercedes was there, somewhere, seen or not, its two occupants monitoring the balloon's descent as it glided slowly in over the field, the two chase men on the ground running with it. Grabbing the trailing ropes, they jogged along, slowing the balloon to a stop mid-field, lowered the basket upright onto the ground, the balloon still vertical above but limp, no lifting power left in it. Stakes were driven into the ground, the ropes tied off. A long whoosh of air exploded from Billy Joe's lungs as Mary Lou applauded, elated.

"Bon travail, les gars!" Hubert complimented the two on the ground as he shut down the burner. Then, to the three in the basket, "Champagne and camembert."

Hubert climbed from the basket, Billy Joe the first out after him, staggering to the ground, Mary Lou following, with no assistance from her husband. Scott remained in the basket and he looked about. The chase men, he saw, had returned to their vans. One was bringing out a portable table, the other a panier loaded with edibles. Nowhere in sight was the Mercedes, which by now Scott knew meant nothing. Suddenly, all he *did* know, was an enormous urge to urinate.

Climbing from the basket, Scott's legs were jelly as he approached Hubert.

"Bathroom?"

Hubert nodded, pointed off. Flanking the field was a bleachers, beside it a small concrete building. Scott made for it. There was one entrance marked W.C. He entered, closed the door behind him, and locked it.

Inside was only a squat toilet, the user having to do just that — standing on footrests over a hole in the floor. Fortunately he had only to do what he'd come for, which he did, with a flow that lasted forty seconds. Shaking himself off, he rinsed his hands in a cold-water-only rusting sink, looked about for paper towels, found none, so settled for toilet paper, which proved to be rough as sandpaper. No receptacle in sight, he discarded the paper onto the floor as his lips tightened, aware of a slow cold rage mounting in his brain, stifling his sense of self-preservation.

When all at once he saw it. A window, high up on the wall above the sink. It was wide, about three feet, maybe eighteen inches high, its lower edge hinged, held closed by a single clasp. Wide enough for a medium sized man to crawl through perhaps if he could reach it, Scott noticed. The only way to it was the sink. Would it hold him? He pressed down on it. It seemed secure enough.

Hands on the sink, arms extended, he pushed himself up off the floor, testing further. Still it held. He tried to bring one leg up onto the sink. Shit! Too high off the floor. He fell back in despair, when he saw the bucket in the corner of the room, a worn mop protruding from it. Discarding the mop, he grabbed the bucket, placed it upturned before the sink. Climbing onto the bucket, he brought first one foot, then the other onto the sink, leaned in, hands against the wall for support, and drew himself slowly to near full height, reached for the window clasp, tried to turn it, to open the window. It wouldn't budge. With all the strength at his command, he tried. The clasp was frozen.

He half fell, half lowered himself back to the floor, barking his shins on the sink as he did so. With his hopes dashed, he stood for a moment, a single sob wracking his body. He turned to the door, unlocked it, pulled it open, and nearly fainted.

Before him stood a brown-suited man, white shirt, and unmatching grey tie. He was tall with a lean, muscular face, a scar across his forehead, and close cropped hair. He wore dark glasses, which gave him a vulturine air. By taking a step backwards, he could have given Scott room to pass. He made no attempt to do so. He stood blocking the doorway, his glasses fixed on Scott, for ten to twenty seconds it seemed. Heart pounding in his ribs, Scott squeezed past, making no effort to look back to see if the man was entering the W.C. or not.

Clenching his teeth to keep from vomiting, Scott stumbled toward his flight companions as the balloon was being brought to ground to be folded by the two chase men. Hubert, he saw, was in conversation with Mary Lou who was peppering the pilot with questions Scott couldn't hear as he approached, Billy Joe left to one side, listening, or pretending to listen, color still trying to make its way back into his face.

The table, Scott saw, was laid out. Cheese, crackers, fruit, champagne, paper napkins, wine glasses. He went for the champagne, pouring himself a glass to its brim, clutching the bottle with both hands to do so. He lifted the glass to his mouth right handed. It was shaking. He switched to his left. Same thing. Downing the drink two-handed, he poured another.

"How'd he *do* that, Scott Fitzgerald?" Mary Lou bubbled, "Bringin' that in like he did? Oh, my, that's stinky cheese," she said, surveying the camembert, helping herself to a cluster of grapes. "At home we go for good ol' American U.S. of A. you know? Tried that duck confitte in Paris. Blaugh! Maybe if they'd had it with down home gravy an' grits."

A surge of bile rose into Scott's esophagus, not entirely from Mary Lou's culinary accounts. He was sweating. He wiped his hands and forehead with a paper napkin, left Mary Lou to her grapes, and approached Hubert.

"I need your help," he said in a voice only the pilot could hear.

"If it is possible, of course," Hubert replied. "Are you ill?"

"I'm afraid…" Scott began.

"Excuse me," said Hubert and turned to the two chase men who were detaching the mouth of the balloon from the basket. "Je prendrai les passagers de retour dans l'autre camionnette. Vous prenez l'un avec la caravane, okay?"

He turned back to Scott who was aware Mary Lou was rejoining them.

"You were saying, Monsieur?"

"Nothing," Scott said. His voice was shallow. "Nothing."

The rain had started again by the time Hubert returned the three to their Beaune hotel. Mary Lou, angrily peeling off her plastic raincoat, headed for the elevator, Billy Joe, still in his blue nylon slicker, was trailing like a truculent child. They'd driven in total silence, not a word between the two until entering the lobby.

"I've never been so humiliated in my life!" said Mary Lou, turning on her husband after pressing the up button, Scott, standing mid-foyer, wet dripping from his raincoat, caught up in their banter.

"I don' do well in heights, I tol' you, Mary Lou," Billy Joe whined.

"Like that night on the thirteenth floor in that hotel!"

"That hotel, it was a one-time thang!"

"Well, keep y'all zipper up in this one!"

The elevator door gaped open, the two disappearing inside.

Scott turned to Hubert who, Scott saw, was filling out papers at the desk. The receptionist, a nineteen-year-old Dutch girl, was coyly trying to engage him in word play. Completing his paper work, Hubert smiled, said something Scott couldn't hear that drew an appreciative laugh from the girl, turned to encounter Scott standing before him, raincoat still on.

"Monsieur Hubert?"

"Oui."

Scott swallowed, nodded toward the receptionist.

"Dutch?"

"When French country girls turn eighteen," Hubert explained, "many head to Paris. Dutch girls come down looking for husbands."

It was not what Scott wanted to talk about.

"Could I leave with you, please."

"Monsieur Fitzgerald, isn't it?"

"Please?"

"Where is it you want to go?"

"I don't know."

"You have your own vehicle, your own transportation?"

"No. I mean, yes. But, no."

Hubert studied Scott. "I asked before, are you ill?"

"I think there are two men…who mean to kill me."

Hubert's face went blank. "Indeed."

"Yes, I…"

"Why would they want to do that?

"If you look outside, across the street, you'll see a black Mercedes."

"A black Mercedes."

"They're waiting for me to try to leave, alone."

Hubert looked through the glass top of the entrance door, through the rain. The Mercedes was there, parked as before, across the street. It was impossible, given the weather, to tell whether or not the car was occupied.

"And why?" asked Hubert, turning back to Scott.

"Because they've been paid to do so, that's why."

Hubert was silent for a moment. Scott's face, he saw, seemed filled with anger. And fear.

"They have very good doctors in the city. The desk can call for one."

"I'm not sick!"

"There is no feeling of motion in a balloon. The lack of motion, yet moving over ground can elicit a dizzying effect on rare occasions, confusing the senses. It passes in a day. But there are medications."

"That's not what..!"

"The desk will help you, Monsieur. Bonne journée."

And with that Hubert turned, moved through the door and was gone.

For a moment, Scott stood, just stood, wet dripping off his raincoat. The bar, he noticed, across from the dining room, was open, no one in attendance, the room unlit, but open. Dragging himself into it, he dropped heavily onto a couch. His mind went back to the man he'd encountered in the doorway to the W.C. at the landing site. Behind those dark glasses were eyes, Scott knew, that regarded him as though he were a mushroom, something to be stamped on, toed aside. In a collage of dark fantasies, Scott imagined a splinter of flame, a millisecond's ear-splitting detonation, then nothing as the bullet ripped through his brain. *God,* how had he let himself get into this? It was going to be nothing, a lark! It had *started* that way. Why hadn't he seen the signs?

Seven

Customs and passport control at Paris de Gaulle, with its trained sniffing dogs, had been an endless line of foreign entrants, and worse moved slowly. To add to Scott's irritation, his flight had taken off an hour late from Kennedy, and his Tumi bag was one of the last off the carousel. Securing it, Scott passed through the inspection process without incident, moved to a bench seat, glanced at his watch still on New York time, reset it to French, 3:30 p.m., an hour and a half since landing. Standing the Tumi upright, Scott settled his carry-on beside him, withdrew his international cell phone, dialed.

"Plaza-Athénée. Bonjour."

"Reservations," Scott said, no effort at a French accent when the operator came on.

Two rings, then a woman's voice. "Reservations. Puis-je vous aider?"

"This is Scott Fitzgerald," he said, then added in a punishing tone, "Where's my limousine?"

"Pardon, monsieur?"

"My name is Scott Fitzgerald," he said, with an impatience as though speaking to a child. "I have just arrived at the airport, Air France 1011 from the States, I have a confirmed reservation at your hotel, as well as an order for a limousine pick up, which is not here!"

There was a pause.

"Monsieur Scott Fitzgerald?"

"That is my name."

"Non, monsieur, there is no such name on our reservation…"

"Which, I'm sure," Scott interrupted, "Mr. Hugo Medlock will be delighted to hear, considering his office *made* the reservation!"

There was what Scott assumed was a moment of shocked silence, followed by a muffled background conversation. A man's voice came on the line.

"This is Monsieur Jardet. May I help you?"

"You are?"

"Directeur des reserves. Reservations manager."

"I have just arrived. I'm tired. More than that I am appalled. I'm here in Paris on special assignment for Mr. Medlock…"

"*Hugo* Medlock..?"

"…who will not be pleased to hear of this outrageous incompetence…"

"Your name again, Monsieur?"

"Fitzgerald."

There was a pause, another muffled conversation, followed quickly by, "Ah! Je suis désolé, pardon, mille excuses, Monsieur. Here it is! J'ai trouvé ici!" He called off to someone in the background, then back to the phone, "Your limousine will be there directly!"

The hour ride in the stretch limo into Paris culminated with two incredible views, the Eiffel Tower looming over roof tops to the south, and Montmartre to the north, neither of which competed with the twenty-year-aged Pierre Ferrand Reserve Cognac Scott discovered in the limo's rear seat bar. He didn't know the price of all the cognacs of France, but he knew Pierre Ferrand Reserve. $189 a bottle! Luxuriating with his second snifter, Scott contemplated. This trip was shaping up! Oh, yeah!

Turning off the Champs-Élysées onto Avenue Montaigne, the limo pulled to a stop before the entrance to the Plaza-Athénée. Two uniformed bell boys hurried toward the vehicle. One opened the rear door for Scott to emerge, the other securing his luggage.

The corridor to the lobby Scott entered was beyond his imagination. White marble floors with inset black marble diamonds, massive vases of flowers, classical art on walls to rival most museums.

"Ah, Monsieur Fitzgerald!" a man in a tuxedo rushed forward, greeting Scott as though he were the Sultan of Burundi. "Bienvenue! Welcome!"

"Monsieur..?"

"Jardet."

"Of course."

"Please," Jardet said, as Scott approached the desk. "There is no need to register. Later. You've had a long flight." And turning to one of the bell boys who stood by with Scott's carry-on and Tumi, "Monsieur Moriel, voyez que Monsieur Fitzgerald est assistée à sa suite immédiatement." Then, turning to Scott, "If there is anything, anything…"

"I'll be calling Mister Medlock directly," Scott offered. "Jardet?"

"Jardet."

"He'll be pleased to hear of your courtesy."

Jardet's bow almost scraped the floor. "We are at your service, do not hesitate."

Scott started to follow the bell boy. "Oh, there's one thing, yes," he said, turning back. "I'll be needing a limousine at eight in the morning to take me to Rue de Bassano."

"It will be waiting for you at eight."

Scott entered the elevator on a high. Jesus, these French! Talk about playing them like a violin! He turned to see the bellhop with his luggage about to enter after him, suddenly pull back, allowing entry to a vision. Dressed in elegant cocktail suit, she was, by Scott's assessment, in her early thirties, slim with a natural allure and beautiful fixed smile. A book in one hand, she pressed the third floor button with the other, stepped back as the elevator began its slow rise. If she had any awareness of Scott ogling her, she gave no notice of it, moved forward as the elevator reached her floor.

"M'amselle," Scott offered, stepping aside as the elevator door slid open.

"Madame," she corrected him, smile still fixed, and was gone.

The fifth floor Royal Suite that Scott was admitted to was not a suite at all. It was a residence. Furnished with antiques, the three bedroom, five room complex, Scott saw in awe as he wandered through, was resplendent with fabrics embroidered with silks and gold threads, white leather chairs and couches, a baby grand piano, and three bathrooms done entirely in Italian marble mosaics and engraved glass. Flowers, fresh cut, were everywhere, along with a welcoming basket of fruit, pate, caviar and toasts, as well as a Noka Vintage Collection of chocolates, compliments of management.

"Voulez-vous que je de raccrocher vos vêtements, Monsieur?"

Scott wasn't certain what the man had asked, but he took a shot. "Oui."

When the Tumi had been emptied, clothes hung up in the master bed room closet, curtains thrown open revealing late afternoon Paris, the bellhop turned, mouth parted to speak, was greeted by a fifty euro gratuity.

"Merci, Monsieur," he said, showing no emotion at the outrageous tip. "S'il n'y a rien de plus, un séjour agréable."

Left alone, Scott didn't know whether to chortle or weep. He chose a third course: drove his fist into an overstuffed pillow with a howl of pure self-congratulatory delight. By God if they could see him back at that fucking magazine! Well, who's on top now? When he suddenly recognized he was exhausted. It was 5:45 in the evening, he saw on the bedside clock, 11:45 in the morning New York time, he hadn't slept on the plane. He was tired. Dog tired. Tomorrow was the beginning. It would start with the Rue de Bassano as he'd been told and go from there, wherever 'there' would take him. Tonight there was sleep. Calling the operator he left a wake-up call for 7:00 promptly in the morning, lowered the curtains, tore off his clothes, threw himself naked under the covers, and succumbed to happy darkness.

Never had he slept so soundly as rolling over in bed he glanced at the clock, and shot upright in alarm. It was 7:30! No wake-up call at seven as asked for, and the limo would be waiting at *eight?*

He jumped out of bed, threw open the curtains. Daylight streamed in. With a curse, he ran for the bathroom, emptied his bladder, shaved and showered in minutes, dove into his clothes, bolted down the emergency stairs, barged through the entrance to the street, and glanced at his watch. It was 8:05. And no limousine!

He paced. Five minutes, ten — *still* nothing! God *damn* these French! His friends were right, his conservative friends! He was *American*, that's what this was about! They *hated* Americans! You could name desserts after the bloody Boche, but *trust* them? He'd never go to another French restaurant again!

When his blood slowly chilled and he felt the sweat of his shirt cold against his flesh, he realized it was getting *darker*. He'd slept an hour and forty-five minutes, not through the night, which was now coming on!

The hotel bar, 'Le Bar,' was blue tinted, trendy, with a subtle musical ambience. And there Scott sat, glowering over a double martini, memorializing the idiocy of his catnap, trying, as usual, to find someone else to blame. He glanced about the room. It was well occupied, a few business groups here and there, some singles, along with one or two couples seated, in shock Scott surmised, with over-priced glasses of champagne, silently wondering how the hell they'd talked themselves into staying at such an extravagant place. And of course, always, forever, the young girl, in her twenties, tears running down her face as she sat with a man old enough to be her father, trying to bear up under what he'd just told her, that he was going back to his wife…

Then he saw her. The woman from the elevator. At a small table, alone, book open, reading, she was wearing the same suit as before, was nursing a wine that seemed to Scott to match the color of her lips. Fully engrossed, she turned a page, draining the last of her wine.

"Excusez mois. Je me demandais…"

She looked up, not so much startled as curious, to see Scott before her.

"All the other tables seem taken," he offered, reverting to English.

She looked about the room and saw he was right.

"Please, s'il vous plait." she said, nodding to the chair across from her, and went back to her book.

Scott slid onto the chair, swirled his martini, and looked her over. The suit she wore was low-cut, not in an obvious way, but enough to show the top of her breasts. Her perfume was subtle, but intoxicating. By any measure she was one of the most alluring women Scott could recall.

"What are you reading?"

"L'Etranger," she answered without looking up.

"Camus."

That caught her interest. She stared at him. "You've read Camus?" Her voice, as her accent, was soft and filled with surprise.

"In English." He nodded at the book. "The Stranger. College lit."

"What question did you find he was asking?"

"Is there a logical meaning to life?"

"Ah!" she said, eyebrows rising in interest as she placed the open book pages down on the table.

"It was on the mid-term test. Thirty points," Scott added.

She laughed, her voice like tinkling glass. Salvo one, mission begun, Scott mused to himself. Though go slow with this one, very slow.

"There are not many Americans who have read Camus," she said in surprising English.

"Well, I've always loved France and the French," he lied.

"You have been here before?"

"Years ago," he lied again.

"What brings you this time?"

"Guess."

"Business?"

"Good," he nodded. "You?"

"Guess."

"Well, let's see. You're not from Paris or you wouldn't be staying at the Plaza-Athénée. So, I'd say, given the way you're dressed, business, too."

"Why not?"

"With a husband at home," he added, nodding at her wedding band.

"A husband. Yes." It had been a beat before she'd answered, Scott noticed, and, he thought, without enthusiasm. It was an opening. Scott took it, thrust out his hand.

"Scott Fitzgerald," he said. She looked at the hand, as though by taking it she'd be crossing a line. She did so, tentatively. "You?" he asked. She stared at him, withdrew her hand slowly. "I've got to call you something," he said.

"Why is that?"

"Because 'Madame' won't work over dinner."

"Dinner," she said, sitting back, with what Scott perceived was suspicion his offer implied more than that.

"Look," he said, his hands spread wide. "I'm just off the plane from New York, I don't know a soul in Paris, I've got to lecture in front of 300 people in the morning, and I'm having a crisis in confidence. I mean, my God, 300 French authors who've come to hear me in my stumbling French, who's read Camus. I'd really like to take my mind off the thing for an hour or two."

It was clear by the look on her face she was buying his bullshit. *Christ,* he could be good when he had to be.

"Just dinner," he said. Then with a grin, "What do I call you?"

"Call me what you wish."

Scott gestured. "Georgette."

"How did you guess?"

Dinner in the hotel's Régence Restaurant in orange-backed white leather chairs, beneath an immense clutter of sparkling crystal chande-liers, was over langoustines amuse-bouche, and lobster with sea potatoes. Dinner over, they'd settled back with coffee and cognac. They'd talked about everything irrelevant. Where he should go, what he should see while here in Paris as time allowed. The Musée d'Orsay with its superb Impressionists. Three of her favorite paintings there, and the Monet Museum in the Sixteenth, a must. And the catacombs, which no American ever saw. And the Bal Tabarin, of course — remarkable staging. Oh! And not to miss Les Invalides. He wrote it all down, pretending interest, on a cloth napkin with a pen she offered him, and stuffed the napkin inside his coat pocket.

"So," she said. "300 authors?"

"I'm a senior editor of an American publication. *New York In Review?* You've heard of it?"

She shook her head, no.

"They've sent me here to assess the possibility of opening a French version, and to assemble a staff of French writers.

Countering her travelogue through Paris he'd been going on and on himself, wherever his imagination took him, fully aware, by the sparkle in her eyes, he was hitting his mark.

"Although," he began, then shrugged it off. "But that's another story."

"What?" she asked, intrigued.

"Nothing."

"No, go on."

"This should be one of the most rewarding times in my life." And he affected a catch in his voice.

"It's not?"

"You really don't want to hear this. It sounds self-serving."

"Please."

"I lost my fiancée three months ago."

"Lost?"

"She caught a virus in Dakar, working with the natives."

"How horrible."

"I was going to bring her on this trip. We even talked of getting married here in this hotel. God, how she would have loved the Royal Suite."

"You're in the Royal Suite?"

"Five rooms, 360 degree view of the city. That's what would have really gotten her: the view."

"The Royal *Suite?*"

"I know. It's ostentatious. It was the magazine's choice. They seem to want to inspire an image."

"You must be very famous. More so than you've told me."

"As long as one keeps a perspective," he answered with a self-deprecating little laugh. "You're welcome to come up and see it for a minute," he said with a glance at his watch. "Though I've got to get to bed." He saw the questioning look on her face. "Not a good idea?"

"For a minute," she made very clear.

"If I don't fall asleep on the ride up."

The view from the balcony off Scott's living room was extraordinary.

"What time is it?" she asked, clutching the railing.

"Ten."

She looked out at the lights of the city.

"Like diamonds on velvet," she said.

"The city of lights. Isn't that what they call it?"

He'd come up behind her, reached up, placed his hands on her shoulders. "Don't."

But she made no effort to stop him and her breathing was heavy. Keep it slow, he told himself. Plenty of time.

"Where's the Louvre from here?" he asked.

"There. Can you see it?" she pointed. "By the river. And there's the Place de la Concorde and Sainte Chapelle…

He lowered his hands from her shoulders, down along her waist. She turned out of his grasp, into the living room.

"I'd better be going."

She picked up her book and purse up from a table, but she wasn't going. She was standing mid room, her back to him. He came up behind her, slowly, put his face close to her hair, breathed in deeply.

"Please...don't." But her eyes were closed and she seemed to be shaking.

"It's been so long," he whispered.

"For me too."

And she was into his arms, pressed against him, her mouth finding his. His hand on her breast, she made no effort to stop him. It was pure and simple surrender as he led her to the darkened bedroom where the bed had been remade from his nap, Patrick Roger chocolate on the pillow, the curtains drawn. The top of her suit fell easily to the floor. Her brassiere followed. He reached for the clasp on her pants.

"Wait," she said. She crossed to the curtains, threw them open to the lights of the city, and came back to him. "Maintenant," she said to him. "Maintenant."

It didn't last long. It couldn't. She was like a banked furnace, relit. Words tumbled out in a pant with his thrusts. "Mon Dieu! Mon *Dieu!* N'arrêtez pas! Incroyable! *Incroyable!*" They came together and it was five minutes, it seemed, before their breathing returned to normal.

He let her have the bathroom first, and followed her in when she returned. Alone in the bathroom, he emptied himself and stared naked at himself in the mirror. *Christ* what a ride. And the night was young. Given his history he could go another two times. Hell, maybe three. And she was worth it. That was the thing about frustrated married women. Light their fuse, and rockets went off! And, man, could he light it. He'd have to be careful, though. In the morning there would have to be breakfast, she'd want to take him on some fucking tour — well, he'd worry about that in the morning. Meanwhile, he smirked at himself in the mirror. Round two. He headed for the door, opened it, and stepped into a totally unexpected sight.

The bed room light was on — full on. And there she stood, all but fully dressed, slipping into her jacket. Her demure expression was gone, replaced by a blankness he had not seen.

"Where you going?" he asked in disbelief.

"To work."

"It's night!"

"I work at night."

"Where?"

"Tonight? Fourth floor. I have an appointment in ten minutes."

He opened his mouth to reply, but stopped, awareness crunching in on him. It didn't take a clairvoyant to know the next thing he'd hear.

"400 euros, s'il vous plait, Monsieur." she said. "No checks."

Eight

Scott shivered. He was still wearing his soaked Eddie Bauer, cold to the bone, slouched on a couch in the darkened unattended hotel bar in Beaune, desperately trying to figure out what to do. Wait them out? Forget it. Slip out unseen? How? There *was* a back entrance to the hotel, he'd discovered, and the one through the kitchen, but both, he'd come to realize, opened onto a courtyard, and the only exit from that was to the street in plain view of the waiting Mercedes.

Heart thumping, his mind continued playing tricks. They'd drive him to a deserted *bois*, force him out of the car, bind his hands and his feet, drag him into the trees, suffering him to the wolves. Or they'd abandon the car, leaving him locked alone inside, the door handles coming off in his hands as he tried to escape, when there'd be a horrific detonation, the car going up in flames, Scott with it. Or...

"My, wasn't that just the most thrillin' thing in the *world?*"

He looked up. Mary Lou was slipping onto the couch beside him.

"You bein' down in Mexico, that revolution an' all, but golly, I jus' never done anythin' *like* that!" Then seeing him in his soaking raincoat, "You poor thing, you look soaked through. You'll catch your death." Just what he wanted to hear. "Lemme get you outa that."

Scott stood, without will, subject to command, lost in a world of despair as Mary Lou helped him out of his coat.

"There, that's better," she said, as he flopped back onto the couch. "You could use a drink."

Scott looked about.

"Where's..?"

"Billy Joe? Bed. You'd think he'd just been to the moon."

"Well, that's what honeymoons are all about," he said.

"The moon?"

"Bed."

"You're *terrible*," she said with a laugh, poking him playfully with her fist. "I bet you've used that 'un before. It surely opens up a conversation. What you *doin'* here anyway? Another book? Bed. You're naughty. I bet you writers jus' have your way with the ladies, all those words you come up with."

He knew what she was. He'd run into them in college. A typical goddamn Tri Delt. They were the worst. Prick teasers. "I can't stop you if you do. But don't. Please don't." Leave you humping air with a smirk on their face. Well, stick her...when it struck him. Another book, she said! *Another book?* That was *it!* His way *out* of this! His whole demeanor changed with the thought. But it called for seduction. Oblique, circuitous. She was country, but she wasn't stupid.

"You're good," he said. "Another book, you're right."

"*Really?* I *was?* What's it about?"

He thought for a moment, thought fast. Across the room, above the bar, was a print of a medieval painting of the ancient Hospice, now the Hôtel-Dieu — Beaune's principal tourist attraction. He didn't know much about it, but he guessed she knew less.

"There's this museum here," he began. "Used to be a hospital hundreds of years ago." Improvise, he told himself! Concoct, contrive! "There's a legend."

"A legend?"

Every town in this fucking country had a legend. Go for it.

"A young nun," he offered, the first thought coming into his mind.

"A nun?"

He glanced at her, sensing her anticipation. Why hadn't he come up with something more outrageous, less cliché? A raid by the Mongolians, a sword duel between two bishops.

"Bet she fell in love," Mary Lou said

Scott looked at her full on.

"How'd you guess?

"They always do. Bet she fell in love with some prince."

"No princes here, just dukes."

"Sound of Music."

"That's where it started."

"Sound of Music? Here?"

"Right here in this town," he said. Christ, she was creating the whole damn thing for him. "They ripped it off."

"The Sound of Music? You're writin' 'bout *that?*"

"The real, true story."

"*Gol-lee*! How'd you learn such a thing?'"

"You know the scene in the movie where they hide from the Nazis in the church graveyard? It was the Visigoths. I was going to run over there this afternoon and research the place."

"Could I..?"

"What?"

"Go with you?"

"It's just research, you'd be bored."

"Gollee, no, I'd never!"

"I don't know," he frowned. She'd taken the bait, was on the line.

"Please? Oh, please?"

"It's a three-block walk," he said thoughtfully. "In the rain."

"Please? I won't be a bother."

She was hugging his arm, her head dropping onto his shoulder, breasts almost fully exposed. He glanced at his watch as though thinking it over.

"Ten minutes?"

"I'll be down in five!"

She started away excitedly.

"Oh," he called after her. She turned back. "This raincoat of mine's a mess. Could I borrow your husband's slicker? That blue one, with the hood?"

"Five minutes," she said, and was gone.

Holy shit, he thought to himself. Could it work, really work? Could he actually walk out of this place in plain view of the Mercedes, arm in arm with her, dressed in her husband's rain slicker? They were both, he and Billy Joe, about the same height. He was more muscular, but inside that slicker who could tell the difference? All they'd see, which they'd seen before, was Mary Lou and her husband off for a stroll.

A wave of sudden doubt swept over him, followed by a surge of panic. Suppose the pair in the Mercedes saw through it. Suppose as he lay there bleeding to death in the street from a volley of shots, the last thing he'd see as she pressed her mouth to his in farewell, were those incredible breasts. It was just too brazen an idea, too ridiculous. He'd tell her when she came down he'd changed his mind. But what other recourse did he have? It was this or nothing, and nothing left no end to this but certain disaster.

She was down in four minutes flat, flushed with the promise of adventure, dressed in her plastic rain gear, Billy Joe's blue slicker in hand. She looked like…given any other circumstance…but his plight trumped all thoughts about that.

"You're shiverin'," she said, as she helped him into the slicker. "You could use a hot bath."

"I don't do well in cold," he lied.

She rubbed her hands vigorously up and down his spine as he zipped up the slicker.

"Ooo, you a strong one."

"Set?"

She nodded she was. He pulled the slicker's hood over his head, involuntarily drew in his breath, moved with her toward the door, hesitated, then pushed through it.

It was cold in the street, the temperature dropping, the rain turned to a thin drizzle. Wind moaned through overhead wires. First a Gaulish center, then an outpost of Rome, the surrounding buildings reflected their heritage with carved door panels and lavoirs. The Mercedes, he saw with a furtive glance, was in position, maintaining its vigil. Slipping his arm into Mary Lou's, trying to act for all the world as natural and normal as he could, he led her off. But natural wasn't easy. His breath was labored, his legs little better than rubber bands. The street they were on, rue Paterne, doglegged to the right thirty yards down, which would put them out of sight of the two vigilantes. *If* he could pass for Billy Joe. *If* they bought it. *If* they could make it. It had come to this. His whole damn world, his life, boiled down to a two letter word!

She was chattering, had been doing so since leaving the hotel.

"They just gonna go crazy 'bout this when I get back, meetin' up with a famous…We big on religion an' spirituality, but nothin' like nuns runnin' off. You suppose they did it while she was still wearin' the veil?"

He stiffened. A car was coming behind them, coming fast. His eyes closed, heart pounding. And then the explosion! His body went ramrod straight, lifting him onto his toes as though from the impact of a shot, followed instantly by the odor, which had to be cordite!

"Ugh, that's smelly!"

His eyes popped open to see a Renault roaring past, the stench of petrol fumes from its backfire trailing behind it. Scott's chin dropped to his chest. He was going crazy, imagining, jumping at shadows.

"We're not really married, you know, Billy Joe an' me. We jus' been sayin' that. Tryin' things out. A trip they say's the way you can tell. Two days in Paris I was ready to take the next plane home, but he starts blubberin' like a baby. So I'm really not, you know…"

He tried to take control of his body, but his mouth kept filling with saliva. His hands and legs were trembling.

"You just shiverin' all over." She clutched his arm, pulled him in, her body close against his, in rhythm with his as they walked, her right leg locked in step with his left. "There, isn't that better?"

They'd reached the angle in the street that cut off view of them from the Mercedes. Ahead was an intersection, the Boulevard Hôtel-Dieu. He was walking fast, Mary Lou almost at a trot to keep up.

"When we get back, I'm puttin' you in a shower, rub you down."

Scott's eyes, as they turned the corner onto the boulevard, were on the museum fifty yards ahead with its sober façade, slate roof, and Gothic spires. What he was going to do when they reached it, he had no plan. All he hoped was there'd be people. It was a Sunday, so there should be. Museums were free on Sundays in France. There'd be safety in people. To his relief, he saw a tour bus outside the entrance. That meant tourists. A crowd. He drew cold burning air into his lungs and glanced at Mary Lou. She'd been waiting for a response to her offer and her face was filled with pout, annoyed that he had not responded in the way she'd expected. His answering smile was rather sickly, but she took comfort that it was agreement.

She reaffirmed her clutch on his arm, clung to him as they hurried along. He knew that if he wanted to he could pull her into any alley and that she wouldn't resist. He thought about it. But his legs, tramping toward the museum's entrance, outfought the thought. Outside the museum a uniformed guard in raincoat stood duty alongside a kiosk selling cold and hot drinks, packaged Danish, Croque Monsieurs, and candy. Reaching the museum, they swept through entrance gates into the courtyard.

Three interconnecting buildings with roofs of red, brown, yellow, and green glazed tiles greeted them, along with a well of Gothic ironwork in the center of the courtyard.

"Ooo, I never!" Mary Lou gushed, looking about in wide-eyed wonder.

Aside from a mixture of sightseers, Nikon Coolpix indiscriminately clicking away, there was a party of English tourists, thirty of them by Scott's guess, surrounding a French Tour Guide. In her forties, she carried an umbrella, held high, as a beacon for her group to follow. She was lecturing in English.

"…was founded in 1443, when Burgundy was ruled by Duke Philip the Good. The Hundred Years War had recently…"

"I want to see the graveyard. Can we see the graveyard?" Mary Lou pleaded.

What graveyard, what was she talking about? Oh, he recalled. *That* graveyard. The Visigoths. Was there one? He didn't know.

"Why was it first a hospital?" one of the tourists was interrupting the Tour Guide's narrative.

"We'll cover that on the bus on the way back to Macon," she answered and continued on about the Treaty of Aras.

"I want to see the *graveyard!*" Mary Lou was insisting.

Scott wasn't listening. He was back in his own thoughts, a jumble of confusion. He was exhausted, but his brain wouldn't stop working. But working toward what? It was as if the needle was stuck in a groove. He tried to hurl his thoughts forward. But there was that throbbing, drowning everything out, all thought, all reason, when...

"We'll cover that on the bus on the way back to Macon," she'd said. "On the bus." On the *bus?*

He was faintly aware of a voice. Mary Lou's. She was mid-sentence, a long one.

"...so I told him I'm havin' my period, which is a falsehood, jus' didn't want him doin' it, so I thought it's time I tell him, go on, go back, catch a plane, go home, I'd just stay on, could see how a writer does it — work, I mean..."

"I'm going to get us some coffee."

"Hunh?"

"Back in a sec, stay here." He reached down, gave her a reassuring kiss on the neck. "Lots to talk about." The last thing he saw of her as he headed out was the low-lidded glow of expectation on her face.

The Euro-Star Tour Coach was parked at the curb outside the Hotel-Dieu, motor running, which fed the heating system inside the vehicle, the driver seated, bent forward, dozing in luxuriating warmth against his wheel. The rap on the right side front door startled him upright. Scott was standing there, saying something the driver could not understand. The better to do so, the driver cracked open the door.

"I'm sick. Have to sit down. I'll wait for the others inside." Scott said.

The driver, a burly ex-trucker, who understood no English, shook his head.

"Les autres sont encore à l'intérieur," Scott pointed. "J'ai obtenu de s'asseoir."

The driver nodded, opened the door wide, admitting Scott, closed it after him as Scott made his way to the back, slid into a seat, ducked low. He looked at his watch. Twelve-forty. Just that? That's all it was? Aside from his meager breakfast, he hadn't eaten in thirty-six hours. Well, that would have to wait. He wasn't out of this, not by a long shot, but there was light at the end of this nightmare.

He glanced at the window, saw his reflection, tried to tell himself it was all a bad dream. He'd had bad dreams before in his life, that gigantic pin cushion, but this was no dream. He tried to write it off as delusional insanity. But it wasn't. From that first night he'd been taken in by Medlock he should have recognized the signs, seen it coming. He was extraneous, superfluous, expendable, sent into a world as secretive and self-protecting as anything in a Dan Brown novel. And yet the assignment had sounded so simple. If he'd only known.

Nine

The limousine, as the Plaza-Athénée had assured it would be, was there and waiting for Scott at eight the next morning. He'd had a bad night, and the time change was only part of it. Awakening at three, he'd stewed over having been taken by that fucking French bitch. He'd never paid for a whore in his life, which was not the worst of it: *400 euros?* He'd been so mad about it, he'd tipped her two hundred more, just to show her who she was dealing with. For an hour before falling asleep, he'd tried to do a calculation, what the night had meant in dollars, always coming up with a different figure, finally settling on something near 800 — *$800?* The French would pay for that. He didn't know how or when, but they'd pay. He'd ordered room service at six, a full breakfast of freshly juiced oranges from Israel, shirred Belgium eggs, Danish ham, Ethiopian coffee, French baguette, Irish butter, with a side order of Russian caviar. The bill, he saw at a glance, was 120 euros. He tipped fifty more, showered, dressed, gathered his wallet, room key, passport, and the small envelope Sykes had given him bearing the key to the bank safety deposit box. Placing all inside his travel jacket, he slipped it on, took the elevator down, and walked out the entrance to the waiting limo.

The ride to the address Scott gave the driver, 17 rue Bassano, took three minutes, which explained the look on the driver's face when he was told the destination. Further, the bank, upon arrival — a Crédit Lyonnais as Sykes had said — was still closed, not open 'til nine. Pretending it was fully expected, Scott told the driver to go on, walked three blocks to the Champs-Élysées, bought an English language Herald Tribune from a kiosk, found a corner brasserie, took an outside table, and ordered a café latte.

The news on the front page was boring — not even a crash at the air show. The President of France was seen at one of the city's leading restaurants, Taivellent, with his wife and mistress, and much was made of their gowns. A waiter brought his latte, which he paid for, over tipping per usual, and then he glanced at his watch — twenty-five minutes to go. He gave up on the paper and occupied himself with passersby.

Virtually every person, man and woman, walking alone, was on a cell phone. Those in a group? Not a cell phone in sight. His attention span on that complexity quickly waning, he turned his attention to the parade of young women passing before him. Scott had a grading system, and he never hesitated to apply it. Zero to three points for their ass. Same for face. Zero to two for breasts. Six points total minimum and they qualified, if barely, to go to bed with him. Sevens were his usual target. Eights? Needle in a hay stack, but they could be found. Like that model in New York.

He sat back, hands clasped behind the back of his head, doing instant calculations. A five passed by. A four. A six. Another four. Hey! This was supposed to be Paris! Where were the sevens, let alone eights he'd always heard about? He was about to give up on the game, go back to his paper, when…

The first thing he noticed was she was walking alone, and not on a cell phone. Dressed in jeans, short sleeved shirt, purse slung over her shoulder, she wore oversized dark glasses, hiding her face. But there was something. He couldn't put it together, but something. Familiar. The way she carried herself, her walk. He rose quickly and moved out onto the sidewalk.

She was walking briskly, as he threaded his way through the crowd, following her along the Boulevard, heading toward the Rond-Point, crossing Rue Pierre Charron, almost losing her at the stop light. Then on again, across Rue Marbeuf. Her stride was long and athletic, and he had to hurry to keep up. At Rue de Marignan she waited out a taxi, crossed, and started to enter the Franklin D. Roosevelt Metro entrance when she heard a voice.

"Tally?"

She turned, lowered her sun glasses to the bridge of her nose, and stared over the rim at the one person in the world she neither expected nor wanted to see.

"What're you *doing* here?" he asked with a grin.

"What're you?"

"Oh. Well. I sold a concept to the *New Yorker*," he lied. "They sent me over. Research. Staying at the Plaza-Athénée."

"Bully for you."

She turned, started to enter the Metro station.

"Can I buy you a drink?" he offered.

She looked back. "It's a quarter to nine in the morning."

"How 'bout coffee?"

She studied him for a moment, narrowed the distance between them. The chill on her face had not dissolved.

"Why?"

"Look. Okay. I acted like an…"

"…ass hole," she finished the sentence for him.

"That wasn't exactly the phrase I'd have used."

"Good bye, Scott."

She started to turn away again.

"Just coffee," he pleaded.

She thought about it a moment, stared off down the Avenue. It was beginning to thin, people heading into buildings, down into the Metro, on their way to work.

"Coffee," she said.

They crossed back over the Rue de Marignan to the corner brasserie — every corner in Paris seemed to have one — took possession of a small outdoor table, Tally ignoring the chair next to Scott, seating herself across from him. Her face remained stone, immutable, a deafening silence between them till a waiter arrived.

"M'amselle, M'sieur," said the waiter, order pad poised.

"Coffee for me. Café," said Scott, as he gestured to Tally for hers.

"Café au lait, s'il vous plait, à la cannelle, si vous en avez."

"A la cannelle, oui, M'amselle."

Her accent was lyrical, perfect, which raised Scott's eyebrows as the waiter withdrew.

"Where'd you learn to do *that?*" he asked.

"You wanted to talk," she said. "About what?"

"Just catch up on good old times."

"We *had* no good old times."

"Yeah, well…" He pushed on, trying to keep things going. "How're things back at the shop?"

"I'm not with 'the shop' anymore."

"They dropped you? They're crazy. You were one of the best they had."

"Scott…"

"So what *are* you doing here?"

She sat back for a moment as though thinking whether or not to answer. Decided with a shrug.

"I'm taking classes." Her voice was flat, expressionless.

"Classes."

"At l'Atelier des Sens."

"What's that?"

"Cooking school."

"Cooking? You're kidding."

"I don't think so."

"Here?"

"Angers."

"Where's that?"

"Loire Valley. I'm here for the day."

"Well, then, maybe we can…"

"No."

"A couple of hours…"

"No."

"I always liked you, Tally," Scott said, defensively. "I really liked you."

She laughed, a low, sardonic laugh.

"What's so funny?"

"Two years out of college I fell in love. His name was — well, it doesn't matter what his name was. We got engaged. On the day of our wedding, I marched down the aisle with my father, and there stood the love of my life in his tuxedo, smiling and handsome as all get out, his four grooms on his side, my bridesmaids on mine. The minister started in with the 'We're gathered here today…' I raised my hand, asked if I could say a few words first. Everyone was sort of startled, but I turned to my friends, told them how I'd loved their friendship throughout my life, told my grade school teacher, Mrs. Johnson, how I'd always remember her encouragement and inspiration, told my parents how I cherished their love and sacrifice. As for my maid of honor, my best friend, Betsy, I turned to her, and thanked her — for fucking the brains out of my fiancé the night before. She ran from the room in hysterics. Not my fiancé. He was looking at me, his face swelling and red. "I always liked you, Tally," he said. "I really liked you.""

Reaching inside her purse, she found a ten euro note, tossed it on the table.

"For the coffee."

She rose, crossed the street to the Metro station, and disappeared inside.

For a long moment Scott sat. The waiter returned with the order, placed the cups on the table. Scott nodded at the note, told him in French as best he could remember, to keep the change, stewed over his coffee, searching a conclusion, till he found one. French women weren't the only bitches in this world. Downing his coffee in a gulp, he pushed away from the table, headed back up the Boulevard.

Returning to the Crédit Lyonnais on Rue Bassano, now open, Scott entered the bank. Approaching a uniformed guard seated just off the entrance, Scott asked, "Safety deposit?"

The guard pointed with a pencil toward a counter. A sign above it read, "Coffres-Forts." Crossing to it Scott waited out the arrival of an attendant.

"Puis-je vous aider, Monsieur?" the attendant asked.

"J'ai quelque chose dans une boite de sécurité je tiens à déposer," Scott replied in the best French he could muster, handing the attendant his numbered key. "Voici ma clé."

"If you'd sign here, please, name printed, then signature," the attendant answered in English, turning a register around for Scott.

God*damn* the son of a bitch! Scott hated that. He spoke the fucking language, give him a break! His temper was nearing the breaking point. He fought to hold it.

"Merci," he mumbled as he printed his name then scribbled his signature where called for.

The attendant verified the name and key number on a computer, nodded.

"If you'd follow me, sir," the attendant said, returning Scott's key.

The safe deposit box enclosure was traditional, floor to ceiling, with metallic locked boxes of varying sizes. The one the attendant led Scott to was small. Stepping aside he indicated Scott was to insert his key. Scott did so. The attendant followed with his, unlocked the box, withdrew, allowing Scott privacy as he opened the box, removed, to his surprise, the sole item secreted within: a ten-by-six inch nylon travel organizer, two inches thick, zipper locked. Looking into the box again, Scott saw that was it. The travel organizer, nothing more. His eyes dropped to it. The one thing he noticed was it had heft to it. Slipping it into the deep side pocket of his travel vest, Scott closed the box, withdrew his key, nodded to the attendant, and made his way out.

The walk back to the hotel gave Scott a chance to resurrect his ego. He was going to allow a hooker, a deposed coworker, a French bank functionary to ruin his day? Like hell! In his pocket, he knew, in that innocuous, nylon travel organizer, was the gateway to…what was it Medlock had said? Complete the assignment and there'd be rewards beyond Scott's imagination! He tried to assess what Medlock had meant by that. $100,000? $200,000? He'd hold out for two. 200,000! Wait a min. Just who was the one in the *cat bird* seat! Hell, why not that Manhattan condo Medlock had put him into just before coming over. Why not that? Along with another fifty thousand! Or hundred! Or two! His head abuzz with dreams of exaltation, he increased his step. He'd get to his room, order a massage, make a reservation at — where had the paper said the

French president ate? — Taillevent! Rested and sated he'd then open the packet and contemplate his road to riches.

Reaching the hotel, he entered, crossed to an elevator, took it to his floor, emerged, crossed to his suite, inserted his card key in the door lock. The door wouldn't open. Twice more he tried, jamming the key in and out, and twice more nothing. Scott pulled back in a rage. This was the Plaza-Athénée, one of the top hotels in Paris, and his fucking *door key* wouldn't work?

Storming back into the elevator, he got off on the ground floor and headed into the lobby, where he found Monsieur Jardet in conversation with a hotel guest. Barging in, Scott waved the plastic card key in Jardet's face.

"The goddamn key to my room…!"

"Monsieur?"

"It doesn't work!"

"It works perfectly, Monsieur."

"Not this key!"

"You are correct."

"Wha..?"

"The lock has been changed."

"Why?"

"Excusez-moi, Madame," Jardet said, turning to the hotel guest. "Je serai avec vous dans un instant." Then, back to Scott, "Because it is no longer your room, Monsieur."

Scott stared at the man, stunned.

"What are you talking about?"

"I favored Monsieur Medlock in New York with a call. He has never heard of you."

Scott's mouth worked twice before words came out.

"That's bullshit!"

"Bullshit?" Jardet asked with a shake of his head, unfamiliar with the term.

"Merde!"

"Ah! Charmant." Reaching inside his breast coat pocket, he pulled out an envelope. "Votre compte, Monsieur. If you would pay at the desk."

Scott ripped open the envelope, pulled out a single sheet of paper, and gasped at the bill.

"This is crap!"

Jardet shook his head, again not understanding the word.

"Merde!"

"Ah. Encore," Jardet nodded.

"I'm not going to pay it!"

"Your valise and personal effects are meanwhile being held in security. Quite safe."

"3,420 fucking *euros?* What *is* this?"

"*This,* Monsieur, is the Plaza-Athénée," Jardet answered, and turned back to his guest.

To most travelers, the Hotel Galileo on Rue Galilée, a few short blocks from the Plaza-Athénée, was the warm, charming, elegant boutique hotel as advertised. "Sophisticated comfort," the brochure in English found at the front desk rightly claimed. "Air conditioning, hair dryer, direct dial telephone, cable and satellite TV, mini-bar, and safe." 275 euros a night for a single, with breakfast. To Scott, as he stood in the small though tastefully appointed room he'd been given with its simple classic décor, it was going from state room to steerage.

Tossing his Tumi suitcase onto the bed, Scott collapsed beside it, along with the bagged possessions he'd left lying about in his hotel suite. Christ, he hated this town. *Hated* it! Couldn't wait to get the hell out! Sooner the better.

Pushing off the bed, he crossed with the bagged items to the small desk by the window, and scowled at the view outside. Though well maintained with manicured shrubs and flowering plants, it was, to Scott, the size of a ping pong table.

Dumping the contents of the bag on the desk, he separated the map of Paris, the Guide Michelin, and the booklet of Metro tickets he'd been given by Sykes from other items, and tossed the bag with the rest onto the bed. Trashing the Metro tickets into the waste paper basket, he reached inside his travel vest, pulled out the organizer, unzipped it, and removed its contents. There was a copy of the original agreement Medlock had had drawn up, notarized, which Scott stuffed back inside his travel vest, an inside pocket, zipped closed.

At first blush, the rest of the contents seemed unremarkable. There was a Michelin map of France, cities, towns, roads, rail lines, airports. rivers, canals clearly marked, as well as a single local untitled map, identified simply with a number: sixty-five. There was a green Michelin paperback designated "Burgundy Jura". A yellow post-it was affixed to page 359. Vezelay. Population 492. 226 kilometers south-east of Paris. Astoundingly the village was accorded three stars. "Highly recommended. Worth a detour," the legend at the front of the book advised. Across the post-it were scribbled three words. "Read and familiarize."

Opening the book to the designated page, Scott immediately saw the reason for the exalted designation. Built on the ridge of a hill rising above the Cure Valley, the town's main road ran up its spine, flanked by two or three restaurants, a small hotel or two, a bakery and florist, along with the usual tourist shops, ending at its aggrandized attraction, the Basilique Ste-Marie-Madeleine. Founded in the ninth century, the text explained, it was at the height of its glory when, legend had it, Richard The Lionheart, King of England, met with the Duke of Burgundy in 1186 to launch Richard's vibrant call for the Third Crusade. "A masterpiece of Burgundian-Romanesque art," the booklet described it, "ranking with that of St Lazare at Autun…"

Scott closed the book and set it aside. Time for that later. Returning to the organizer, he culled out what remained. There was a voucher for a mid-sized car from Alamo Car Rental. And another for an open reservation at the Compostelle Hotel in Vezalay, eighteen rooms, no restaurant, "assez confortable," according to Michelin, 260 euros a night.

The final was an unmarked envelope. Tearing it open, Scott found a single sheet of type-written paper, headed by the words, "Read and destroy." He read it over. Twice. The "procurement" he was to thieve, if that was the word and it was, had already been described in detail by Medlock, and now was again. The *how* of that procurement was left to Scott.

But a mid-sized car and an "assez confortable" hotel? He glanced at the Michelin listings for Vezelay again, noticed the Hotel L'Esperance, three stars, accommodations and restaurant. He'd heard of it. It was famous. More than famous. Had one of the great kitchens of France. Three kilometers outside of the town, 1,500 euros a night for a suite. Reviewing the vouchers for the mid-sized car and hotel one final time, he balled them up, tossed them after the Metro tickets, picked up the phone, called the receptionist at the front desk. She was African and spoke perfect English, he'd noticed when he checked in. More than that, she was a fucking knockout. He wondered what time she got off work, what plans she had for the evening, The wheels were already grinding in his head about what he could do about that when she came on the line.

"Monsieur Fitzgerald, bonjour."

"It is indeed."

"May I help you."

"Yes, if you would. . . sorry, never got your name."

"Veronique."

"Beautiful. Where from?"

"Nigeria."

"Always wanted to visit."

"A spectacular country — if you're in oil."

Scott laughed

"How *can* I help you?" she asked.

"Three things."

"D'accord."

"I want an open reservation at l'Esperance in Vezelay, beginning tomorrow night. A suite."

"If possible. It *is* their high season."

"Whatever the rate. I mean that. Whatever. And who would I call for a luxury car rental?"

"My suggestion? Auto Europe."

"Could you get them on the line?"

"Of course. And third?"

"What time do you get off work? I was thinking Taillevent."

"My husband picks me up at six."

"Ah-ha."

"But there are escort services, Monsieur. What price range were you considering?"

Ten

Another storm cell had settled in, this one accompanied by lightning and thunder. From his seat, crouched low and alone in the back of the Euro-Star Tour Coach, Scott watched in cold sweat through a rain-streaked window. Finally, there they were: the English tourists hurrying from the Hotel Dieu, some with umbrellas, some with papers held over their heads. True to the indomitable spirit of the British, none complained, patiently waiting in line — to Scott's teeth-clenched exasperation — climbing onto the bus, one by one, past their hooded French guide who stood in the rain, counting their number as they boarded.

Come on, *come on!* Scott silently urged them up and on, the veins in his neck like wire cables. Get your fucking asses!

Satisfied all were accounted for, the guide boarded herself, nodded to the driver, took her front row jump seat as the door was drawn closed and the bus thankfully began to roll. Ten minutes and they were on N47, headed south out of Beaune toward Macon.

The rush of air pouring from Scott's mouth lasted eight seconds. He closed his eyes, rocked his head side to side in pure relief. He was out of it, safe, it was over. *Christ*, what a day, and it was not even half gone! He'd never been to Macon, knew only that it was a mid-sized city, and mid-sized cities throughout the country had rail stations, leading to an interlocking system that could take you anywhere in the country you wanted to go. Just get him to Macon, that's all he asked. Then on to Nantes. There was that airport in Nantes, with flights to London. And it would be done, over, finished! Pray they had a TGV in Macon that could make the trip in two hours. But he'd take what they had. That was *two* for the French. Their fucking bread and their trains.

Staring out the window, through lessening rain now, Scott saw through half-lidded eyes the rolling hills of Southern Burgundy, undulating and green. Ten more minutes and they were running alongside a canal, boats of all sizes, lock houses brimming with mini-vegetable gardens and geraniums. Poplar and plane trees lined the banks above ancient long abandoned hard-packed dirt paths where barrel-bellied Selle Français horses once lumbered along, hauling barges. On through a tiny twelfth century village. Then rolling hills and farmland again, Beaune mercifully further and further behind.

Never in his life had Scott felt so tired. He'd been going on adrenalin, and now it was seeping away. *Jesus*, what an ordeal. But he'd licked it. Beaten the bastards. Finally. He guessed it was an hour to Macon. Maybe he could catch some sleep before they arrived. He sat back, closing his eyes, only half aware, caring less that the tour guide was on her feet, wireless microphone in hand, her voice amplified through speakers.

"The Hundred Years War had recently been brought to a close," she was saying. "Massacres, however, continued with marauding bands, pillaging and provoking misery and famine. The people of Beaune were declared destitute. Nicolas Rolin, Duke Phillip the Good's Chancellor, and his wife Guigné de Salins, reacted by deciding to create a hospital and refuge for the poor..."

The tour guide's voice, which was close to putting Scott to sleep, suddenly stopped. Mid-sentence. Just stopped. Scott's eyes snapped open. She was standing, he saw, at the front of the bus, microphone in hand, staring at her complement of tourists. Something was bothering her. She started up the aisle, pointing left and right with her mike, mumbling in French. She was counting heads!

Reaching Scott, she stood a moment, brow furrowed, perplexed. She turned, began to retrace her steps, counting heads once again, Scott watching with a growing sense of dread. Reaching the front of the bus, she thought for a moment, turned, and brought the microphone to her lips.

"Would you hold up your vouchers, please," she said. "Everyone, each of you. Vouchers."

The tour bus pulled off the road and braked to a stop. Its door gasped open, discharging Scott. Stumbling to keep from falling, he turned back to the 230-pound driver who stood in the doorway.

"I'll pay! I've got money!" he protested, holding out his wallet as the driver drew the door closed.

"I'll pay, I'll pay!" Scott screamed, running alongside the bus as it pulled back onto the road and away.

Slowing his run to a stop, Scott stared after the disappearing bus in disbelief.

"Shit! *Shit!*"

He turned to see where he was and saw he'd been deposited at a service area. Signs told of fast food and a cafeteria in a single, low-lying building. Also refueling and shopping facilities. Two or three cars were in the immense gravel parking area, but mostly trucks. Twelve- to eighteen-wheelers. Three or four of them. Scott tried to get his bearings. Across from a woods, he was out in the middle of nowhere. He thought about trying to hitchhike. He didn't know if they did that in France, had never seen anyone trying. It was then he realized where he was standing. At the edge of the road, exposed, to any and all passersby as cars whizzed past. Fear — an emotion he was becoming more and more familiar with — began to grip him. He began to back away from the road toward the building, when there was a shout, a man's voice.

"Non, non, monsieur, arrêtez, ne vous déplacez pas!"

Scott spun about, froze. What he expected was not what he saw. Directly before him was a family of four, a man, woman, two preteen children, down on all fours, turning over pebbles in the parking area, one by one.

"Pardon, excusez-moi," the man apologized. From the look on his face he was in deep distress. "Nous étions ici il y a deux heures. Ma femme a perdu le diamant de son anneau de mariage."

Scott shook his head, not understanding.

"Ring," the man tried in English. "Diamond." He showed the setting on his wife's ring. Its diamond was missing. He gestured, trying to find the word to explain. "Disparu. Disparu. Dans les pierres," the man said, pointing to the gravel.

"Oh," Scott answered. "Sorry."

He turned, took a step, and stopped. Six inches from the toe of his shoe was a small glistening object. He picked it up, turned, and handed it to the man whose mouth fell open. As did his wife, who slowly rose, incredulous at the sight of her lost diamond. Never in a million years, their expressions said, had they ever expected to retrieve it.

"Je ne le crois pas. Je n'ai pas estime! Incroyable! *Incroyable!*"

The man dug into his pocket removed his wallet, pulled out a handful of euros, and looked at Scott with reverence. Scott threw up his hands, palms out in refusal as he backed away.

"No, no. Glad to have helped."

He turned and walked quickly into the building.

Inside, to the left, was a shop, its merchandise eclectic. Regional specialties, foodstuffs, newspapers, magazines, and books. Even clothing and electronic equipment, and an ATM. Across from him, two or three travelers sat at a fast-food and sandwich counter. To his right was a cafeteria.

On the wall between the shop and sandwich counter was a sign. "Toilettes." With an arrow.

The restroom was unisex — men to one side, women the other, with the two areas separated by wash basins. Hurrying in, Scott entered the men's side, moved to one of the two urinals, began to relieve himself — a hot, long stream — aware he had not done so since the balloon landing, and found himself staring at his image in the mirror above the urinal. His face he saw was flushed. Panic, fear? He pitched his head forward, forehead against the mirror as the flow poured from him. His breath was shallow, his pulse was racing. He was in an isolated outpost from all he could see, no transportation, a fucking sitting duck if they caught up to him, no place to run, no place to hide.

"Allemand?"

Scott pulled back, looked to the adjoining urinal, saw a short, thick man with an agreeable smiling face, rough clothing, an obvious trucker given the truck design and "Interglobal" stitched on his cap.

"Vous êtes allemand?"

He was asking, Scott realized, if he were German.

"No."

"Ah," the man answered. "J'essaie de deviner. Comment puis-je dire?" He seemed disappointed. "I try to guess," he said in English.

No interest in conversation, Scott shook himself off, zipped up his pants, and moved on to the wash basins.

The cafeteria, Scott found, slumping into a chair at an isolated corner table, was loaded with truckers, sitting quietly by themselves, sleeves rolled up to reveal a gallery of tattoos. Hungry though he was — he would have eaten anything — the menu that was placed before him brought him upright. There were three options that day. Beyond a choice of two starters, there were main course offerings of a charcuterie, a pork rillettes, or poulet Basquoise, along with fromage blanc or assiette fromage for dessert. A penned note at the top of the menu listed, in French, a shower for two euros, three euros with towel. For one brief moment all thoughts of impending disaster gave way to the poulet Basquoise, which he ordered with a glass of Sancerre.

He was half way through an unexpectedly delicious meal when a second, half-eaten plate clattered onto his table. Startled, he looked up to see his grinning companion from the urinals dropping onto a chair before him. He'd not only brought his lunch, but his wine and utensils.

"If you vant to eat vell en route en France you look for trucks, vere zee routiers stop." the man said in surprising if heavily accented English. "Relais routiers. Vy not. Ees hard life behind zee veel."

It took an instant for Scott to assess the intrusion as a blessing. Seated across from him, his back to the room, the trucker's wide body screened Scott off from view.

"Vous parlez Anglais," Scott said.

"En France? Everyone speak English. Zay jus' don' like to."

You could fool me, Scott thought, but answered, "You thought I was German?"

"Zee pink face. All Germans haf pink faces."

For an instant Scott didn't get it. Then he did. He'd seen it himself, in that mirror. He looked warily over the trucker's shoulder, instinctively on guard.

"You're here viz someone. I intrude," said the trucker.

"No. No, I'm alone."

"Driving vere?"

Scott thought about that. "I don't know."

"Pardon?" the trucker asked, eyebrows raised.

"I'm without a car."

The trucker's eyebrows raised higher in question.

"I got a lift this far."

"Lift?" asked the trucker, not understanding.

"Some people drove me from Beaune. It's as far as they could go."

"Vot do you do in Beaune? For zee wine?"

Scott nodded, yes. Why not? "I was there for a tour of the vineyards."

"Romanée Conti?"

"Yes."

"You saw it? Zee most famous in Burgundy. Napoleon made hiss troops salute ven zey marched by."

"Yes, they mentioned that," the lies went on.

"And vere do you go?"

"Macon, if I can get there."

"Ah," said the trucker with a hand slap on the table. "I go to Lyons. Iss trou Macon."

"Jesus, you're kidding. I'll pay."

"Non, non."

"Fifty euros. A hundred!" Scott reached for his wallet.

"Un plaisir," the trucker replied with that grin. "I practice my English."

With a relief Scott hadn't experienced since the tour bus vacated Beaune, Scott bolted his food, washing it down with his wine, looked across to see the trucker had finished just as quickly. The lunch bills paid, the trucker rose.

"Vee go," he said, rising, Scott rising with him.

"What are you driving?" Scott asked as they crossed to the exit.

"Ten tons," the trucker replied, pushing through into sunlight, the door held open for Scott who emerged nose to nose with the fleet of parked trucks.

"Which one's yours?" Scott asked.

"Behind zee Renault," the trucker said, grabbing Scott's arm, leading him around an eighteen wheeler. It was not a light touch, Scott realized. The man's grip was iron. In seconds Scott saw why. Behind the Renault was not a truck. It was the black Mercedes. The man in the brown suit and dark glasses Scott had encountered at the balloon site stood by the rear door, holding it open, as the trucker led Scott toward it.

Eleven

The rental Scott had leased at the Paris Auto Europe agency, with extras, was 1,133 euros a day, plus tax. 490 horse power, thirty-two valves, six-speed transmission, the sleek red Ferrari F430 Scuderia passed everything on the auto route south as though imbedded in stone. A police car, lying in wait for speedsters at a turn out, gave up any thought of trying to catch it as it hurtled by.

It wasn't boyish delight with a new toy that had Scott's foot jamming the accelerator to the floorboard. It was anger. Pure, unadulterated outrage. Paris had been a disaster, a humiliation, and it left him in an ugly mood that the Ferrari could only partly assuage. For the most part his ire centered on Tally. He'd tried to be nice, given her every opportunity to make amends. What had he gotten for it? A verbal finger. Well, there'd be a day. Knock this thing off for Medlock, then home to his promised rewards, that condo among them, he'd damn well insist on that. He'd throw a party, invite her, invite them all, shove his newly acquired opulence and notoriety up their noses. Yeah. That was it. That sounded right. Way to go, and damn if he wouldn't!

He slowed, approaching an off ramp, D944, took it, southeast off the auto route through Voutenay sur Cure. With the growl of the downshifted engine, the Ferrari wound along a country road now, through verdant hillocks, dotted with chateaux and watermills, then south on D951 to the outskirts of Vezalay.

Pulling to the side of the road, Scott stared up at the long, narrow hill town on a rising ridge of land, surmounted by its eleventh century Basilique Ste-Marie Madeleine. Less a town, more a village, there within sight was the object of his mission, the means to a lifestyle long dreamed of, and, more sweetly, revenge. If there was one thing Scott understood, it was revenge. He saw himself as a black belt in revenge.

Slipping the car into gear, he drove on a kilometer more, turned in at an elegant entrance flanked by white walls, each adorned with a large M, lettering above spelling "L'Esperance" on one side, "Marc Meneau" on the other. At the chateau-like three-story building at the end of the white cobble-stoned parking area, Scott pulled the Ferrari to a stop between a Maserati and a Rolls.

The check-in lobby off the entrance was simple, its unattended desk opening into an opulent lounge beyond. There was a button. Scott pushed it, setting his Tumi on the floor at his feet. A remarkably attractive young woman in a blue business suit, came smiling from an office behind the desk.

"Bonjour, monsieur."

"I've a reservation," he answered in English, not even bothering to try his French. "Scott Fitzgerald."

"Yes, of course, Mr. Fitzgerald," she replied, not even checking her register as he handed her his credit card. "We had that cancellation, regrettably not a suite as you requested, but are delighted to be able to accommodate you."

God, she spoke better English than he did. And, no wedding ring he noticed. Something for the file.

"We have a lovely room for you: 600 euros a night. Do you know how long you'll be staying?" she asked, running his credit card through.

"A day, I'd guess, two at the most."

"If you'd let us know, when you can."

He acknowledged he would.

"Your room is just up those stairs, number six," she said, "with a view of the village. We've held a dinner reservation for you, eight o'clock, if that's convenient. I'd suggest the terrace at seven-thirty for hors d'oeuvres and an aperitif."

She held out his card and his room key. She was holding her smile.

"If you'd like assistance with your luggage…"

"No, I've got it."

"Anything else I can do for you, my name is Huguette."

He held his tongue on that one, lifted his Tumi.

"Enjoy your stay, Mr. Fitzgerald."

The room Scott found was small, but well appointed, antique furniture, parquet floors, with the promised view of Vezalay and its crowning basilica. He unpacked his Tumi then turned to Medlock's instructions, read them over as he had a dozen times. They were limited, but clear, and he sensed the rant with which they'd been written. He looked out the window that overlooked the parking area, up at the village again. A chill went through him as in his sightline, he realized, was his target. But that was tomorrow. Tomorrow it would all happen. At worst, the day after. He'd plotted it out, how it was going to be done. All it took was cunning and personality, and that he had in spades!

At seven o'clock, following nap, shower, shave, and change of clothing into casual evening wear, Scott entered the terrace. Leather-backed chairs were situated about round glass-topped tables across from a bar. Mid terrace was a large embossed Grecian baignoire with a ten inch high white marble statuette of a naked woman, posed in thought, perched among blooming white flowers.

Ushered to a solitary table, Scott was presented with a menu for the evening. One could order a la carte if they chose, but the featured recommendation was the fourteen course dinner at 600 euros. While considering his options he was offered the promised apéritif and hors d'oeuvres, a strip of raw seasoned tuna, a disk of lamb, and a vegetable fritter.

Settling back in his chair, his eyes swept the room. It was almost filled now, with enough diamonds and pearls, he saw, to give Cartier a run for its inventory. A sense of wellbeing swept over him. This was the life. This is where he belonged, and tomorrow he'd not only *be* in their company, they'd be in *his*. Then his eyes came to a couple seated two tables away. They were not a match. He was in his early fifties, she, no more than twenty-five, both French from what little he could hear. In a low-cut dress showing off her superb breasts, she was, by Scott's calculations, a six and a half, maybe even a seven. There was a sense of urgency in her gamin face as she seemed to be making a desperate appeal, clutching her companion's arm to his stoic, silent response.

Scott put it together in seconds. He'd seen it before, in the bar at the Plaza Athenee. He was her boss. Paris, probably. She was his secretary or a girl from his office. It had likely been a coy flirtation at first, then a few lunches over which he'd told the long sad story of his deteriorating marriage. Drawn in, she'd bought his line, dreamt of their future together, leaped at the offer to go off for a weekend. And now, the weekend ending, it was all crashing down as she heard the cold hard words that he was going back to his wife. Hell, Scott realized, he'd played the same scene himself. No wife, but who knew?

The summons to dinner brought Scott to the conservatory-like dining room, floor to ceiling glass windows overlooking the garden where a family of ducks waddled around at the edge of a pool. White table cloths stretched to the carpeted floor, which was a tapestry of green and white leaves. Settling into a green leather backed chair, Scott chose the six hundred euro fourteen course dinner, bluffed his way through the wine list, ordering a white Montrachet as well as a 1988, 250 euro, red Burgundy Echezeaux, principally to show that he could pronounce it.

The size of the entrée courses when they began to arrive were modest. They had to be. Among them was poached langoustines in consommé with a spoonful of cream and caviar floated on top. Sea urchin baked in shell. Seared rare foie gras in a pool of creamed sweet corn. Oeuf de poule a la Florentine. Roasted pigeon on a bed of sweet vegetables. A small dish of raw oysters in a puree of sorrel. And glazed carrots stuffed with vegetables flavored with cumin.

It was during the latter that Scott noticed the two from the terrace. Seated across the room, their conversation, he saw, had suddenly turned heated. The man was shaking his head, no, no, as she sought to plead a point. Still no, no, with an unrelenting grimace.

The word *opportunity*, one of Scott's favorites, instinctively began to take shape in Scott's brain as multiple courses of desserts arrived. Nougats and handmade bonbons, followed by a dish of berries, then soft meringues. A small dish of nuts with dried fruit and melon balls, followed by Fraises 'Marie-Antoinette'.

He was struggling through the final entry, petit dark chocolate tarts, when it happened. Tears streaming down the girl's face, she burst from her chair, knocking it over as she ran from the room, leaving her escort sitting alone, stone faced, unyielding, and with no effort to go after her.

Calling for *la note,* Scott quickly signed, went on a search. In the deserted lounge off the check-in desk he found her. Seated at the end of a corner couch, clutching her purse, face streaked with tears, her head moved slightly side to side as though in disbelief. She wore, Scott saw, a diamond bracelet watch. Her dress, he guessed was Prada or Balenciaga, the purse by Gucci. What some guys will do to seal the deal.

"Est-ce que je peux vous faire quelque chose?" Scott asked.

"No, merci. Il ne serait pas," she replied.

"Vraiment? Rien?"

She looked up, saw him standing before her. The look on her face said he was not what she expected. Handsome as he was, well-groomed, well-dressed, there was a look of such sympathy and caring on his face.

"English?" she asked.

"*New* English."

"American."

"I couldn't help noticing you were in distress," Scott said in sympathy with a nod toward the dining room.

"There's nothing you can do," she said with a shake of her head, her English perfect.

"It's not my nature to pry…"

"Broken promises."

Scott had to hold back a smirk. Had he called *that* right. He gave it thirty minutes to his room.

"Look," he said. "I can walk with you in the garden, it's a lovely night, and you can talk about it or count the stars."

She studied him a moment, seemingly assessing his sincerity. She held out her hand.

"Monique," she said.

"Scott," he answered, taking her hand.

The walk in the garden took them around the pond. Bordered by flowering shrubs it was a world of its own, white pebbled pathways subtlety illuminated by muted ground-level lighting. The moon was full, outlining Vezalay's basilica two kilometers off at the top of the town, dominant, brooding. He made no effort to touch her as they walked. His hands were tucked into his pockets, as though that was the last thing on his mind. Sooner or later, he knew, she would lead herself into his web. Didn't they always? Christ, he thought to himself, he ought to write a book. Seduction for Dummies. Two weeks it'd be on the best seller list.

They walked in silence, the unseen web between them. She looked at him, and flew right into it.

"What are you doing here? By yourself, with no one."

"I don't want to talk about it," he said, his face seeming to fill with grief.

"I'm sorry."

"No. No, I should. It's time." He paused as though whether to go on or not. "My wife and I spent our honeymoon here. Four years ago. This week." He paused again, went on, a choke in his voice as though the memory was beyond bearing. "It was just before going on to Africa. We'd both finished our internship at Boston Medical…"

"A doctor?"

"We decided to take a year off before our residency. They had a project in Rwanda, making a water-purification system and desperately needed volunteers. She contracted Ebola. The nearest hospital was two days away. The roads were washed out by rains. And there were the rebels. She never made it."

For a moment, he stared straight ahead as though seeming to wonder if he'd betrayed some private inner grief better left unshared. He looked at her. She was staring up at him, seemingly trembling.

"I'll give you my coat," Scott said, starting to slip out of it. "You're shivering."

"It's not that kind of shiver," she said. Her hand, he noticed, had taken his arm. "It must be irreplaceable, that kind of loss."

"Nothing's irreplaceable, they say. They didn't know Tanya."

"You mean it can really be like that?"

"I shouldn't have come back here, too many ghosts."

"You had something beautiful."

"I guess it's because I try. What would we be if nobody tried to find out what was beyond? But if you talk like that, people call you crazy."

"No," she said, "that's beautiful.

It ought to be, he thought to himself. He'd ripped it off from Mary Shelley's Frankenstein.

She was holding him closer, he realized. He could feel the sway of her hip against his as they moved.

"Where do I find someone like you?" she said.

"I'm just a doctor with an absurd ambition to discover cures for the world."

"If I could just discover one for myself."

"I remember, we were in Paris…"

"I live in Paris."

He looked at her. "Really?" he said.

"I leave in the morning…"

"I love Paris…"

"But not 'til morning."

There was, he saw, what appeared to be, utter adoration on her face. Thirty minutes? Hell, make that ten.

"If I only had someone like you in my life."

"I think…" He broke off, as though what was in his mind was best left unsaid.

"What do you think?"

"…I'm there now."

What she said next came out almost in a breath.

"My room is twenty-two, third floor."

Scott opened his mouth to reply when his heart gave a great leap into his throat and was choking him. "My room," she'd said. "*My* room?" If she had a room, alone, then who was this guy with her? Definitely not what he'd supposed. Then what? What was she doing here, what *was* she? What was *he?* It was then that it struck him, the whole façade, the act, performance, the Plaza-Athénée all over again. Christ, how these French hookers worked, this one with her pimp, no less. Well, fool him once, shame on France. Fool him twice…Yet how to get out of it without igniting the rage of a Gallic prostitute scorned. Hell, he decided, go with the flow.

"I can't. Not that I don't want to, you understand, you know that I want to. I can't. Not here in this place. It'd be desecrating my wife's memory. I'm sorry. I'm terribly sorry."

With that he turned — take *that* and stuff it and you know where, he thought — and walked away.

The following morning, Scott awoke to the smug conviction he'd won one, prouder still how he'd fleshed it out and bested the — what'd the French call them? — Putains? She might be a pro. Well, so was he.

Ordering room service, he brushed his teeth, washed his face, shaved, wrapped himself in the provided hotel robe, crossed to the window with towel draped around his neck, looked up at the town, his charge, his pursuit that would eventuate in a total change in his life, when something in the parking lot below caught his attention. Monique and her pimp were in heated discussion. Hands on his hips he was shouting into her face and she was shouting back! Scott imagined what it was about and he had to smile at the thought. The pimp had brought her here to engage a rich John, and she'd wasted the night on some mid-level mourning sap from whom she got nothing!

The next thing Scott saw was the two angrily splitting off from each other, he turning to the Rolls, she, to Scott's surprise, the Maserati flanking his Ferrari. He watched as she entered the car, slammed the door closed, fired the engine, floored it, spraying white cobble stones, nearly colliding with an oncoming truck as she went through the entrance gates, roaring away. But a *Maserati?* Business had to be good!

Scott turned at the knock on his door, opened it to the arrival of his breakfast, had it set on the terrace outside his room. Less in quantity than the dinner the night before, it had its own delights. Freshly squeezed orange juice, strawberries with crème fraiche, an assortment of croissants and pastries and chocolates, a silver pot with enough coffee to float the Titanic, and, of course, champagne, as well as the ever present English language *Herald Tribune*. Downing the juice, he poured his first cup of coffee, propped his feet up on a vacant chair, holding the coffee with one hand, and opened the paper. The first page had little to offer. He turned to the second and his coffee fell out of his grasp and into his lap. The first thing he saw were their pictures, the two of them, Monique and the man he'd seen with her. They were Pierre and Monique Honfleur. The headline below their photographs said it all.

"Billionairess And Father In Fight Over Dubai Petro Oil Purchase."

The paper slipped from his fingers. God, he hated France.

Twelve

In the back seat of the Mercedes, travelling south now on the AutoRoute, the tall man in the brown suit beside him, Scott knew that unless some wholly unexpected means of escape presented itself his chances of surviving the next hour were non-existent. Soon, he knew, the car would turn off onto a side road. He'd be taken out and shot as methodically as though he were a cornered fox. He tried to clear his head, but the pounding in it made thinking difficult. He glanced at the man beside him. His head was back against the head rest. His eyes were closed as the other, the 'Trucker,' drove. Scott's lips tightened. He became aware of a slow cold rage mounting in his brain. They were going to kill him, and they didn't care whether he knew it or not!

He tried to breathe, but the muscles in his chest seemed incapable of making the effort. All his life he'd found a way out. In college, too indifferent to prepare for tests, he'd perfected a system of cheating, foolproof, undetectable. Hell, why not? What was college anyway but a proving ground to *beat* the system. Plagiarizing papers, he'd wisely abstained from the usual contemporary, shop worn sources, pirating instead from the far away and little known. The 'incident', which is all it was, at *New York In Review* Publications, had led him to Medlock, hadn't it? So how was this different? It *was* different! *Christ* was it different!

The car purred steadily on, the windows tightly shut. They'd been driving about twenty minutes, had passed through a small straggling village with a single roadside drab café, then out into undulating forested country again, when the two lane highway south narrowed to one, traffic slowing to a crawl past workmen repairing a hazard. In that second Scott acted. His self-control, seized by blind fury, suddenly left him. Before he knew what he was doing, he'd thrown open the door, hurled his weight against it and hit the road.

Half-stunned by the impact, Scott rolled clear, stumbled to his feet and made for the woods flanking the highway. Plunging through oak and beech and chestnut trees slapping at his face, he ran 'til he couldn't run any more, fell to the forest floor, gasping for breath, waiting, listening for pursuit. A red deer, flushed by his presence, bolted past, through the underbrush and was gone. Still he listened, not daring to move. A soft wind rustled tree limbs, and, too, there was the far off sound of traffic. But nothing more.

Had he done it? Had he beaten the bastards again? When just as suddenly he realized where he was. There were more than deer in these woods. There were wild boar and snakes, he'd read. Large snakes, like the asp viper. The green Michelin paperback in his packet on Burgundy had said so. And ladder snakes, and the western whip! An Egyptian vulture, that had found its way north, suddenly swooped down from a tree limb sending Scott bolting back in dread as it flew past him and away.

Choking back a surge of bile, Scott tried to take stock. His pants, he saw, had been ripped at one knee. There were scratches on the back of his hands. The dread of the forest and what could be waiting for him outside it sent him into a bout of despair. But he had to take action, to choose. Which one of the two? Lifting himself onto shaking, unsteady feet, he opted for the road. At least to see.

The route back, through shrubbery and low exposed roots he didn't see that caused him to trip and sprawl was longer than he realized, his terror of unearthing a snake adding to his fear, which was now nearing panic. Reaching the edge of the forest he peered through branches. He'd come out below the road-repair workmen and vehicles were accelerating back onto the two lanes south. Poking his head through the last of the branches, he surveyed. No sign of the Mercedes. But he'd gone through that before. Still there was no choice. He had to get to Macon, to the train station in Macon. Everything was Macon. No! God, no! It *can't* be Macon! They know about Macon. He'd told them! Then *where?*

With all the courage he could muster, which wasn't much, Scott vacated the forest, edged his way to the side of the road, did the only thing he could do, stuck his arm out, thumb emerging from his fist, begging to hitch a ride. Whether this was not the symbol for hitchhiking in France or the fact that no one cared, cars raced by him without notice. When suddenly, fifty yards down, a Citroen was pulling off the highway and stopping. Scott stared, open mouth. It was a ride? He started toward it, broke into a limping trot as a man emerged from the driver's side — and just as quickly, Scott saw why. Circling the front of his car, the driver approached a tree, unzipped his pants and urinated. Scott could only watch, hopes dashed, as the man completed his mission, zipped up his pants, returned to his car and drove away.

All hope deserting him, Scott's will gave out. Dropping to the weed-covered bank at the side of the highway, his shoulders sagged, his head dropped down between his knees. The sun, fully out now, was past its zenith. A glance at his watch told Scott how far. One thirty. *One thirty?* That was it? That was all? What did it matter. He was out in the middle of God knew where, no transportation, maybe a few kilometers back to that last so-called village they'd driven through. *Then* what? Did they even have phones? If they did, who'd he call? The Mercedes would catch up to him long before then, wherever it was, that he knew. He lifted his head, looked off into space. Maybe he'd just give up, sit there till they found him. He'd never thought about death before. What would it be like? Would it be quick? Over in a moment? Would there be suffering? A moment of astonishment and then it would be done? He fantasized the obituary again. "The Remains Of David Scott Fitzgerald…"

When all at once he was staring. A Peugeot was slowing to a stop thirty yards past him, and now, incredibly, was backing up along the shoulder. Scott slowly rose, mouth agape as the car came to a stop before him. The front passenger door opened. Inside the car he saw the family of the lost diamond he'd encountered in the parking lot of the service area.

Thirteen

Showered, Scott sat in his underwear on the edge of the bed in his room at L'Esperance reading, for the final time, Medlock's terse and commanding instructions. The spilt coffee had left a reddening welt on the inside of his thigh, but thankfully the robe had gotten the worst of it. He glanced at his watch. It was half past eleven. Folding the sheet of paper, he placed it back inside the travel folder and rose. It was time. Slipping into a cotton Smart Care raspberry shirt and tan gabardines with matching coat from Barney's in Manhattan, as well as alligator loafers by McAfee of London, extravagantly acquired for the occasion, Scott gathered car keys, room key, wallet, passport, looked at himself in the mirror. For one brief instant he had to blink as he saw a matador, primped and ready for the ring. Well, how was it different? All it lacked was cheering crowds.

The drive up the picturesque vine grown narrow spiny ridge through Vezelay, flower boxes alive with late summer geraniums, took Scott into well-preserved antiquity. Past ancient wine growers houses and Renaissance dwellings, boutiques and galleries, cafes and restaurants, and there, at the top, towering over the village, the ninth century Basilique Ste-Marie-Madeleine.

Finding an open parking space, half on, half off the sidewalk, Scott left the engine running, sat a moment in contemplation, looked toward the ancient Abbey at the top of the hill, its massive length supported by flying buttresses, with narrow bays decorated with statues of Christ, the Virgin Mary, Mary Magdalene and angels. For the first time butterflies began to dance inside his chest. A slight touch of wet broke out on his brow, and it didn't come from the late morning sun. A wave of sudden insecurity gripped him, Was he ready for this? Really ready? It all came down to now. Had he underestimated the difficulty of what he was being asked to achieve? Nothing had gone right so far since landing in France. Why would this be different? Maybe he should just take what was left of his advance, his fifty thousand, have himself one helluva joy ride, go back to New York, get a meeting with Vanity Fair, tell them about this whole thing with Medlock, get an assignment to write it up like he'd been under-cover all along, get on their staff if he could. But, Jesus, "*Riches beyond his imagination!*," Medlock had said? He shook off the furies, bolstered by bluff and greed, cut the engine, climbed from the Ferrari.

Locking the car, Scott looked about. Across the street, a half a block down from where he stood, was the Musée de l'Oeuvre-Viollet-le-Duc with its medieval sculpture and castings from the Basilica. Next to it, Maison Jules Roy, home of the exalted French writer and friend of Camus. The Musée Servos with its famed modern art, Scott saw, was one block up, across from the Galerie d'art St-Père, showing the celebrated con-temporary French artist, Georges Hosotte.

Drawing a deep breath into his lungs, Scott expelled it, crossed the street to a low swinging gate, a simple plaque on it reading "Chez Gaillard", pushed through into a flowered courtyard. Crossing, feet crunching on gravel, he came to a glass inlayed door, which was opened from the inside by an attentive waiter, admitting Scott to a well-appointed restaurant done in rose wood, indirect lighting and rose-colored table cloths. It was early and deserted.

"Bonjour, Monsieur," Scott was greeted by an arriving Maître d'.

"Etes-vous ouvert pour le déjeuner?" Scott asked.

"Of course, Monsieur. Would you like a table by the window, a view of the valley?"

Shit! Again! English!

"Merci," Scott replied, trying to force French. "Ce serait bien."

Ushered to a table overlooking the valley below with its sloping vine-yards, Scott took a chair at a table for two.

"May we offer you something to drink, Monsieur," the maître d' asked, setting a menu before Scott.

"Un verre de Margaux, si vous l'avez," Scott answered, determined.

"Margaux, of course," the maître d' replied and left Scott to the menu.

Bread was provided, along with a thin slice of pate as Scott opened the menu, his eyes traveling down the entries. They fixed on one.

"Je suis prêt," Scott told the waiter who was pouring Scott's water. "Les médaillons de gibier."

"The venison, excellent choice, Monsieur," the waiter smiled with a nod and withdrew.

Scott simmered. He was going to get the bastards for that, oh, yeah. God, did they have it coming.

Fourteen

Seated in the rear of the Peugeot along with the family's two sons, fighting nausea unrecognized as self-loathing, Scott looked out on the Gare de Lyon Part-Dieu as the car pulled up before the entrance to the station. They'd asked him where he was headed and he'd told them the train station in Lyon, avoiding the airport, fearing it would be watched. They'd asked no further questions, had taken him where he wanted to go, reassuring him, in what French he could decipher, it was not out of their way, which he doubted. The man reached back and took his hand.

"Bonne chance, Monsieur," he said, and there was a look of deep concern on his face.

The woman took his hand also. "Dieu soit avec vous," and she kissed it.

A feeling of great discomfort ran through Scott. He was unfamiliar with sincere expressions of affection, had little to draw on how to respond. He settled on a tight smile and nod of his head and climbed from the car.

Watching the Peugeot drive away, he had a sudden sense of abandonment. He looked about, seeing unseen threat among the countless passengers moving in and out of the station, many of whom were staring at him, strange looks on their faces as they passed him by. It had been a horrible day. More than that his entire experience in France had been a disaster, and all he wanted, could think about wanting was to get out of the country. Now. As fast and far as he could.

Entering the station, he sought out the scheduling board. The next train to Nantes was in forty minutes, 15:45 it read, a four-hour twenty-minute trip, thankfully by a high-speed TGV, with stops at Massy, Le Mans and Angers, getting him into Nantes a little after eight that night. A brochure found from a kiosk mid-hall told him the first class fare: 274 euros. A taxi to the airport in Nantes should deliver him from the Nantes rail station by eight thirty. Whatever the next flight to London, he'd take it and be *out* of this nightmare.

Wondering why people continued ogling him, he saw why upon entering the men's room. Scratches on his face from his run through the woods were caked with thin streaks of dried blood. Most of the bleeding, though, seemed to be from a superficial scalp wound now crusted over, coming most likely when he fell to the pavement escaping the Mercedes. The sum total made him look stupid and grotesque. Running warm water over his face and hands he washed away the blood, reducing the scratches to welts, the scalp wound buried under his hair. Drying off his hands and face with paper towels, he secluded himself in a stall, took out his wallet, dropped to the seat in exhaustion, and counted his cash. 447 euros. More than enough to get him to Nantes, he calculated, as well as taxi fare to the airport. He'd stupidly left his open return ticket to the U.S. in his Tumi suitcase, but no matter. He'd use his credit card for the flight to London, then on to New York. In his travel vest was all else that was needed: his passport.

Purchasing first class fare at a ticket window, Scott was told, "Voie trois, voiture quatre, siège vingt-deux." Track three, car four, seat twenty-two. He asked if they were boarding yet, was told that they were, but there was a first class lounge available for waiting if preferred, which he did not. Going directly to track three, Scott boarded the first open car, walked through the train to his, found his seat, a welcoming note on it informing all first class passengers were offered a meal of hot food, salads, sandwiches, desserts in the bar-buffet car included in the price of the ticket. Other than that there was not a great deal of difference, Scott saw, between first and second class except for price. The seats, two rows on one side, one on the other, were wider, reclining, had headrests, footrests and fold down tables. Aside from the inclusive meal, that was it.

Dropping onto his aisle seat, one away from the window, Scott was immediately aware of other persons in the car so far. A ten-year-old French boy stood fidgeting at a window staring at the train on an adjoining track, his parents, squabbling over who knew what. A man in business suit was setting up a lap top in one of the single aisle seats. A young couple, head phones on, were thrashing about in their seats to unheard rap. Others, too, were boarding now in increasingly benign order, their very insignificance lending an air of normality, which seemed absurd. He lowered his head, not wanting to make eye contact with anyone, tried to convince himself he was no longer in danger, that he was only a little more than four hours from salvation. But his body was tingling and he was short of breath.

At 15:45 precisely, the car half filled, the boarding door slid silently closed. Ten seconds later the train began to move, so effortlessly it seemed at first as though the adjacent train was moving, not Scott's.

The TGV travelled slowly at first, north through the industrial center, then the outskirts of Lyon, turned west across the first of two rivers flowing through the city, the Rhone, then the Saone, then began to accelerate. Fifteen minutes out, through lush green countryside, it reached its cruising speed, a hundred eighty-six miles per hour.

For a few minutes, Scott stared out the window, realizing everything within proximity of the track was a blur. A conductor came through, punched Scott's ticket verifying his passage to Nantes. An inbound TGV passed with what sounded like an explosion, then was gone. Scott dropped his head back, eyes closed, trying to relax. Finally, at last, he was safe. There was none of the previous exhalation at beating the bastards. He was much too tired for that. He tried to think how he would play it when he got home. God knows he had a tale to tell. But his mind was mush, too much so to create a scenario.

"Pardon, M'sieur." A man's voice, followed by a large body edging past Scott to occupy the window seat next to his, which Scott ignored, not even opening his eyes, until, "Haffing a good trip?"

The voice went through Scott like a shot. Before he looked, even before, he knew who it was.

"I am into zee mos' interesting book," his new seat companion was going on. "Un man iss attempting to elude assassins out to keel heem. Ee makes un fatal mistake. Ee tries to do so by train. Picture ziss yourself. Zee assassins could get on and off at any stop. Imagine, sitting zere, hour apres hour, fearing sleep, zee fear of being knifed in un corridor. To try to escape by train is zee worst ee could do."

It was the trucker, the one who drove the Mercedes. For a moment, Scott sat frozen.

"Mille excuses," the man then said. "You haff paid for your ticket. You are entitled to some comfort."

Scott exploded! You son of a bitch! You want to make something out of this? You really do? You don't know who you're fucking with! Let's go! Come on! Now! All of which was in his head, Scott settling for:

"There're railroad police on this train."

"Not in *zis* book," the man said.

Scott was out of his seat as though shot from a canon, heading toward the rear of the car, through the door into the next, through that into the bar-buffet, already crowding with travelers. His relief was slight but there was relief. There was safety in numbers, had been all day. He ordered a Scotch, straight up, further realized, in paying for it, he was decreasing his already dwindling supply of euros, carried his drink with two shaking hands to a chair at a small window-side table. He tried to feel better, he couldn't, though there was a faint reason to do so. It would really be difficult to kill a man on this train without anyone knowing it. You might be able do it if you could get him alone. But Scott had no intention of letting that happen, not once, not ever on this ride. The bar-buffet was where he was and where he'd stay till Nantes. The real danger he knew would be when he got off the train. Then, suddenly, Scott's heartbeat drummed sickeningly at the base of his skull. Standing at the end of the bar was the man in the brown suit.

Scott looked away, the blood leaving his face. He had only glanced, but it was enough. The man's eyes had been staring into Scott's coldly, inspecting Scott as an executioner might inspect a doomed man. Draining his glass, his hand shaking so badly half the liquor spilled onto his travel vest, Scott willed himself not to look back, but the need was too great. He did so and came as close to a heart attack as ever in his life. Pointed directly at his head, no more than two feet away, was the muzzle of a gun!

True to near-death experiences, Scott's life flashed before him. In that most of it had been fraudulent there was a collage of encounters, relationships, rules, strewn by the wayside, bringing Scott in this moment to God whom he'd forever denied, when a strong voice interceded.

"Gustave! Que pense-tu que tu es en train de faire?"This accompanied by the sound of a hand slapping the side of a head. "Mettre ce jouet!"

The gun, Scott saw, his life surging back, was not an actual gun at all. It was a plastic toy, in the hand of the boy he'd seen in his car staring out at the adjacent train.

"Pardon, Monsieur," his father was saying, "Il est impossible," and the boy was dragged away.

Drained of strength and resolve, Scott sat shaking his head side to side as near to capitulation as ever in his life. No. He was beyond that. He was doomed and he knew it, time to acknowledge it, to surrender. Who would miss him? Barry? Barry, maybe. The rest? They'd stick pins in his corpse at his funeral to make sure he was dead. He looked up, ready to give himself over to the man in the brown suit at the bar. His mouth fell open. The man was gone.

When Scott was a boy growing up in San Francisco, he snuck into a theater through an unlocked exit door where they were showing old black-and-whites, anxious to see the 1950s "Thing From Another World." Scientists at an Arctic research station discover an alien spacecraft buried in ice. Upon closer inspection they see inside it the frozen pilot. All hell breaks loose when they take him back to their station encased in a block of ice and he is accidently thawed out and gets loose, appearing and eviscerating, unannounced, anyone caught in an open doorway. It was during one such incredibly tense moment some wag sent an empty 35-mm film can bouncing down over the theater's concrete steps that sent Scott, along with the audience, four feet into the air.

It was that film all over again. Every time there was a champagne cork popping, a door gasping open, a cough, a sneeze, the bark of a laugh, for nearly four hours Scott sat reliving that moment, awaiting the reappearance of his two assassins. Even as the train pulled into the station in Nantes, he waited. But nothing. No sight of them. Nor had there been at stops along the route. Where they were, he didn't know. But they were there. That, he knew. And he had to get off that train. That *they* knew.

The Gare de Nantes was split into two stations, Gare de Nord and Gare de Sud, separated by a pedestrian subway running between the two beneath the tracks. Arriving at the north station the train disgorged its passengers into fading daylight to a line of taxis drawn up along the Boulevarde de Stalingrad. Buried within the largest clump of passengers he could find, Scott drew back under an overhang at the sight. Taxi drivers, each looking more menacing than the next, stood by their vehicles awaiting fares, when Scott saw it. A bus was drawing up to the curb. "Express en Navette l'Aeroport," it read. A bus to the airport!

A half dozen people were boarding. It would take Scott into the open to make it. Willing himself to do so, he seemed incapable of will. The last was boarding, Scott saw. With a scream in his head, he went for it, cut through the crowd, clambered aboard. He didn't even ask the fare, shoved a handful of euros, all he had left, at the driver who called to him as he started toward the back of the bus, "Monsieur!" Scott turned, fear on his face. The driver was holding out Scott's change.

Hunkering down in a back seat, Scott waited for the door to close. Another passenger boarded. And then another. "Close it! Close the fucking door!" he silently screeched in his head, collapsed back into a fetal ball when at last it did so, the bus pulling away from the curb. He checked, 123 remaining euros, and looked about at his fellow passengers. None was looking at him. None was among the two who'd chased him across half of France. Clenching his teeth to keep from retching, he did not at first realize what was happening. Nothing. For thirty minutes it remained so, the bus crossing the Loire, taking D145 southwest out of Nantes to the Nantes Atlantique Aeroport.

Arriving at the edge of night, Scott looked out onto the departure zone and his heart skipped a beat. For the first time that day, a positive one. The place was swarming with police, some even with dogs. Alighting, he entered the arrival concourse quickly. The largest airport in southwestern France, it was packed with travelers. Scott looked at the departure board. British Air to Gatwick, London, 22:20. He converted quickly in his head. 10:20 p.m. Two hours. A sign indicated British Air was in Hall Three. One over. He made for it, a quickness to his step, also lightness he hadn't experienced in memory, it seemed.

Arriving at the British Air counter, he waited out two passengers applying for tickets, bellied up to the counter, slapped his passport on the desk before the ticket agent.

"One way to London, the 10:20, please," he said.

The agent finished some paper work, looked up. Dressed in a light blue uniform, British Air stitched to her tunic, she was, Scott immediately saw, pert and rosy cheeked, small but firm breasts, lithe, no wedding band. A solid six, he thought.

"We can accommodate you, sir, it's not a full flight," she said in one of those English accents that always turned him on. "May I see your passport, please. Ah." She saw it was already out as Scott shoved it toward her.

"You'll be travelling by yourself, sir?"

"Just me. First class if you have it."

She busied herself running his request through her computer. He watched her. Shame he wasn't staying in Nantes. A dinner, maybe two would do it, along with the old story about his wife dying in Africa. This one could be a couple of nights, he was certain.

"That will be seat four, a window seat," she said as the ticket came through. She placed it before her on her desk, along with his boarding pass. "And how will you be paying for this, sir?"

"Visa." He fished it out, handed it over.

"575 euros, first class one way."

"Whatever."

She ran his visa through, waited for its acceptance. Ran it through a second time. Frowned.

"There seems to be a problem, sir."

"A problem? What problem?"

"The card's been denied."

"You're kidding."

"No, sir."

"Why?"

"I don't know, sir. Just that's it's been denied."

A short, sharp laugh escaped him.

"That's ridiculous. I've got ten to fifteen thousand in that account."

"I'm not the one to argue with, sir."

"There's a mistake. Where's a phone?"

"Across the way, sir."

Crossing to a bank of phones, Scott read, 'Cartes de Crédit Acceptées,' suddenly realized his card was of no use, thankfully found on the back of it a number, 'Customer Service Outside The U.S. call collect.' Which he did, reaching a recording. "Due to the high volume of calls, yours will be answered in approximately six minutes."

Welling with rage, Scott glanced at his watch, fought for calm. Okay. Plenty of time. Time was on his side. He looked across at the agent, already involved with others. A search dog on a leash passed by, pausing to sniff at Scott, then moving on. Finally the phone began to ring. A voice came on the line.

"Customer Service. How may I help you?" India, for Christ's sake! Scott hated that.

"Look, there's been a fuck up..!"

"Sir?"

"I'm in Nantes, France. I tried to use my card for a flight — it's got thousands on it — it was denied. I want to know why?"

"I'll do what I can to assess the problem, sir. Your name as it appears on your card?"

"David S. Fitzgerald."

"Card number, please?"

Scott gave it to him.

"Security code?"

"What security code, what's that?"

"The three numbers listed on the back of your card, sir."

Scott turned his card over, saw what the agent was asking for, gave him that, too.

"Your mother's maiden name?"

"Oh, for Christ's sake…"

"Your mother's maiden name, please, sir?" the agent repeated.

Scott growled out her name.

"One moment, please."

The moment was twenty seconds that seemed like an hour.

"A hold has been put on your card, sir. By Auto Europe."

"I rented a car from Auto Europe. A Ferrari. It's in Beaune, across from the Hermès Hotel. They can find it there, pick it up whenever they want."

"Apparently they *have* found it, sir. It was broken into, virtually dismantled."

Scott stood immobilized, turned to stone.

"Sir?"

He clutched the receiver as though by doing so it would keep him from fainting.

"Sir?"

If Scott heard he gave no indication of it. A look of utter disbelief, turning slowly to panic etched his face.

"If there's nothing else we can help you with, sir, thank you for calling Visa."

Fifteen

It had been a long day, Tally starting at the open air market in Angers off the Boulevard M. Foch at 6:30 in the morning. It was her turn to prepare a meal at the école de cuisine, and she'd chosen a goat cheese appetizer, stuffed artichokes, rabbit in Vouvray wine, Tarte Tatin with a Chenin Blanc.

The class was made up of ten people, mostly British, a German widower and an Austrian couple, the husband spending more time trying to flirt with Tally than on the program. Her presentation went off beautifully. Only the celebrated owner-chef of the school, Mme. Morille, suggesting the Tarte Tatin might benefit from a touch of lemon.

In the final of the four-week course, Tally found herself at the head of her class. Socially, however, she fell between generations. The widower, in his late fifties, had invited Tally to dinner, Tally making certain their conversation and relationship remained on topic, their lessons. At night, students at the local Catholique Université de l'Ouest, come from around the world for a late summer course in *la langue Francaise*, would hail Tally on her way to and from her class from their curbside tables on the Boulevard. College age for the most part, she'd occasionally join them where they reacted in awe at her knowledge of French. But there too it was as far as it would go, Tally eventually retreating, always with a smile it seemed, when she'd had all she could take of their cannabis.

It was this night, the next to last, as Tally prepared to leave following her culinary success, that Mme. Morille asked her to stay behind. In her mid-fifties, bearing the remnants of a once considerable beauty, Mme. Morille had a manner some thought haughty and intimidating. Establishing her school, l'Atelier des Sens, within the past decade, she was known to be a long time member of the Culinaire Institute de Paris. She was also known to have left half a dozen suitors by the wayside for, some locals whispered, a lesbian lover in Nice.

"What is it you want from this?" Mme. Morille asked. Tally started to reply in French, but the woman waved her off. "English. I need the practice."

"To make a proper Tarte Tatin," Tally laughed.

"Beyond that."

"Dreams?"

Mme. Morille said nothing, but a gesture of her hand suggested she was waiting for an answer.

"To have my own restaurant in the Languedoc," Tally answered.

"Why not?"

"Two reasons. I'm not sure how accepting the French would be for an American in their domain."

"One of the best vintners in France today is an American."

"And money."

"Ah."

"Yes, 'ah,' I'm afraid. I've talked to people who've tried. Endless paper work, enormous costs. I've heard as much as 350,000 euros. Where do I come up with that? Unless I find a sugar daddy."

Mme. Morille shook her head, not understanding the term.

"A Santa Claus. A Père Noel."

"So what are your plans?"

"After this? Back to New York. I walked off a job. They don't like that. I'll find another."

Mme. Morille pursed her lips, studying Tally a moment.

"I need an assistant," she said.

Tally stared, incredulous.

"I'm not qualified."

"More than you know. You have what we call, 'le nez'. The nose. What you don't know, you can learn. Perhaps one day, that dream of yours…"

Tally sat back.

"I don't know what to say."

"Think about it."

Tally thought for a moment, then nodded. It was a nod more out of respect than commitment.

"I'll think about it."

It was after ten, daylight long gone, when Tally, purse slung over her shoulder, walked down the rue des Lices, two blocks off the Boulevard, which she'd cross to her rented apartment on rue Boreau. The street was ill lit and deserted, neither of which bothered her, having taken it so often now. She thought back to her meeting. It was true what she'd said. Madison and Fifth Avenues were closed to her now. You just didn't walk away from those people and word would spread. But a restaurant here in France, her own? Even a modest one? The rent or mortgage payments alone, not to mention licenses, counters, tables, silverware, chairs, shelving, refrigeration, ovens, ranges, fryers, cookware, computers, registers, staff. She shook it off. She had friends at *Mother Jones* and *People* and *The Planet* at home. She might get employment with one. The pay would not be the same, but at least it would be something.

It was then she first heard it. Footsteps. Ten, fifteen yards behind her. Without alarm, she quickened her pace. The footsteps behind quickened also. And they were closing, almost on top of her. Tally was not one given to panic, but her heart rate was soaring. She reached inside her purse, spun about and let loose a spray of mace directly into the face of her pursuer.

"Jesus, Tally, for *Christ sake!*"

Tally stared incredulous at Scott as he dropped to the sidewalk, hands to his face, writhing in pain.

"What are you doing here, how'd you find me?"

"I'm *dying!*"

"You're not dying.," she said. "Hold your eyes open. Don't take deep breaths." Reaching inside her purse she pulled out a couple of handi-wipes, handed them to him. "Pat. Don't rub. It'll be gone in a few minutes."

"It *hurts!*"

"You didn't answer my question."

"You *told* me where you were, in *Paris.*"

"And?"

"Jesus!" he said, shaking his head side to side.

"What *are* you doing here?"

"I got no place else to go. I got thirty-six euros to my name. They're trying to *kill* me!"

Tally pulled back as though she hadn't heard correctly.

"What are you talking about?"

"These two guys. Aw, hell, I can't even think about it. I'm done, I'm finished, it's over!" he whined.

For the first time, even in the dark, Tally saw it. The welts on his hands and face, the torn, ripped clothing. She turned, looked up and down the street, empty except for the two of them, finding no help. She stood for a moment, fighting a decision she clearly did not want to make.

"Get up, come on."

He sat for a moment, staring up at her in confusion.

"Or stay," she said and started away.

Scampering to his feet he followed.

The bells in the high tower of the Basilique Ste-Marie-Madeleine in Vezelay tolled through the town and across the valley where all work ceased in honor of the occasion. Lying in open casket in the nave of the abbey, where two thousand people crowded to pay their respects, Scott lay in state, arms crossed over his lifeless body. In an elevated altar above the transept, Barry, dressed in cardinal's red vestments, was concluding his eulogy.

"Few things carry more pain, disturb more, than watching a great man brought to his end. But over the past days it was happening as the devils of darkness converged upon him. Never once did he flinch from their pursuit, nor sought sanctuary against their mendacity, but faced them with the courage of ten lions, only to be overcome by the sheer weight of their numbers. May his final words echo through these halls. 'Laissez le bon et le juste mourir pour une juste cause!' Rest well, my friend. Rest well."

It was at that moment that a great beam of light played in on Scott's face, his eyes opening to. . . heaven? Then why was he staring at a large window filled with panes, flanked by curtains, blinding sunlight pouring in. Further aware, he found himself on a couch, a blanket draped around him. Sitting up he looked about. He was in a small room, maybe ten by twelve. There was an arm chair, across from the couch, a coffee table between them. Two upturned wooden packing boxes stood against a wall, one with books, the other with neatly folded clothing, no television. No TV? Was he in *hell?*

When suddenly a daemonic figure loomed before him, one hand holding what appeared to be a chalice emitting curls of steam, the other a ceramic disk; the first, as his eyes and reason unclouded, proving to be a cup of coffee, the other a plate of toast and scrambled eggs. Setting them both on the coffee table before Scott, with a paper napkin and fork, Tally lowered herself to the arm chair across from him. Dressed in slacks and cotton shirt, she was backlit by the sun so all he could see of her was her silhouette, no sense of her expression, though he could guess what it was.

"What time's it?" he asked, and had to repeat it, clearing his throat as his voice had been garbled.

"Does it matter?"

He dropped his eyes to the food and attacked it, then the coffee, downing half of it in a gulp.

"I need a shower. I smell."

She let that one slide, nodded, and pointed.

"Through that door. Empty your pockets, throw your clothes out. There's a washer and dryer downstairs, I'll get them started. You can put on my robe 'til they're done."

The shower was tiny, curtained off, barely enough room to turn around, with a hand held shower head attached to a flexible hose. No matter. Never had anything felt so luxurious as he ran hot water over his body. The soap was liquid, from a plastic container, which Scott usually hated. He loved it, lathered himself head to toe, between the toes, under the arm pits, crotch, between the smile of his buttocks, foaming his head. Soaping his face, he shaved off a day's growth of whiskers with a pink Quattro razor he found in a tray, then leaned back against the shower wall, letting the hot water drench him till it began to give out, turning cold. Drying himself off, he tried to figure it out. The only time he'd expected to see Tally again was at his funeral. Then it hit him. She'd been rumored to frequent the pound on Third and 101st, finding homes for rescue cats and dogs. *That* was it. He was a fucking *rescue!"*

Slipping on Tally's robe found hanging on the back of the bathroom door, Scott saw that it was sheer, exposing him fully. Wrapping the damp towel around his middle, he tucked it in at the ends, drew his fingers through his hair and opened the door.

In what passed for the living room, Scott found Tally standing at the window, arms crossed, back to the room, looking out at the park across the street. Dropping to the couch Scott stared at his passport, watch, car keys, wallet, hotel key on the coffee table, looked up at Tally's back. Despite all she'd done, rescuing him, feeding him, washing his clothes, the shower, old feelings began to creep in. For all their word play at the publishing house, he'd never liked her, hated women who had power over him, control. The vulnerable and the wanting, that was his hunting ground. The Tallys of this world? Spare him. The wider the distance between them the better.

"Who's out to kill you. Start there," Tally said.

She turned, facing him.

"It didn't start there."

She said nothing, waited for him to go on.

"Nobody would hire me after. . . you don't know what that's like, what you fucking did! You could have handled it better, you know! You didn't have to do it in front of two fucking thousand people!"

Still she said nothing, stood waiting. His shoulders sagged in recall.

"I couldn't get in a door. No e-mails answered, no letters, no calls. Four weeks, six. And then I got a hit."

"A hit."

"I was down to broke, canned crap for dinner, furniture repossessed, my plasma TV. I could paper the room with rejections."

"A hit. You said."

"Hugo Medlock."

For the first time, Tally exhibited surprise, her eyebrows arching in astonishment.

"Hugo Medlock?" she said in disbelief.

"He had an assignment for me."

"Hugo *Medlock*?"

"In France."

"What assignment?"

"There was something he wanted and couldn't get. He hired me to nail it."

"Why you?"

"Because I'm fucking good at what I do, that's why!" he came back at her defensively.

"You're a thieving little shit, Scott, without an ounce of conscience about how you get what you want."

"Yeah…well…"

"Which is why he went for you, my bet. Go on."

"What're you so Goddamn hostile for? You got your pound of flesh. Cushy fucking job to go back to, kissing their asses to put the waste on me!"

"I said, go on."

"He sent me to Vezalay."

"Southern Burgundy."

"$50,000 down against more than I could imagine if I got him what he wanted."

"Why Vezalay?"

"There's a restaurant there. Chez Gaillard."

"I don't care where you ate, I asked why Vezalay?"

"I just told you."

"What?"

"Chez Gaillard."

"A *restaurant*."

"Yeah."

"Why, what's there?'

"What's usually at a restaurant?"

"Scott," she gestured with growing impatience, "I'm about to put you on the street."

"A recipe."

"A what?"

"It was a recipe. It's what he wanted. He wanted a recipe."

Tally stared at Scott in disbelief, her brain trying to compute.

"I don't believe you."

"Believe what you want."

"A *recipe?*"

"He'd been there, he said. Said it was the best venison medallions he'd ever eaten in his life. But there was something unusual about it, something he couldn't decipher. Usually the dish was Teutonic or Belgian, he said. Those he knew. This one was different. Improvised, improved. He asked for the recipe. They told him no. He offered to pay. No deal. Upped the price. Still no. You don't tell Hugo Medlock no."

Tally's shoulders suddenly were wracked with laughter.

"You think that's funny?"

"He paid you $50,000 against 'God knows what' you said for a *recipe?* Come on!"

Scott reached inside his travel vest, unzipped the inner pocket, removed the copy of Medlock's agreement, handed it to Tally, who read it, incredulous.

"How..?"

"You ever met the guy?"

"In the papers."

"He's a nut. But he's a billionaire nut."

"So what happened?"

"There was this girl there, at the restaurant."

"Why am I not surprised."

"You want to hear this or not?" he shot back. "The one that brings you the water and bread. Five three, blond, nice ass, maybe a six..."

"Scott?" It was warning shot across his bow.

"Anyway, I said this was a helluva dish, how'd they make it? She said there was a chef who'd come up with it. I said I'd like to talk to him. She said he was gone, six months ago, had a family or something in Moldova."

"Moldova."

"Yeah, I hadn't heard of it either."

"Between Romania and the Ukraine."

"'Kay, so you're a fucking cartographist."

"Cartographer."

Shit! But he went on.

"Guy's name was Chernivtsi, she said. I wrote it down. Googled him back at my hotel. A chef, he'd been around, retired to this town. Pelivan, no address or phone number, just Pelivan outside Chisinal..."

"Chisinau."

His face reddened. He'd had just about enough of her fucking amendings.

"I flew there from Paris."

"To Chisinau."

"Forty minutes on the tarmac waiting for a fucking gate…"

"How'd you get a visa so fast?"

"You don't need a visa with a U.S. passport."

"And?"

"Rented a car, got a map, headed for the town. You want to see cabbages, that's what they got, *fields* of it…"

"Scott..!"

"Half way there I'm run off the road by this fucking black Mercedes. Okay, locals, ass holes, I figured. Poorest country in fucking Europe, I'm told, and they got *Mercedes?* That's not the way it turned out. Got to the outskirts of the place, there it was."

"What was?"

"The Mercedes, blocking the road. Listen, you got any bourbon or something?"

"No."

"A beer?"

"Blocking the road," she said, trying to keep him on course.

"It was a Mexican standoff, like a pair of bulls. I'm staring at them, they're staring at me. I guess they're staring, I couldn't see."

"What'd you do?"

"What am I supposed to do," he said in exasperation, bounding to his feet, unaware the towel around his waist fell free. "They got horns, I don't have any."

"I can see," Tally nodded, staring.

"Turned the car around, headed back to Chisinol…"

"Chisinau."

"Jesus *Christ*," Scott said suddenly aware of his exposure. Grabbing the towel he dropped back onto the couch, the towel in his lap.

"What then?" she asked.

"Flew back to Paris."

"That's it?"

"*It* my ass! When I got to my car — I'd left it in the airport parking garage — it'd been broken into. Nothing taken, but searched."

"What were they looking for?"

"You tell me! I didn't have anything to find!"

"So?"

"I panicked. I should have gotten on a plane for the States right then. I didn't, I panicked, drove the hell out of there as fast as I could, headed for

Lyon to get a flight out of the place, when this storm came in. I mean you couldn't see the nose of your car. I got to Beaune, checked in at this hotel for the night. When I woke up in the morning, there was the Mercedes, out in the street."

"What then?"

When he'd brought her up to date, from balloon flight to mace, she nodded her head in understanding, shook it at the idiocy.

"What?" he asked.

"Nobody was trying to kill you, Scott."

"Yeah, right, you were there."

"If they'd wanted to, you'd never have gotten out of Moldova. Restaurants are big business in France. So are their recipes. They guard them like diamonds. But they don't go around killing people."

"You didn't meet these guys."

"They picked up on what you were after, decided to run you out of the country. That's all."

Scott drew in his breath, held it as though about to explode. All that came out was a defeated little "Shit."

"How'd you plan to get home?" she asked.

"Round trip ticket, Air France. But I left the damn thing in my suitcase at the hotel in Beaune."

"You've got your passport," she nodded at it lying on the coffee table. "Yeah."

"The airline'll have you in their computer."

He groaned, realizing he could have done that earlier.

"I've got a class. I'll toss your clothes in the dryer on my way out. I'll drive you to the airport in Nantes when I get back."

"It could wait till morning," he offered.

"It could. It won't."

And she was gone.

Sixteen

It wasn't the first time Scott had done it. That was when he was nine.

His father, a gastroenterologist, mild-manner, non-confrontational, was at the hospital visiting patients before eight in the morning to avoid running into their families. His mother was off for her bi-weekly early morning tennis lesson with her bronzed twenty-eight-year-old Latin pro. It would be several years later that Scott would come to realize tennis wasn't the game they were playing. But still, even then, he would find himself often as not alone in the house, going through his mother's room, closets, dresser drawers, bathroom, in an effort to find out who she was.

"George!" Scott would hear her voice sometimes at night when in bed, "It's ridiculous for you to even *think* about coming along. It's my French club. You'd be nothing but bored. I'll be back in three days," she would say before a trip to Santa Barbara, Scottsdale, or Palm Springs.

Go with her, Dad, Scott would scream to himself. *Go with her!* Which he never did.

Her room, separate from his father's, always had the smell of lavender, her closet filled with enough pants suits and dresses to open a dress shop, shoes to match each outfit.

"George, I'll be late tonight. It's bridge. Don't wait up."

Dad?

The most perplexing thing was the compact he found in the folds of a soft silken case deep inside one of her dresser drawers. Or what looked like a compact. Opening it he found it filled in a circle with tiny pills. It became a fascination to him. Each time he found it, it had less and less pills, or was filled completely at the start of each month.

"George," he'd hear his mother say, "I'm just not interested in *that* anymore! No! I'm dried up!"

Dad? Dad!

Or the nights when his father would come to Scott's room to kiss Scott goodnight as he and his mother were going out to dinner.

"George!" he'd hear her from the foot of the stairs, "leave that child alone!"

Over and over he'd go through her room. And now he was going through another.

Tally's bedroom was far from the opulence of his mother's. It was small. Ten by eight. Small, even by European standards. There was a bed, which was a single, neatly made up. A closet and dresser. Atop the dresser were a couple of small slate blue ceramic containers. Royal Copenhagen. Seconds from the look of them with slightly flawed embossing. He opened them. One held pins and sewing needles and thread. The other loose coins.

Closing them, he opened the dresser's top drawer. Panties, socks, t-shirts, carefully folded. He closed it, opened the second. Pajamas, jogging pants, and a couple of sweat shirts, along with a small unlidded cardboard box containing several pieces of costume jewelry. He started to shove the drawer closed, to move on to the next, when something caught his eye. Beneath the night clothes was a blue cloth 'secretary.' The sort a traveler might carry for brochures and documents. He pulled it out, aware it had little heft to it, unzipped the first of three zippered pockets, dropped to the edge of the bed, removed its contents.

Tally's robe tucked between his legs, he began to go through what he'd found. There was her passport, and an open Air France ticket home to New York. There was a copy of her apartment rental agreement, and Xerox copies of each. There was also a letter-sized envelope, unsealed. He dug inside it, pulled out a single sheet of paper, unfolded it. It too was a Xerox copy, type written on *New York In Review* official stationery. It was addressed to Dan Randall, Executive Director, *New York In Review* Publications. It read:

Dear Dan: Effective this date, be on notice that I am resigning my position with the Publication. You do not need me to cite the reasons why. You will understand or you won't. Know simply the position you put me in at last night's awards, exposing Scott publicly, was beyond humiliation. Not only for Scott but for myself as well. While I wish you and the publication continued success, I can no longer, in conscience, be a part of it. Respectfully, Tally.

It was dated, Scott saw, the day he was fired.

Scott read the letter twice over, lowered it to his lap. The normal response, by any standard, had to be contrition. Such should it be, discovering the ignominy, the degradation at the night of the Ellies was *not* Tally's invention, but *theirs*, the fucking thirty-third floor, that Tally had been ordered, *made* to do it, thereafter sacrificing her career because of it.

Except Scott was not given to normal response. If there was one thing he thrived on it was objurgation — blame. It was a life force. He had thrived on his rage against Tally. Fuel for the tank. Tally, who had destroyed his career, sacked him in front of two thousand people, no warning. And now that was being uprooted, taken away? He didn't know how to respond. For minutes he sat there, trying to assess his feelings. All he encountered was confusion. He had nothing to call on, no history of penance, remorse.

Stuffing the letter back in its envelope, he returned all else to the 'secretary', replaced it where it was found, closed the dresser drawer, smoothed down the bed cover, returned to the front room, dropped to the couch, tried to gather his thoughts. He had none, they were numb. He thought he knew what there was to know of Tally. He looked about the room, as though by doing so all would become clear and plain. It was basically barren, clearly its occupant temporary. There was, he noticed for the first time, a glass jar filled with a small grouping of wild-picked flowers. There was a Sunday edition of *Le Monde*. The place otherwise looked as though it had never been moved into, offering him no clue as to what and who she was. About the only thing he had to go on were the two upright wooden boxes, one with sweaters mostly, the other with books. He went to the latter.

There was *A Little Tour Of France* by Henry James. *A Year In Provence* by Peter Mayle. *The Flavor Of France* by Narcissa and Narcisse Chamberlain. What the hell was this crap she had about France. He hated the place. Couldn't wait to get the hell out. His feelings of anger against the country and all he'd gone through supplanted his feelings of confusion over Tally, gave him direction. He'd wait for her return with his clothes, get dressed, give her twenty euros for driving him to the Nantes airport and be out of this shit country and on his way!

He curled up on the couch to catch some sleep, knowing sleep on the plane was impossible. Only sleep wouldn't come. He tried every trick he knew, counted the women he'd seduced at the Publishing House, earlier too in college, fantasized pitching a no-hitter for the Giants against the Yankees. Nothing, only churnings he couldn't escape. It was as though something had been taken from him, an energizing force, and he wanted it back!

It was the last day of class at the l'Atelier des Sens and, as was custom, there was pate, cheese, crackers, cakes, and champagne. Some were going on, some were going home. The Austrian couple had booked a week's cruise aboard the four-masted Star Clipper, sailing the islands out of Athens. All were making their farewells, new fast friends who would never see each other again. As Tally, glass in hand, bid her adieus to one after another, it was Mme. Morille who sensed her distraction.

"You're conflicted about my offer," Mme. Morille said to Tally.

"Yes," she answered, which wasn't the case.

"Eh bien, it still stands."

"Merci, Madame."

"I'll hear from you."

"Of course."

The woman went on to others, leaving Tally, for the moment, alone.

Lowering her glass to a table, Tally looked off. It had come on slowly, but now her mind was a swirl. *More than Scott could imagine if he got Medlock what he wanted?* That's what Medlock had told him? More than he could *imagine*? Scott was not the most reliable source when recounting events, though it had taken her a while to learn the signs as she reflected on the first time they'd met. It was eighteen months ago that she'd been called to the thirty-third floor to Dan Randall's office, six weeks after being elevated to Articles Editor, three years after arriving at the magazine.

Fresh out of the University of Pennsylvania, she'd gotten a job due to her fluency in the language, with the French consulate in Philadelphia, found herself languishing at the front desk greeting arrivals. She'd written an article, mostly for herself on her work experience, entitled "A Recipe For Ennui." Friends encouraged her to send it out, which she ultimately did, getting an immediate call from *New York In Review* Publications. Assigned a desk at $500 a week, she was told to come up with whatever enticed her, with a view toward their twenty-something readership. Her success was immediate, her rise in the company meteoric.

Then, that day.

"Dan wants you," her assistant, Warren, had told her over the intercom. "His office. ASAP."

She'd taken the elevator to the thirty-third floor, passed through reception to the hallway, walked its length to Dan Randall's corner suite, acknowledged the nod from his assistant, Thelma, that she was to go right in, opened the door and stepped inside. The first thing she saw, rising from the couch across the room, was, her heart skipping a beat, the most physically attractive man she'd met in her life. Sandy haired, handsome to a fault, with a seductive disarming smile, he'd worn a brown jacket over an open-throat shirt, gabardine trousers and loafers.

"Tally," Dan said, "meet David Fitzgerald."

"Scott," the vision corrected, thrusting out a hand in greeting. "They call me Scott."

The hand, she recalled, was soft, callous free, but the handshake firm, and seemed to linger.

"We're bringing him aboard," Dan was explaining, "assigning him to your department. He's in from the coast. Wrote some damn good stuff for *Parade*. He asked how he should play it here, I told him to go after your job." He laughed. So did Scott. So did Tally. "Take him to lunch, he'll fill in the blanks."

Twenty minutes later, they sat facing each other at one of the simple wooden tables at La Bonne Soupe on West Fifty-Fifth, Tally with French onion soup and salad, Scott with a hamburger slathered with ketchup.

"I love this place," Tally exuded.

"Ketchup. I could eat it on ice cream."

"Great value, great neighborhood. For less than $20 you can get soup, salad, bread, drink, dessert. You can't go wrong. If you read the reviews you'll see a pattern. Especially if you're going to the theater. Never disappoints, crepes large and light as a feather. Walk along Fifty-Fifth you'll pass restaurants and they'll be empty when this place is jammed. There's a reason."

She was prattling, she knew it.

"Well that's me. Your turn," she said.

"I'm a simple guy with a simple dream," he answered.

"Which is?"

"Learn from the master. I've read your articles. 'Recipe For Partners,' 'Recipe For Genetics.' Tally's 'Recipes.'"

"I like cooking. It's a hobby," she laughed lightly.

"Look, I'm here to serve. Whatever you want, however you want it, just tell me, I'm on it," he said with winning charm.

"Tell me about yourself," she said.

"Modestly or otherwise?"

"Whatever."

"Phi Beta Kappa at Berkeley," he'd lied. "Editor of the *Daily Californian* on campus." More lies. "Single. Looking."

"Meanwhile?"

"Meanwhile, love to take you to dinner."

It was an initial meeting that took her by storm, soon to decay in a tide of erosions as she came to realize it was all a ploy. Judgment trumping attraction, she'd kept him at arm's length, often, at first, condemning herself for doing so, trying to fight off a niggling sense there was more, or less, to Scott than revealed. She was right. Agenda set, Scott was soon detected going for whatever pleased him or stood in his way. Shielded by the thirty-third floor, indifferent to his proclivity for seducing any assistant he could convince to work after hours, he managed a genuinely successful patchwork folio of work, which some thought suspiciously familiar, if not flagrantly the work of others, which it often was, but which no one could prove, not until that fateful night of the Ellies.

So as Tally stood staring off, the buzz of the class farewells diminishing behind her, her mind thrashed about in a swirl with all Scott had told her. To believe him or not? There was certainly that. And yet, if what he'd told her were true? His value to her, his entrée to Medlock, her participation, which could lead to fulfilling her dream, her restaurant, was simply too huge to ignore. She had to get what Medlock wanted, of course. Without that all would be wasted. But as far as Scott's conviction it was entering deep waters, who knew the French better, he or she?

At six o'clock in the evening, footsteps on the wooden stairs outside the apartment heralded Tally's return. The first thing Scott noticed, rising as she entered, his hands bunching the folds of her gown to hide his crotch, was the foot long baguette of bread she carried. The second was she didn't have his clothes.

"Where..?"

Offering nothing, she entered the kitchenette, opened the refrigerator, took out a plate of brie, secured a half-empty bottle of Breton red from the counter, a spreading knife and two glass jars, brought all to the coffee table.

"Where're my clothes?"

"In the dryer."

Scott started toward the door.

"Two flights down, out the front door into the street, left to the alley," she explained, uncorking, pouring wine into the jars. "It's kind of a zoo out, everyone going home."

He stopped turned back to her.

"Just what the hell…"

"First rate brie," she said, nodding at the cheese. "Can't vouch for the wine, it's four days old, but the bread's fresh baked."

"You were driving me to Nantes, couldn't wait to get me the hell out of here!"

She broke off a piece of bread, layered it with cheese, shoved bread, brie and wine toward Scott. He lowered slowly to the couch again, forgetting to cover himself. Something was going on and he wasn't going to like it.

"Tell me about it," she said.

"What?"

"Vezalay. Chez Gaillard."

He sat back with an awakening awareness. "Holy shit!"

"What."

"Don't fucking 'what' me!"

"You've lost me, Scott."

"Like hell I have. You want to go for it."

"Is that what I said?"

"That's *just* what you said."

"Just for a hypothetical…"

"You're crazy!"

"What happens if we do?"

"*We?*"

"I know food, you know Medlock…"

"I'm not going back there!"

"Just for conversation…"

"I'm not going to do it, Tally! No!"

She opened her mouth as though to argue the point further.

"*No!*"

She thought that over a moment, nodded. It was a nod of submission, and, Scott sensed, regret. She rose.

"I'll get your clothes."

The ride to Nantes in Tally's rented two-seat 2003 Renault Clio was made in silence. Pulling to a stop at the Air France Departure Terminal, Tally left the car running, waited for Scott to get out. He sat for a moment, glanced at her. She was staring straight ahead, lips parted as though she had something to say. She nodded at the airlines sign.

"Air France, you said."

He turned from her, stared into the night. His head was throbbing.

"Scott?"

"A fucking moment, okay?" he said irritably.

"All the moments you want."

"You haven't a clue what you'd be getting into."

"This is France, not Sicily, Scott."

"I just got out of the fire, you want me to dive back in? These guys aren't meeters and greeters."

"You've said."

"Give me one reason why I'd go along with this?" he challenged.

"'More than you can imagine,' isn't that what Medlock told you? Unless you've got something you can't wait to get back to."

He began rubbing his forehead, the pain coming on. It was true. He had nothing.

"What do you get out of this?" he asked.

"I get half."

"*There it is!*" he bellowed, throwing up his hands.

"Scott, get out of the car, go catch your flight."

Scott made no move to leave. He sat rubbing harder, the pain getting worse.

"A recipe. A fucking *recipe!* Christ!" He shook his head as though unable to believe the idiocy of it. "How's this going to work?"

"Haven't thought that far."

"That's wonderful, great! What makes you think you can get what Medlock couldn't."

"Don't know that I can."

"Then why…?"

"The opportunity."

"For what?"

Tally's chin came up. If she had an answer, which she did, she was keeping it to herself.

"That tells me a lot," Scott grumbled.

"Scott, I'm burning two liters of petrol just sitting here," she said over the Renault's idling engine.

"What're the fucking rules?"

"Two. I'll handle the costs, decide what they are."

"And?"

"You start looking for synonyms."

"Partners," he said, uttering it as though it were a pejorative.

"Yeah, I kind of gag on the word myself."

He nodded, desperately trying to find a way out of the pain.

"This is going to be the biggest fu…effin mistake of my life."

Seventeen

"J'ai une réservation pour une personne a douze heures et demie. Le nom est Garner."

"Bien sûr, madame," the maître d' said, confirming her name on his reservation pad. "Cette façon."

She'd arrived at Chez Gaillard alone and on time in a smart, if casual, suit. The luncheon crowd already filling the restaurant, Tally was ushered to a center room table. It was a Saturday, and tourism in Vezalay was active.

"Madame serait comme un verre de vin?"

"Café glace," she answered, and was handed a menu.

She opened it and found at once what she was looking for as bread and a small plate of pate and cornichons was put before her.

The server was replaced by a waiter who started into his routine.

"Nous avons certaines spécialités du jour…"

"Les médaillons de gibier," Tally interrupted, handing him her menu as her ice coffee arrived.

"Excellent choix, Madame," the waiter nodded in condescending affirmation.

It had been a bizarre thirty hours. Awakening at three a.m. following their return from Nantes, unable to sleep, Tally sat cross-legged on her bed in her apartment, dressed in unrevealing cotton pajamas, reading glasses on, laptop computer open, typing by the light of a side table lamp when there was a light tapping on her door.

"I'm up," she said.

Scott pushed the door open slowly. He wore her robe, but this time it was over underwear.

"I saw the light. What are you doing?" he asked.

"Notes."

"Notes," he repeated. "What kind of notes?"

"Getting you some clothes for one."

"After that?"

"Hotel Saint-Père. It's two kilometers outside Vezalay. First thing is the Galeries Lafayette in the morning. You can't go around in those pants and loafers. They're shot."

"Tally…"

"Don't worry about it, they're having a sale." He was wavering, she was sure of it. "You're going to need a razor and stuff," she said. "I've an extra toothbrush in the bathroom, brand new, top right drawer. Take that."

"Listen, there's something…"

"400 kilometers, I checked it out, a five-hour drive. No worries. Separate rooms."

"Right, yeah well…"

"Get some sleep," she said, closing conversation. "It's going to be a long day."

He stood a moment, as though to leave. He didn't, lowered himself to the foot of her bed, shoulders bunched.

"What?" she asked.

"I'm not that guy," he said, staring down at his hands.

"What're you talking about?"

"That day, your wedding. Your, whatever you called him, fiancé. I'm not that guy."

He turned, he looked at her. Whatever she'd assumed he was here for, expected to hear, that wasn't it. She was staring at him over the top of her glasses as though trying to fathom his intent. Sincerity or manipulation? Or something more. She gave it a long hard thought, came to a conclusion.

"Good night, Scott," she said.

He held a moment, nodded, rose,

"Night." And left, closing the door gently behind him.

She lowered her glasses, looked after him, silently establishing another rule. He was not to get within ten feet of her, figuratively speaking, or any other measurable proximity if that's what this was about. She couldn't, wouldn't let it happen. His value to her was his entree to Medlock, that's what it was, that's all. But she had to get what Medlock wanted. Without that all would be wasted. As far as Scott's warning she was entering treacherous waters, again, who knew the French better? She went back to her computer, typed in Chez Gaillard, Vezalay, requested a reservation for lunch, twelve-thirty, the day after tomorrow. She typed in her name where required. Number of reservations? She typed in that too. For one.

The following morning she'd taken Scott, as promised, to the Galeries Lafayette. As his gaze fixed longingly on Versace and Armani tailor-mades, he found himself led to the sale in the basement. Two pairs of cargo pants, two poplin shirts, three pairs of underwear, chino socks, a pair of canvas deck shoes, and a light canvas duffle bag. Toiletries secured from the Pharmacie Joly Poirier on the rue de Ville Morge, the entire outlay cost less than half what Scott once paid for a Gucci belt.

"Vos médaillions, Madame."

Brought out of her reverie, the first thing Tally noticed was the aroma as the dish was placed before her, along with a serrated knife replacing the standard one. Two slices of backstrap venison, she saw, surrounded by pomegranate seeds floating in a sauce, pungent, her nasal senses immediately captured, with rosemary and something else she couldn't decipher, like the smell of pines.

"Bon appétit, Madame," the waiter offered with a perfunctory smile and withdrew.

For several seconds, Tally stared at the dish, marveling at its influence over her destiny. Her mind was racing. *If* Scott were telling the truth, if he *knew* the truth…'More than he could *imagine?*' This was not exactly the Holy Grail or Golden Fleece, and yet to her…

Okay. Ease up. Slow down. Deep breaths. She reached inside her purse, removed a small pad of paper and pen, placed them on the table, picked up her knife and fork and cut into the venison, dipped it in the sauce and brought it to her mouth. A deep dark flavor, balanced, yet. . . what was that forest redolent fragrance? *Juniper berries*, that's what was blending with the rosemary, explaining the subtle taste of pines. But with a hint of alcohol? She wrote it down. The venison, she noticed, had been seared with a touch of salt. In olive oil, butter? Doubtful. The meat was lightly caramelized, deep brown, not the product of olive oil and butter, which could not have withstood the high heat of searing. Yet both, she sensed, were apparent in the sauce. Safflower oil, most likely, that's what was used for the searing, with olive oil and butter tossed in at the end for flavor. When it suddenly struck her. It *wasn't* juniper berries. It was but it wasn't. It was gin! *Made* from juniper berries! *Gin!* To deglaze the pan. With *gin!* She wrote that down too.

She sat back, assessing what she so far had. The sauce, which was everything, was beginning to materialize. Tart, sweet, peppery. Something deep? The pomegranate seeds, of course. And lemon. She'd picked that up easily. And the rosemary and now the gin. A touch of brown sugar, too, she was certain. And onions. Her sense of smell and taste told her onions. But was it? They'd be overpowering, which they weren't. Yet that flavor. Shallots? Minced shallots? Shallots! As well as a slight hint of tomato and vinegar. Tomato and vinegar. Her note pad was beginning to fill.

What was she missing? Stock, of course, was the base of the sauce. How made, reduced from what? Beef? She doubted that. There was no cutting corners for what she was tasting. Venison! The stock was made from venison bones, reduced, she was sure, with crème fraiche or sour cream. Which one? Not sour crème, it curdles. Crème Fraiche, she guessed, she'd go with that. Again she wrote on her pad, when from the corner of her eye she saw her waiter in intense conversation with the Maître d'. He was listening intently, and then they were both staring across the room. At Tally.

Tally wasn't through. There was something she was missing. Very subtle, vaguely familiar, but what? The Maître d', she saw, was crossing the room toward her table. She made no effort to return the pad to her purse, rather left it in plain view, had resumed her eating when the Maître d' reached her.

"Is there anything the trouble?" he asked in English upon arriving.

"I beg your pardon?" she said, looking up as though in surprise to see him standing there.

"You are making notes, Madame. Perhaps there is a problem?" His English was very formal, though he seemed proud of it.

"Quite the contrary," she answered with a welcoming smile. She reached into her purse, took out her wallet, and removed a card, which she handed over. "I'm Articles Editor of *New York In Review* publications in the States." It was an old card she'd kept that still had her name and title. "We're doing a survey of leading restaurants here in Southern Burgundy for our October issue. Our readership is rather upscale. It travels. Monsieur..?"

"Naniche."

"Please, Monsieur Naniche." She gestured to a chair at her table. "I'd like to conduct an interview for the article, if you've the time."

Whatever wariness he'd had instantly dissolved as she picked up her pen.

"Arnaud Naniche," he said, spelling it out for her as he slid onto a chair, galvanized by the anticipation of fame.

It had been the worst night's sleep of Scott's life. They'd arrived at the Hotel Saint-Pere at six the evening before. The hotel, a once mid-nineteenth century hunting lodge, with hanging baskets of Dusty Miller blue-grey flowers, backed up against a stream, was, for all its surrounding woodland beauty, a one-star at best by Scott's assessment. A light dinner of unusually good truite meuniere in the hotel's rustic dining room changed little of his appraisal of the place. Especially when he awoke in the morning.

His back was a mess. His slab-like bed, he judged, was a left over from days long past for fileting game. Little accounting was given to the tension he felt. No, it was the bed. Pulling himself to a sitting position with muffled cries, he made it to the bathroom, relieved himself, shaved with one hand supporting his weight on the basin, managed to get into the shower, hoping the long hot stream of water would relieve the pain. It didn't.

Drying himself as best as could, he returned to his room. On the wicker armchair next to the bed were his clothes of yesterday. Dragging them to the bed, he lay back on it, naked, still half wet, tried to slip into his underwear. Twice he tried. He couldn't make it, waited several moments, breathing heavily, tried again, assisted by a stream of curses, couldn't do it, lay back as though the next breath would be his last. Giving up on the underwear, he reached for the chino pants, managed one leg on, then, with all the will at his command, fighting pain, the other. It was as far as he could go. He lay back, exhausted, chest heaving so violently he thought he'd break a rib. And there he lay, three hours, four, dozing fitfully, till there was a rap on his door.

"Scott?" It was Tally. "*Scott?*" More rapping.

"Wait a minute. Wait a goddamn minute! Jesus!"

He glanced at the clock on the night stand by his bed. It was four o'clock in the afternoon. *Four o'clock?* He pushed himself upright on the bed with the speed of a sloth, breathing heavily, buttoned the top of his pants with shaking fingers, raised the zipper, brought his feet to the floor, crawled along the edge of the bed, bare chested, lunged for the door. The bolt turned easily, but his strength was expiring. Turning, he made it to the arm chair, dropped into it as the door was pushed open and Tally looked in. The sight of him brought a sincere look of concern.

"What happened?"

"My back's what happened. That fu…goddamn bed."

"Get on the floor."

"Yeah, sure."

"Get on the floor!"

"I can't."

"Give me your hands."

He reluctantly held out his hands. She took them, pulled them toward her till he dropped to his knees with a howl.

"Sit back, butt on your heels, lean forward, hands on the floor, reach, arms straight, stretch it out."

"Damn!"

"Dog tail in, head back, stomach in, stretch! Don't give up on it, hold it! Stay there, just like that. I'll be right back."

She was back in two minutes with a glass of water and two Aleves. "Any better?"

"I don't know."

"Take this." Which he did, swallowed the pills. "Roll over."

"How?"

"The flat of your back on the floor."

It was a minute before he'd accomplished it.

"Put your arms out to the side, bring your knees up, far as you can."

He tried to do so, was startled when she threw the top of her body against his knees, pressing them into his chest to stretch out his back.

"Christ!"

But it wasn't just the stretch. He could feel her breasts against his knees, her hair falling over her face, gleaming fair hair. The muscles of her stomach, against the lower part of his legs, were flat and firm. And there was an odor about her, clean, like spring.

"Hold that, long as you can, knees to your chest," she said. "Bring your hands up, grab your knees, hold them there." She backed off. "Give it half an hour, it'll be better. Come down to my room. First floor." She gave the number and left.

For a long while Scott lay on his back, knees held to his chest, went over and over what had just happened. There was nothing flirtatious in her manner, no promise of anything beyond what they'd come here for. She had done what she usually did. She had come to the rescue. Again. A rescuer. And yet? Yet what? Had he read the signs wrong? Was there more to it than that? 'I mean, Jesus,' he thought, recalling their first meeting, that lunch. She'd been stumbling all over herself in front of him then. Now? 'Come down to my room,' she'd said? "*Down to my room?*"

True to her prediction thirty minutes brought the pain to a manageable level, enough so he was able to dress. Primping before the bathroom mirror, he ran a comb through his hair, checked himself out, right side, left, and went over the signs. He was pretty good at that. He'd made a *career* out of signs. And the more he thought about it, the more it solidified in his brain. '*Come down to my room!*' Maybe. Just maybe, maybe!

Taking the stairs to the first floor, Scott came to her door, hesitated, affected his most beguiling grin, and knocked.

"It's unlocked."

Pushing open the door, Scott was immediately met with a familiar aroma as well as the farthest thing from what he'd expected. The room he saw was larger than his, had a kitchenette, its counter brimming with condiments, a bottle of gin, and chopped herbs, Tally turning from the stove with a sauté pan, nodding Scott to a chair at a small round dining table.

"Sit down. Taste this."

He sat, Tally removing half the contents from the pan onto a plate, two medallions, spooned over with juniper berries and sauce. There was a fork and knife already in place. He picked up both, a growing excitement running through his bones like never before, sliced into one of the two medallions, dipped it in the sauce, brought it into his mouth.

"Well?" she asked.

A great beam spread across Scott's face.

"Medlock, you son of a bitch, did you pick the right guy. I've *done* it! What?" The look on her face brought him up short. "*We* did it!" he corrected himself. "*You* did."

"Shit!" She was looking into the pan.

"No shit, what shit..?"

"We haven't got it," she told him.

"We *do*, you've *got* it!"

"No." she said, still staring into the pan, still shaking her head. "No."

"No shaking head," he blurted out, panic in his voice, "No 'no', it's there…"

"It's not," she said. "There's something missing, something…"

"No, nothing missing. We'll call the airline. Be out of here, back to. . . cook it up for Medlock, more than I can imagine, he said…" He stared at her still shaking head. "Oh, God." It was a total capitulation, his world, his future, all thought of it, shattered into a pile of lost delusions. "What're we going to do?" he asked in barely a whisper.

She seemed to think for a moment, though she'd come to the answer well before.

"Moldova."

His head drew back, his face turning white.

"What Moldova?"

"What was the name of that chef?"

"No, no chef."

"The one who invented this?"

"You're crazy!"

"Chernivtsi."

"No Chernivtsi!"

"In that town you went to. Pelivan?"

"You're nuts!"

"Pelivan."

Scott fought for something to say, found nothing, so dropped his head into his hands. The pounding in it was coming on again. This time with a bout of nausea.

"Look at me."

He shook his head, side to side.

"Scott, look at me!"

It was an order, not a request. He lifted his head, looked up at her.

"I can't do this without you," she said.

"You're saying I owe you!" he challenged as though the wounded party.

She stared at him.

"Why would I say that?"

"You damn well know."

A look of bewilderment crossed her face, then realization.

"You went into my *room?*"

He drew in his breath to reply. She waited for it. She'd wait forever.

"Get out. Pack your things and just get out."

"Where am I supposed to go?"

She reached inside her purse hanging from the back of a chair, pulled out four fifty-euros notes, slammed them on the table before him.

"Taxi to Sermizelles, train to Paris, bus to the airport. Just go."

It took Tally forty-five minutes to clean her room, pack, call Vayama Air Lines for a one way ticket, 9:25 p.m. out of Lyons to Chisinau, Moldova, through Munich, check herself and Scott out and head for her car in the parking lot. It was close to five o'clock; the trip of 230 kilometers should get her to the Lyon-Saint Exupery Airport no later than seven-thirty if there were no delays. Reaching her car with her bag and carry-on, she stopped dead in her tracks. Scott stood by the passenger door, his duffle bag at his feet. His hand came up, holding out the 200 euros she'd given him.

For a moment she stared at him, with the growing conviction she was involved in a nightmare. Opening the car door, she tossed her bag in behind the narrow opening behind the driver's seat, dropped her purse at her feet, slid in behind the steering wheel, sat clutching it.

Her gray eyes rose to the rear view mirror. She stared at herself. She was a woman who had always been inclined to think well of her fellow creatures, but the first involuntary thought that came into her head was that she must have done something reprehensible to be tied to this one. Her head came up as Scott opened the passenger door, dropped his bag behind the passenger seat, got in, and closed the door.

Still she sat clutching the wheel. He opened his mouth to speak, but she held up a finger, a single warning finger, which clearly said, "Shut up. Just shut up." A moment more to think things through. She reached into her bag, pulled out her cell phone, hit the redial button, which connected her to Vayama Airlines. In three minutes she'd changed the reservation to Chisinau to two, closed her phone, dropped it back into her purse, started the engine, threw it into gear and peeled away, spitting gravel.

Eighteen

"Why does a Yugo have a rear window defroster?" It was Scott at his self-anointed worst. "To keep your hands warm while you're pushing it."

They'd arrived in Chisinau at eight in the morning after a five hour delay in Munich. The cheapest car rental service at the airport was Europcar, and the cheapest car to rent was the Yugo, long since voted one of the worst automobiles ever built. But its rental was sixteen euros a day, making it affordable, and inviting Scott's running commentary as Tally drove east from the capital city toward Pelivan.

"What do you call a Yugo with a flat tire? Totaled."

They hadn't spoken to each other much since leaving Vezalay, and now, as they approached Pelivan, Scott's stomach turning to knots, he tried to bury his anxiety with blather.

"What's included in every Yugo's manual?"

"Scott…"

"A bus schedule."

She shook her head almost imperceptibly.

"Come on, that's funny," he said.

"Sorry. I must have been dozing."

How she'd been taken in that first day they'd met in New York she still couldn't fathom. That lunch they'd had, as she sat there fantasizing — what? She didn't even want to go there. She'd seen what happened to women that did. She shook her head again, this time a little fiercely, trying to rid it of even *thoughts* of what if. A sign, black on white, riddled with bullet holes, someone's target practice, came into view, indicating a road off the highway to Pelivan, four kilometers. Tally took it, the sixteen-year-old grey, box-like, rattling, rusting Yugo chattering in protest as it bounced along the rutted dirt surface past fields of cabbage. In the near-distance Tally could see hills crowned by woods. But here the land was flat. Arable, but crudely cultivated.

"What do you call a Yugo that breaks down after a hundred miles?" Scott asked, but the muscles in his face were growing tense at the familiar but threatening terrain.

"An over achiever," Tally answered in irritation. "Old as the hills."

He dropped back against the seat.

"Just trying to be friendly."

The rest of the ride was driven in silence, but Scott's heart was hammering, his head craning, looking about for lingering disaster as they arrived at the village to find two dozen single story homes scattered about like tossed dice. Most had outside toilets. Most, too, with small vegetable gardens, cultivated, from what one could see, by primitive tools. A wooden dray, two men aboard it, was being drawn through the street on oversized balloon tires by a pair of horses. Tally slowed the Yugo, rolled down the window.

"Do you speak English?" she called out to the men, unfamiliar herself with Romanian, the spoken language in Moldova.

The two men looked at each other, no idea what she was asking.

"French?" she asked. "Français?"

One of them, the older of the two, nodded.

"Un peu."

"Nous cherchons un homme, Monsieur Chernivtsi?"

"Non," he said.

"Chernivtsi," Tally repeated.

"Chernivtsi," the man repeated, started to shake his head again when, "*Chernivtsi!*" he said, but with a totally different pronunciation.

"Savez-vous où il vit?" she asked.

"Deux kilomètres!" he pointed down the road. "Une maison rouge. Par verger." His French was guttural, not easily understood, as well as improper. But she got the sense of it.

"Merci, monsieur," she said, rolling up her window against the dust, then throwing the Yugo into gear, driving it through and out of the town.

"What'd he say?" Scott asked. "Verger. What's that?"

"An orchard. A red house by an orchard."

Two kilometers further on they came to it. A dirt but leveled lane ran off the road past a well-maintained orchard of peach and apricot trees. Circling a half acre-sized pond, Tally brought the Yugo to a stop before a two story, red painted, equally maintained farmhouse. Cutting the engine, which ran on before dying, they stared at the place, an oasis in the otherwise coarse landscape. Firewood, an axe buried into a chopping block beside it, was neatly stacked before the entrance. A tractor with rotary tiller blades stood by a shed. There was a well, a smoke house and a barn. No wires could be seen carrying electricity or telephone lines to the house, but from somewhere there was the soft purr of a generator.

The driver's-side door emitting a painful screech, Tally emerged from the car, looked about as Scott joined her. Whatever they'd expected to find, this wasn't it, when:

"We grew up with Kolhoz and Sovhoz, Soviet collective farms before our independence, and it's difficult for the government to part with these huge associations, where people used to work for nothing."

At the sound of the voice, Tally and Scott had turned to face a tall, clean shaven man, with lean muscular cheeks and grey close cropped hair, perhaps fifty. He was dressed in rough but clean work clothes and high ankle boots, with a body well-adapted to labor.

"I think the government is not keen to help the farmers," he continued in excellent English. "They don't even pay attention to us. They refuse to come to our meetings, though we invite them. They want to export grapes and wine only from huge farms, which are the same as Kolhoz."

"Monsieur Chernivtsi?" Tally extended her hand. "I'm Tally Garner, this is my associate, Mr. Fitzgerald. We're here…"

"I know why you're here," he interrupted, ignoring her hand, but nodding them toward the house. "There's tea."

The main room directly off the entrance, or common room as it was called, was nineteenth-century original, wood-work, doors, floors, latches, furnished with scrub-top tables and country chairs, most if not all seemingly came from flea markets, but in excellent repair.

There they sat, Scott on the edge of a vintage cottage loveseat as though ready to bolt, Tally, hands folded on top of her purse on a companion chair as Chernivtsi entered, cups and steaming pot of tea on a tray. Setting it on the larger of three nesting tables, he poured three cups, picked up one for himself, sat in a wicker chair across from them. Thirty seconds went by in silence, sixty. It was clear he was not going to be the one to break the silence.

"How *did* you know?" Tally asked.

"Your 'associate' has made things rather obvious. A recipe. So, why?"

"I can't tell you that," she answered. "I'd lie if you asked me again."

He nodded as though appreciating her candor.

"An expensive pursuit," he said.

"We're budgeting."

"I am not talking about money."

Questioning frown lines creased her face at the line, Scott looking wide-eyed from one to the other as though watching a ping pong match as Chernivtsi went on.

"I'm sorry, lady, you have wasted a long trip."

"Why?" she asked.

His eyebrows rose at her question.

"You aren't still in Vezalay," she continued. "Which raises the question. Why not? Chez Gaillard has become a star-rated restaurant. You were its chef."

"I'd lie if I answered that," he said.

"Of course," she replied wryly.

"But, why not. Moldova is a very poor country."

"We've seen."

"Many from here cross into other European states illegally looking for work. As did I, six years ago, into France. The French government took homage. It was prison pending deportation. I left."

"Your recipes left behind."

"Of course."

"Then it's unimportant to reveal the contents of one."

"The venison medallions."

"Yes."

"Again, why?" he asked.

"I've told you…"

"So the two of us are shrouded in mystery." He thought a moment. "What have you determined of its ingredients?"

Was it hope? She plunged into it, told him all she'd discovered, or thought she'd discovered. The backstrap venison, pomegranate seeds. The sauce with its shallots, gin, ground juniper, rosemary, crème fraiche, brown sugar, and lemon.

Chernivtsi nodded, impressed.

"But I'm missing something."

"Correct."

"Would you tell me what it is?"

"If I want to lose a hand."

Tally sat back slowly. "I beg your pardon?"

"Tell me you've not heard of the Union Corse."

"We're talking about a *restaurant*."

"A criminal organization operating out of Corsica and Marseille. Far more secretive and paranoid than any Sicilian Mafia. Money laundering, racketeering, drug trafficking, extortion, contract killing of persons or organizations attempting to infiltrate or obstruct any activity or possession."

"What have they to do with Chez Gaillard?"

"They own Chez Gaillard."

"Jesus fucking Christ, I knew it, I *knew* it!" Scott exploded.

Tally's face was in shock. "I don't believe this."

"Believe what you want. You have put yourselves in great jeopardy. Myself as well, should they believe I have told you anything, which I have assured them I would not."

It took Tally several second to absorb what she'd heard.

"This is nonsense," she said. Then, "If I told you my reasons..?"

"No, lady, I think not. But understand. Let your excellent brain grasp what I'm trying to tell you. It is perfectly simple. Continue this endeavor, perhaps even if not, they will try to kill you."

Five minutes later Tally and Scott sat in their Yugo in frozen silence, internally blundering toward a switch that would turn off everything they'd heard. There *was* no switch. There was only the vague perfume of apricots and peaches and the faint buzzing of bees. Inserting the car key, Tally was about to turn on the engine when there was a rapping on the window beside her. Chernivtsi indicated she was to roll it down. When she'd done so, he pushed his face into the opening.

"It's been banned," he said.

"What?" she asked in bewilderment.

"Your missing ingredient. It's been banned."

With that he pushed away from the car and walked back to his house.

Nineteen

They'd returned to the main road, were heading west toward Chisinau past a stand of trees colorful in their autumn robes. Scott glanced at Tally. Her face was rigid. Her hands, gripping the wheel as she drove, were white-knuckled. And then she was turning off the road, onto a patch of scrub grass beneath the shade of a hornbeam tree. The motor left running, burnt-orange leaves floated in a light breeze.

"I'm sorry," Tally murmured in a voice so low Scott could barely hear. Her chest, he saw, was heaving, and her eyes were at the edge of tears. "I am so, so sorry," she said.

Scott had never, in his adult life, allowed himself to be a feeling person. There was too much vulnerability that went with that. He'd gone through it as a child. But it was now, for the first time since the long ago loss of his father, leaving him with an uncaring mother, at which time he promised himself he would never, ever go through the pain of that again, that he felt a discernible sensitivity and concern for another human being.

"When we get back to Lyon," she was saying, "you can get a flight to London."

"You?"

"I've got to go back to Angers."

"You *can't* go back to Angers. What's in Angers?"

She offered no answer, dropped her chin. On total impulse, no thought behind it, Scott reached across, took her face in his hands, his lips on hers. Instinctively, she pushed him away.

"Don't do that!"

He obeyed her instantly, sat back staring out the windshield as she said in a voice more bewildered than condemning, "Why did you do that?"

Scott said nothing, in fact had no answer. But the taste had been sweet, lips soft if unyielding.

"Well," she was saying, "don't do it again."

They sat in silence for a moment, the tension all but crackling.

"What are we going to do?" she asked at length.

"When I get out of this? Going to Alaska," he said.

"Why Alaska?"

"Get me an Inupiat Eskimo woman. They don't speak English, can't talk back and do what they're told."

Tally shook her head, looked ahead up the road. But her heart was beating fast and so was his.

"Okay. Okay, what are the givens." she said. "They don't know we're here."

"Oh, they know we're here."

"Shit!"

"Sorry," he said.

"Well, come up with something!"

"They'll be waiting for us in Lyon."

"You know that," she said sarcastically.

"Though maybe not."

"Jesus."

"You got a better thought?"

"Why Lyon?" she asked.

"Your car's in Lyon. They know we haven't got what we wanted or we wouldn't have come here. They know what's-his-name wouldn't give it to you, he told you why. Maybe they want to see where you're going to go. Back to that restaurant, maybe."

"*God*, I'm glad you never thought about writing fiction."

"Hey, listen...!" he started to object to the sarcasm.

"Go on."

"Why'm I the guy doing all the work here," he replied irritably.

"They'll be waiting for us in Lyon," she conceded. "What do we do?"

"As a thought?"

"I'm listening."

He sat for a moment, deciding any sort of stealth was out of the question. His eyes wandered to the street, drawn to a farm worker on a bicycle trudging past. Otherwise, no traffic.

"We don't go to Lyon," he said at length.

"My *car's* there!"

"Is it going anywhere?"

"Go ahead."

"If we can just get somewhere to think things through."

"You've a plane to catch."

"They fly daily."

She turned and looked through the windshield again.

"Montpellier."

"Where?"

"Montpellier."

"Why Montpellier?"

It was as though her mind had taken three steps and stopped.

"Montpellier," she said.

The Lufthansa Fokker 100 from Munich set down without incident at Montpellier's Mediterranee Airport. It was six o'clock in the evening and customs officials were as anxious to be on their way as were arrivals. A cursory glance at passports, a quick stamp of entry, and everyone, Scott and Tally among them, were through.

Twenty minutes later, the rented Peugeot 107 with its hand-cranked windows and no air conditioning was headed toward the city, Tally driving. From his passenger seat Scott checked the highway. Most of it was late day traffic, people on their way home. If there was a trailing black Mercedes, Scott couldn't see, which accounted for nothing.

Located in the Languedoc of southern France just off the Mediterranean coast mid-way between Nice and Toulouse, Montpellier had long been a university city of a quarter million people, with a centuries-old history of intellectual advancement and social tolerance. It was also the worst city in France for driving into without a clear knowledge of its insane spider web one way cross-stitching streets. Best to avoid if possible, which Tally did, taking the coastal route east from the airport south of the city.

It was a Mediterranean autumn sunset, the water dancing with color, pinks and reds, the slight breeze blowing in from Africa not enough to churn white caps. Elegiac as it was, Scott could still not shake a deep apprehension. He kept looking at the side view mirror at trailing traffic, no sign of anything suspicious. But he'd felt secure before only to discover, to his alarm, there was no such thing.

"Where we going?" he asked, suddenly aware it was not Montpellier.

Tally gave no answer, but thirty kilometers further brought them to Sete, a seaside small boat harbor fishing village. Canals gave it the look of a miniature Venice, Scott saw, neck craning as Tally turned down a quai, past apartment and commercial buildings, drawing the Peugeot to a stop before a canal-side restaurant.

Time had not been kind to the place, its wooden facing weathered, all effort to keep it up seemingly abandoned, even the name across the entrance, "Vieux Logis." Colorful fishing boats, brightly painted every hue of the rainbow, floated at their tie-downs thirty feet away. On the darkening horizon, just inside the harbor entrance, a forest of masts bobbed at their moorings. A sign before the restaurant entrance read, "A Vendre."

Entering, they found it empty, perhaps too early for diners if any were to arrive. What drew most attention was the run-down look of the place. There was a counter, a zinc trough behind it for shucking oysters. Several circular chipped wooden tables filled the room, each attended by wooden chairs. A pair of ceiling fans rotated slowly offering nothing much in the way of comforting air.

"What is this place?" Scott asked looking about as they seated themselves. "It's a dump."

"Good oysters. Mussels and oysters," she said, draping her purse straps over the back of her chair.

"What's that sign outside?" he asked. "Something vente."

"A Vendre. It means for sale. The place is for sale."

"Good luck with that," he answered dolefully.

Said as Le Patron, the restaurant's sole staff and owner, arrived. He was medium height, mid-seventies, dour, close-cropped white hair giving him a look more Prussian than Gallic, a bad back keeping him from standing upright. Placing a plastic basket of bread, paper napkins and two cheap wine glasses on the table, he wiped his hands on a soiled apron around his middle.

"Madame, M'sieur."

"Up for it?" Tally asked.

"Sure," Scott shrugged.

"Deux ordres d'huitres, une douzaine chaque," Tally said. "Et un demi-bouteille du vin blanc de la maison."

The man nodded and withdrew. Silence, neither for the moment finding words. Scott looked about the room in disdain, trying to deceive himself they'd at least found an oasis.

"What do you suppose he could get for a place like this?"

"175,500."

"Dollars?"

"Euros."

"What's that in dollars?"

"227,500."

"That's crazy."

"That's what he wants."

"He'll never get it."

"So long as I don't have the money for it, he won't."

"You'd *want* this place?"

"You want an Eskimo."

"Where would you start?"

"Patch, repair, but preserve the rustic nature. Gut the interior, brand new kitchen, replace the counter, tables, chairs, get rid of those fans, inlay the counter top with old menus when oysters were ten francs a dozen, if I could find them. Two people could run it." The words sounded normal, but her teeth were chattering.

"You've thought about it."

"Thoughts don't cost a dime."

"When'd *that* start?"

"I was down for a weekend, saw that sign."

"What could you do with it?" Scott asked, looking about.

"The oysters would stay. Mussels, too. That's what people come down here for. But I'd bring in my own creations. Nothing served that wasn't raised or grown within fifty kilometers of here except the wines. They'd be exclusively from the area, though, Languedoc-Roussillon. I think that would be an appeal. To locals as well as tourists."

"I got a name for it," he said, still ogling the place.

"What?"

"Nobody Knows The Truffles I've Seen."

She tried to stifle a laugh, she couldn't, the first laugh he'd seen from her to anything he'd had to say in months.

He watched her toy with a piece of bread. "Listen. About what happened in the car…"

"What do you suppose he meant," she said immediately. "The missing ingredient, something banned."

Scott sat back, accepting her deflect.

"Steroids?" he answered.

A look of annoyance crossed her face.

"Sorry," he said.

"What're they doing right now?" she asked, coming back to what was most on her mind.

"Who?"

"Them, they, your pursuers."

Scott held for a moment.

"For a guess?" he said.

"No fantasies."

"They've given up watching your car. They know by now we didn't come in through Lyon."

"What else do they know?"

"These guys? I've given up guessing," Scott said.

"Okay. What then?"

"What if we went to an American consulate?"

"And told them what?" she asked.

"That we needed safe passage."

"To where?"

"Home, for Christ's sake, where else?"

Tally said nothing. Scott's eyebrows raised in realization.

"You're not going," he said.

"If we get it, get what we're going for, and your man comes through…"

"You'd buy this place?" he stared incredulous.

"And you could take your Eskimo bride on safari."

"You're crazy, you're out of your mind."

They ceased conversation as their oysters arrived. Reaching under his arm pit, Le Patron produced a half bottle of a cheap local white, screwed in a cork screw. A pop as the cork was pulled and wine was poured. A deep frown furrowed Scott's brow.

"What's that?" he asked.

"What's what?"

He was staring at the small metal container half-filled with a greenish, blackish, yellowish liquid in the middle of his platter of oysters.

"That!" he pointed.

"Mignonette sauce," she answered. "Goes with oysters."

"What's it made of?"

"Minced shallots, cracked pepper, vinegar."

"M'sieur," Scott called with a snap of his fingers. "Ketchup!"

The man turned back, a look of utter horror on his face.

"Quoi?"

"Ketchup!"

"Avec les *huitres?*" The man was appalled

"J'ai dit que je veux ketchup!" Scott repeated.

The man looked at Tally, who appeared to share his dismay, threw up his hands, disappeared into his kitchen, returned with a half empty bottle of long since opened ketchup, and slammed it on the table in disgust. Uncapping the bottle, Scott slathered it on his oysters. A look of disbelief crossed Tally's face.

"You're kidding."

"I told you. Ketchup…"

"…on ice cream, I know."

"Chacun son gout."

Defiantly spearing an oyster, Scott raised it to his mouth. . . and froze.

Tally had started to reply, instead saw the look on his face. She turned, following his gaze. Two men were standing just inside the entrance to the restaurant. Nothing distinguishing about their dress to set them apart in a crowd, the first was large, thick, of indeterminate age, hair, topped by a hat, falling in straggly black masses. The other was medium height, blond, seemingly wily, with an intense pallor about his unshaven face. Crossing to the bar, they slid onto seats, back to the room, Le Patron greeting them with no recognition.

Their order was muffled, neither Tally nor Scott able to hear. Scott slowly lowered his oyster. He felt blood leaving his face. He had only glanced at the men, but the whole picture filled his mind.

"Out," he whispered.

"What?"

"Out of here."

She sat frozen, overcome with inaction. Reaching inside his travel vest, Scott pulled out the last of his euros, dropped them on the table, rose, took Tally's arm, lifted her to his feet, grabbing her purse from the back of the chair.

"Don't look back, just walk," Scott murmured. His voice was toneless and husky.

Reaching the door, they went through it. Night had fallen, muted lights along the quay were on, playing a weird dance on the canal's waters. His grip on her arm was firm as he led her quick step toward the Peugeot, forty feet away. Reaching it, they split, Tally to the driver's side, electronically unlocking the car doors, Scott to the passenger's with a final look back. He stopped, Tally with him. No one was following. Still they stared. No one was coming from the place, the two men seen through the restaurant window still seated at the counter. Scott glanced across the top of the car at Tally, then back at the two men, neither making any effort to leave or pursue.

Air exploding from his lungs, Scott collapsed against the side of the car, shaking his head in relief. There was a step behind him and he swung around, nerves jumpy, into a rain of blows.

"You bastard!" Tally railed at him. "You scared me half to death."

"Yeah, well…"

"Well, what?"

"Just…"

"…all the paranoids are out to get you, right?"

"Christ, you always had a mouth!" he seethed, shoving her purse into her hands.

"*I* did?"

"Everything a fucking judgment!"

"The pot calling the kettle?"

"Where's it written you're the monitor of everyone's ass in this Goddamn world? Well, that time's past, baby!"

"Get in the car," she said.

"Fuck you!"

"In your dreams."

Tally started to circle back to the driver's side, Scott opening the passenger side door as though to get in, then, like hell he will, slamming it closed, when there was a shriek.

"Scott!'

He hurried to her quickly, stared at what she was seeing. The Peugeot's two rear tires had been slashed.

Twenty

The fishing boat reeked of dead tuna, washed down though it had been, as Scott and Tally huddled beneath its gunnels. Secured to its quai-side mooring, the boat was limited sanctuary, protected by dim lights coming from buildings along the quai. The only sounds were the water lapping against the hull, and the measured, deliberate footsteps of the two men from the restaurant, walking, looking, rattling gates, searching alcoves and entrances to buildings.

At the sight of their shadows, Tally drew in a quick breath, Scott's hand immediately across her mouth. The two men stopped, not thirty feet away, alerted to the sound, decided they'd heard nothing of importance, consulted in muted conversation, then split, one moving up the quai, the other down, searching, searching.

For a time they crouched there, listening, hearing only the rippling water now, Tally looking at Scott, beseeching decision. He tried to think and found that he couldn't. The things he was used to, artifice, calumny, self-assurance had ceased to exist. He was in a land he hated with annihilation on its horizon, alone but for the one person to whom he might speak of his terror, but couldn't and wouldn't, though she was sanity, and substance.

Raising his head above the gunnels, Scott saw the quai was deserted. But not entirely. A hundred feet down was a delivery van. In semi-darkness two workmen in blue coveralls were removing what appeared to be boxes and baskets of food from the rear bed of the van, carrying them to and across a gangway down into a tethered barge. A name was faintly visible on its bow. "Escargot." Lit from within, the two men were depositing deliveries, then returning to the van for more. For a moment Scott remained motionless, then grabbed Tally's hand.

She opened her mouth to question, but Scott was hauling her to her feet, over the gunnels, onto the quai, half-dragging, half-running her at a crouch toward the barge. Reaching it, almost stumbling across electrical hookups from the quai, Scott dragged Tally onto the gangway, headed down.

Aboard they saw it was no ordinary scow, but a converted luxury floating hotel, food being brought on, stored in a massive refrigerator and cupboards, along with table linens and wines. With the soft purr from an onboard generator, the workmen ignoring them as though they belonged, Scott and Tally glanced about. The aft section, they saw, opened past a twelve seat dining table to a lounge of comfortable cushioned couches and chairs. Stairs, forward off the dining area, led topside, a hatch cover slid closed and locked from within eliminating access. The forward lower section, past the stairs, led to a companionway past six numbered doors.

Still grasping Tally's hand, Scott led her into the companionway, opened the first door they came to, pushed Tally in, entering himself behind her, closing, locking the door behind them.

It was a cabin, illumination from the quai filtering in through windows providing enough light to see. Furnished with a single double bed, there was a closet with built-in drawers, a chair and desk, a corner door opening into a small, but well-appointed bathroom containing toilet, cabinet, sink, a curtained-off shower as well as more than usual traveler's amenities. The bed was freshly made. Fresh towels hung on the bathroom rack.

Lowering to the bed Tally looked up at Scott and all he could think of was did she know a frightened man when she saw one. But he'd gotten them there, he'd done that. And then she was on her feet and her arms were around him, holding him close, her body pressing against him. The next moment his arms were around her. He did nothing more, nor did she invite him to, the two just clinging to each other till she leaned back, half against him, looked up into his face as though trying to discern something. Letting go, she disappeared into the bathroom, lit solely by a night light, and closed the door.

Dropping into the chair, Scott was aware his legs were shaking. And not only from fear. He was being drawn into a totally new state of mind with this girl, and he had no history to call upon how to handle it. She'd given him no encouragement, that was for certain, and he'd made a fool of himself in the car with that kiss. He'd had women that were gone from his mind in an hour, impersonal, dispassionate encounters. Yet that kiss? Why did it linger?

On the other side of the thin partition separating the cabin from the bathroom, Scott could hear the toilet flushing, followed by running water. Moments later the door opened. In the dim light Scott could see Tally was down to her panties and bra, her clothes hung on the hook on the back of the bathroom door, her shoes and socks in hand, which she set on the cabin floor. Without acknowledgment, she turned to the bed, climbed in, pulled the covers up over her shoulders, tucked herself into a tight ball and closed her eyes.

Scott made no move. Instead he sat there in the chair listening to the faint throb of the generator. Through the cabin window, he could see the workmen had finished their deliveries, heard the entrance door to the barge being closed and locked, following which he could see the rear of the van slammed closed, its occupants boarding and the van was driven away. His eyes lowered to Tally, already nearing sleep. His thoughts went to her face, her voice, to her, so different from others he'd known. He got up, wrapped himself in a light blanket taken from the foot of the bed, and returned to his chair. He would, he decided, spend the rest of the night like that, forced a yawn, tried wandering into an uneasy doze that wouldn't come. He reflected on the moment she'd pulled back from their embrace and looked up into his face. What was it? 'How nice you suddenly are?' Or simply, 'Thank you?'

For a while he watched the gentle rise and fall of her body beneath the covers, when out of nowhere his stomach turned over. He was not used, he suddenly realized, to people out to kill him. He tried to force anger. He couldn't. He was, quite simply, scared. And so was she. Further it was becoming more and more clear she was looking to him to get them through this. *That* was the look he'd seen on her face. It was on that thought, far into the night, Scott finally fell asleep.

When he awoke, sunlight was pouring in through the window, and the barge, he saw, was under way, cutting slowly across an inland expanse of water, past land a hundred feet away. He looked toward the bed. It was empty. The door to the bathroom was open, swinging slightly on it hinges with the light roll of the barge. Tally's clothes were gone and so was she!

Discarding the blanket, he moved into the bathroom. One of the towels, he instantly saw, was damp, droplets of water still collected at the base of the shower. It was then he caught a glimpse of himself in the mirror. Usually when he did so, he'd see a more virtuous, elegant version of himself. Not this time. Whatever her reasons for rising, showering, quitting the cabin could well have been him. He looked like crap.

The amenities, he saw, included two travel tooth brushes, one of which had already been opened and used, a small tube of tooth paste, a plastic handled razor, and a small tube of shaving cream. Availing himself of all, Scott brushed his teeth, shaved, showered quickly, dressed, slipped on his travel vest, checked its belongings, passport, wallet, still the room key from his hotel room in Beaune, strapped on his watch. It was nine o'clock.

Opening the door, he stepped into the companionway and came face to face with a tall ash blond woman, lithe, mid-thirties, with a perpetual, toothsome grin. In her hand was a cup of steaming coffee.

"Good *morning*, Mr. Fitzgerald." Her accent was English, her greeting so cheerful one would think they'd known each other forever. "I'm Lynn." She handed him the coffee. "I'd take this, if I were you. You're going to need bracing. She's very upset."

Accepting the coffee, Scott stared at her, his face growing blank and stupid. By the time he reached the lounge the expression was set.

Seated in a deep back chair was Tally, one leg jiggling up and down as though in uncontrolled tension, a glowering look on her face. Across from her sat the barge's captain. Also mid-thirties, likeable, tousled head of red hair, scratchy patch of red beard, he was dressed in tan short-sleeved shirt and trousers and Sperry boat shoes, no socks. His name was Tim, and he was listening in doleful sympathy to Tally's rant.

"I *told* him," Tally was fuming, "you don't *know* this is our boat! 'Yeah, I do, I *know*,' he said. 'How can you *know?*' I said." Then turning to Scott at the sight of him. "Tell him!"

"Wha…"

"You don't even have the reservation confirmation!"

"Because?" he said, trying to figure out where this was going.

"You packed the damn thing in our *luggage!*"

"Which?"

"The airline lost," she said. "I *told* you not to pack it away!" she said, seemingly fighting tears. "Does he listen? He never listens."

It had taken a bit for the bulb to go on. But now it had.

"So now it's *my* fault," Scott jumped into the game.

"Shoe fits!"

"So where the hell *are* we?"

"Tell him," she said, turning to Tim.

"Lor', mate, you're on th' Escargot," Tim told him. He was Cockney, in word and accent.

"The what?" Scott asked in apparent shock.

"*See?*" she said.

"That wasn't our boat," Scott said in forged dismay.

"Oh, really!" she said in slashing mockery.

"Use your loaf, lad," Tim tried to cut in, calming things.

"I'm going to cry," Tally pretended to fight back tears.

"Oh, fine! Good! Go on! That solves the solution!" Scott answered.

"The *one* trip I ever wanted! Ever since I saw *Murder On the Orient Express!*"

"That was a train!"

"Hang about," Tim forced his way in. "Don' 'ave a bull about it. We'f got six people comin' aboard at Agde. Couples. Tha' leaves free cabins. Yew wiv us ter Bezier, two days. Then maybe yew can catch up wiv yew barge. Nuff said, yeah?"

"You'd do that for us?" Tally pleaded.

"Straight up."

And he was up the ladder to the deck hand on the wheel.

"We'll be in Agde in half an hour." It was Lynn. She'd been standing by with a sympathetic smile. "It's a lovely day. You can see it all topside. The others will be boarding at four. If there's anything my husband says you don't understand, tell me, I'll translate."

With that she turned, followed Tim up the ladder.

For the moment, Scott just stood, then dropped into a chair, looked across at Tally. Her leg was still jiggling.

"Hey," he said.

Realizing, she placed a hand on her knee, cooled it, but not the tension.

"The Orient Express?" he asked.

"Always a fantasy of mine when I was a teen."

"Being on that train?"

"Being seduced on it by Leonardo DiCaprio."

"He wasn't in *Murder On The Orient Express*."

"He was in my fantasy."

"Yeah, well…"

"Yours?" she asked.

"Halle Berry."

"I could go for that too."

Scott looked at her.

"What am I, getting a new side to you?

"Only men have fantasies?"

The conversation was forced, the tension real. He tried to read what was behind her expression. A continual exercise. He couldn't. But he knew what was behind his. And she read it.

"You think they know where we are?" she asked.

"How can they?" he said without conviction.

"Maybe they didn't walk away the way it looked. Maybe they saw us board."

Another pause, all the more intense because Scott didn't refute it.

"What happens in Bezier?" he asked.

"There're trains."

"Forget trains."

"Buses."

"Maybe."

"Ought to get us back to Angers overnight," she said.

"Wait a minute. Angers? There's no going back there."

"Yeah, there is."

"They're waiting for us! Angers? You're crazy!" Scott said, disbelieving. "Why?"

"The école's there."

"École, what école?"

"The cooking school."

"Oh, shit," he said, realizing where she was going with this.

"She's got every condiment, herb, and spice there."

"You're still going for it."

"Yes."

"The fucking recipe."

"Yes.'

"And then?"

"I don't know about then," Tally said, evading what both of them knew.

"Like hell you don't! You heard what we were told in Moldova!"

No answer.

"Jesus Christ, Tally, why?"

Still no answer.

"You're *crazy!* You *are!* You're fucking nuts!"

She rose abruptly, bolted from the lounge area, past the dining table, disappeared into the companionway. For a moment Scott sat, his jaw set tightly, the veins in his neck like wire cables. Pushing himself up off the chair, he followed her quickly, reached the door to the cabin, found the door locked.

"Tally?"

No answer.

"Open the door, Tally!"

Still no answer. He banged on the door. A single, tight-fisted rap.

"Open the goddamn door!"

There was the turning of the lock and Scott pushed his way in, closing the door behind him as Tally dropped to the still unmade bed, sat there. A single tear coursed down her cheek, and this time it was real.

"What the hell are you doing?" he demanded.

"Don't yell at me."

"I'm not yelling!"

"You're yelling."

Scott dropped into the chair, shoulders drooped, hunched forward.

"Tally, look at me," he said. "*Look* at me!"

She lifted her head, turned to him.

"These guys. There's no *logic* to them. They got their own laws, their own commandments! Thou shalt have no recipes of mine. Thou shalt not make for thyself a recipe…"

"Scott, go home. Get your hair cut by Sharon Darran-Krause, put on your Armani and Guccis, splash yourself with Clive Christian Number One, shine the Rolex, hit the offices and watering holes on Madison and Fifth. They've got short memories. Just ask them how they want it, pro-homeless, anti-homeless, pro-abortion, anti-abortion, don't take a position, you can't make a mistake, no good comes from being an identity, be a cipher. You'll have a corner office in a week. When I find what I'm looking for, I'll call you."

Scott sat a moment, mouth parted as though to respond. He found nothing to say, rose, quit the room, found his way to the stairs leading up to the sun deck. The barge was making its way through the Bassin De Thau, a large inland salt water lake. Empty lounge chairs occupied the fore deck, along with a rack of bicycles. Lynn was forward, wiping down cushions, the deckhand on the wheel in the aft section. Behind them was Sete. Scott turned to the railing, clutched it. 150 feet off the starboard beam was Marseillan: a would-be St Tropez with its eighteen restaurants and cafes and flamingoes. The sun was out, light breeze, gulls circling in hopes of a discarded morsel or two.

"Lor' luv a duck." It was Tim moving in beside Scott leaning with him on the railing, taking in the surroundings. "Wonerful go'in' away from i' all. No worries, no cares, know wha' I mean? Jus' serene."

Serene, Scott thought to himself as Tim pushed off the railing, went about his way. *Serene?* His mouth was filling with saliva so that he was swallowing repeatedly. His face was clammy and so were his hands. He was, quite simply, a man who didn't know who he was anymore being asked to face a terror he couldn't precisely define nor see but knew was there. With that, as he stared out at the passing serenity, came the question. Was he seeing his old self for the last time?

Twenty-One

"Built in da seven'eenf century, its aim was 'orse drawn transpawtashin by barges ov wheat, wine, textiles an' silk."

The Escargot was underway, the barge meandering inland along the Canal du Midi, past old Roman fortifications and vineyards, the Pyrenees vaguely outlined in the distance, cyclists coursing along the abandoned tow paths flanking the canal. Over an aqueduct, through a tunnel, under a bridge from which two adolescent preteens sat in blue shirts and shorts, feet dangling over the side, looking down on the slowly passing barge, cigarettes drooping from their lips.

On the sun deck, Tim was holding court in the late afternoon sun, the deckhand aft on the wheel, Scott and Tally on opposite sides, apart from each other, as Lynn passed around wine and hors d'oeuvres. Scott tried to read Tally's face. She'd discarded the anger and replaced it with a vacant stare.

"Fallin'in'er disarray, i''ad its rebirf in da nineteen sixties, no small part due ter taahrists such as yerselfs who fell i' love wiv da canal's beau'y an' nature."

They'd come aboard at Agde. Six of them. Four were Americans: the Finnegans and the Houghs if Scott had caught their names properly. One, the Hough woman, seemed familiar, Scott thought. An actress? He was certain he'd seen her before. The other two, both men, were Frenchmen from what little Scott had heard them speak on arriving. But a guttural French, the sort most spoken in North Africa. The first of the two was dressed in outdoor clothing, very new, a sandy-complexioned man in whose face artificial geniality seemed the salient characteristic. The other, too, was dressed in relatively rough wear. There the similarity ended. He was older, by twenty years, a thin stoop shouldered man with a narrow vulturine face, a large silk handkerchief held to his perpetually runny nose. It was this pair, as Scott watched them, that brought him an overwhelming sense of foreboding.

"Thus," Tim was going on, "all barges, as well as new 'uns, was turned into floatin' 'otels ov which de Escargot is one. We 'ave bicycles if yew wan' ter ride da parfs from lock to lock. Or yew can walk it. I'll be tellin' mawer as we travel along. There're maps on da coun'er below if yew wan' ter follow da route. Nuff said. Questions?"

Scott looked across the deck at Tally and caught her eyes. She too had felt alarm at the sight of the two Frenchmen and was looking to Scott for evaluation. Tim was answering an array of usual questions from the four Americans. How long before they reached the first lock? How long was the canal? How many locks were there? To what height did the canal eventually rise? The queries ran their course and Lynn stepped forward.

"It's six fifteen…" she started to speak when interrupted.

"I do not speak English very well. It is a very difficult language. I do not understand it well." It was the thin, stoop shouldered Frenchman. "My friend does not speak English any. But he is good backgammon player. You have backgammon aboard?"

"Yes, we do," Lynn said.

"Good. Good. It is a game of options as all games should be. To crush an opponent. You play?"

Lynn waited for the man to continue, but that was it. Though not for Scott. A chill went down his spine. The man had directed his question at him.

"Dinner at eight," Lynn resumed. "Cocktails and appetizers in the lounge. Plenty of hot water for showers if anyone wants. We'll be mooring for the night in an hour at Vias. The last town with street lights we'll see before Beziers," she grinned. "It's saumon beurre blanc for dinner."

The deck was quickly cleared, everyone going below except Scott and Tally lingering behind, 'til Tally rose, moved forward to the prow of the boat. Scott sat for a moment, then followed. She was standing on the forward port side of the barge amid cushioned deck chairs, the rack of bicycles behind her, each tagged with a metal plate dangling from the center bar, 'Propriete d'Escargot', as Scott approached. Pale green water swept away from the bow in fan-like ripples. Plane trees along both banks formed a bower over the barge. A woman sat at her easel on a bank painting wild yellow irises. A pair of lovers walked hand in hand along the pathway almost keeping pace with the slowly moving barge. Fifty meters ahead was the first lock since leaving Agde. The silence between them went on 'til Tally finally broke it.

"What do we do?"

Scott thought about that a moment, then answered, "They're probably just what they said. A couple of hustlers making their way with backgammon. Paranoia's going to kill us."

Tally looked at him. "Us?"

"If anyone asks, we're just two freelance writers on our way back to the States with a mystery we couldn't solve."

Tally looked forward again. The barge was entering the lock. For the moment the process seemed to hold their attention as huge gates swung closed behind them, capturing the barge in a fixed chamber. On the ground above, a lock keeper spun a wheel. Water rushed in, lifting the barge slowly five feet, ten. Reaching the desired height, forward gates opened, the barge moving slowly out of the lock, into the continuing canal.

"And then what?" Tally finally asked.

The question had more to it than a casual inquiry. Scott gave no answer. But fighting every instinct that had gotten him through life, he knew the girl standing there in the golden checkered light of the setting sun was someone he could not abandon.

The saumon beurre blanc, prepared and served by Lynn, proved the equal of any three star restaurant in Paris. And now seven of the eight guests sat about the dining table over crème brulée and coffee. The eighth, the sandy-complexioned Frenchman, had retired to the far end of the lounge, backgammon board open, playing a game against himself. His companion pushed back from the table.

"Madame, je vous remercie. Mes compliments."

With that he rose and disappeared up the stairway to the sun deck. An oppressiveness seemed to dissipate with his departure. Conversation and histories broke out spontaneously. The Finnegans, Bill and Pat, were a husband-wife television production team from Los Angeles, the Houghs their close friends, Stan a TV producer, a physical six-four rawboned powerhouse, his wife, Jean, a semi-noted actress of the eighties and nineties, now retired.

The Finnegans, it quickly became clear, as the four reminisced, had purchased a forty foot French sloop — a Bénéteau — and the Houghs were invited over as crew for its maiden voyage from Hyères, east of Marseille, to Sete where the yacht would be winter quartered, and from where they caught the Escargot for its excursion up the canal. As the Beneteau had headed into Sete, Pat on the wheel, Jean beside her, the two reflecting on Hollywood's better days, Bill, laying back in the transom, hands behind his head, had been heard to say, in a voice, laconic, almost sleepy:

"Pat? I think I'd come about. You're just about to go up on the rocks."

Laughter. Little of which Scott reacted to nor had heard. It was the man with the vulturine face that blocked his mind from all else. He'd seen enough spy movies to know if ever there was a cliché for an assassin this man was it. He glanced across the table at Tally. She appeared to be occupied with the Finnegans and Houghs, though he knew she wasn't. Scott's face began to turn volcanic. Wherever they'd gone, they'd been discovered, shadowed. Well this, Goddamnit, was *it! Enough!* On impulse he rose, offering no apology, made his way to the stairway and climbed.

Emerging from the cabin below, Scott stepped into the night. The barge, he saw, was tethered to a quai, along with a half dozen other canal boats, smaller than the Escargot, rentals likely, lights on in some playing out on the water. From somewhere a disco was blaring. It was then Scott felt the sweat prickling out all over his body. Foreword, at the quayside railing, in silhouette, stood the vulturine-faced Frenchman.

Scott turned, clutched the railing. He had never been a courageous person. Bravery was not a word in his personal thesaurus. With all the will at his command, he opened a file.

"Bon soir," he said. "It is very nice tonight."

He waited for a response. None came. He decided any sort of equivocation was out of the question.

"Look, suppose we talk this out."

"Is no good," the man replied. His voice was toneless, husky. Small tired eyes stared out at the quai. "He's made up his mind."

"He?" Scott said, a slight croak in his voice.

"Is no use making a complaint."

Scott flinched, suddenly sick with impotence and fear.

"I don't feel well," Scott said. "Excuse me, please." He started to turn away.

"You seem to view it with disapproval," the man said.

Scott turned, looked back. The man was dabbing at his nose with his handkerchief. His lips were twisted and in his eyes was the bitterness of years.

"I was just going to say…" Scott started to explain.

"On the other hand, you may find humor in the situation."

Too many people about, Scott thought. They couldn't do anything with so many people about. Well, he'd defend himself, if that's what it came to. And just as suddenly, Christ! He'd never been in a fight in his life.

"Perhaps it's my fault, I'm too old," the man was going on. "Perhaps too old to afford the luxury of despair. What I cannot understand is why he did not approach me as soon as he knew. Though when I think of the times we had together in Vienne…"

Scott's mind was suddenly short-circuiting. What the hell was he talking about?

"Vienne? Vienna?"

"I thought perhaps I could dissuade him. Perhaps this trip to reconsider. His mind and heart are gone."

For a moment Scott stood immobilized. It was then it came to him. Holy Shit! Scott wanted to pound the railing in exaltation. *Shit!* So much for a book by its cover! He heard himself pouring out a tale of this boy he'd known at school, this gay, one of his closest friends, and how he'd stood up to three guys, fought them off in his friend's defense, a stream of empathy and understanding, none of it true.

"Is better." The man was looking at Scott with almost tearful gratitude. "Is not best, but is better."

Scott drew a deep breath. For a few moments he stood enjoying the gradual un-gnarling of his muscles.

"Well. Good night, sir." It was all he could think to say.

The man's answer was a nod, followed by a turn to the stairway leading down, out of sight. Alone on the deck, Scott made up his mind to walk it five times, to bring his heart rate back to normal, made the tour only once. A drink. Never had he wanted a drink so much in his life. He turned to the stairway, pulled back as Tally blocked his access, stood half out of the stairway, eyes asking the question.

"They're lovers. Or were."

Her eyebrows arched in disbelief.

"It's a break-up."

For several moments she stood there, gripping the railing, a light breeze tossing her hair, lips parted as though about to speak, but saying nothing. He fantasized she was coming close to him. His hand grabbed her belt, to pull her to him. No need to. Her body moved suddenly, pressing against him. His arms were around her and he was kissing her hair...

Except his fantasy was just that, fantasy. She was gone, back down the stairway. His stomach turned over. And this time it was not from fear. When at length he followed her to the main salon, he found her nowhere in sight. Lynn was washing dishes. Tim, gone since before dinner, was in the town on some errand. At the far end of the salon the sandy complexioned Frenchman was in a game of backgammon with Finnegan, Hough looking on. The two women were engaged in what they would do their last day in Paris. One thought the Hall Of Masters in the Louvre, the other the Monet in the sixteenth.

"You've never seen it?" Pat Finnegan was pressing her choice. "In the basement the room's circular, the walls entirely painted. Stand close it looks like blobs of nothing. Back away to the center of the room it's suddenly water lilies. How'd Monet *do* that?"

For a while, Scott stood watching the game from a distance, no involvement in it nor interest. Turning to the bar, he took down a bottle of Scotch, poured himself a third of a glass, replaced the bottle, picked up the glass, paused, slowly lowered it to the dining table, looked toward the companion way leading back to the cabins.

"Can I do something for you, Mr. Fitzgerald?"

Startled, Scott looked about. It was Lynn.

"Would you like something? Coffee? Cookies?"

"No. Nothing. Thank you. Nothing. Good night."

"Good night," she answered with her unalterable smile.

Moving into the companionway, Scott came to the door to their cabin, found it unlocked, entered the semi-darkened room. As at Sete light from the quai provided faint illumination. Tally, Scott saw, was already in bed, under the covers, not yet asleep, she couldn't be, but seemingly so. Moving quietly so as not to disturb her, he pulled off his shirt, lowered to the chair, removed shoes and socks, slipped out of his pants down to his underwear, hung pants and shirt on a hanger in the tiny closet, pulled the folded blanket off the end of the bed, placed it on the chair in preparation for spending the night there, slipped into the bathroom, closed the door, flipped on the light. As before, he saw Tally's pants and shirt were hung on the back of the door. Relieving himself, he flushed the toilet, washed and dried his hands, brushed his teeth, turned to flip off the light switch, stopped cold in his tracks. On a rack, draped over one of the towels, washed and left to dry, were Tally's panties and brassiere.

For an instant his brain seemed to have lost touch with reality. Slowly thought rearranged itself. He switched off the light, which brought on the night light, drew a hand across his mouth as though pausing to gather in what was happening, opened the door, stepped into the cabin.

Tally, he saw, lay motionless. Eyes open or closed he couldn't see. Circling to the opposite side of the bed, he stepped from his underwear, lowered it to the floor, slipped slowly naked under the covers.

"Move over," he whispered.

"I can't," she answered, "I'll fall off the bed."

"I meant this way," he said.

She turned to him, almost with a lunge, found him aroused, pressed against him, when his mouth was over hers, and this time there was no resistance, no pulling away. He lowered his lips down her neck to her shoulder, then to a breast. His hand moved down her back to her buttocks, pulling her close. Then one knee was separating her legs, neither of which made an effort to stop him, and he was on top of her, guiding himself into her. He found he was entering more than her — no way to describe it. It was as though for the first time in his life he was entering a new discovery, the most incredible feeling, and not just in his groin as she surged beneath him. Her eyes, he saw, were open, wide open. Her legs came up, wrapped around him, drawing him closer. She moaned, not in protest, but responding to his thrusts. He'd been high before. Psychedelic drugs. But this was a natural high he'd never known. Her body tensed, grew rigid, suddenly arched as she cried aloud.

"Now!"

Twenty-Two

Through the window, by the early morning light Scott could see the barge was under way. Small smoky clouds ventured in and out of passing plane trees. Slowly easing himself from the bed, he looked over his shoulder to make certain Tally was still asleep. Shaving, showering, silently slipping into his clothes, it was just after six that he reached the salon, empty, except for a basket of baguettes and Danish on the dining table, still warm and fragrant from a local bakery. There was an urn of freshly made coffee, orange juice, butter and jams. He wasn't hungry. The pit in his stomach negated all thought of food.

Turning to the stairway, he climbed to the sun deck into the chill of crisp morning air. As before, the deckhand was aft at the wheel. Crossing to the railing, Scott leaned against it, his mind reflecting on the night just past. And that was the problem. He'd encountered something he'd never experienced before. He couldn't even put it into words. His feelings were a jumble, tumbling, and he didn't like it! Feelings were the enemy, to be locked up, the key thrown away. He turned to old reliables. He guessed that his absence when she awoke would be puzzling to her. It was going to be difficult to avoid encounter. He would have to forestall that.

He pushed on to more immediate thoughts. Time to think clearly. For the first time since the beginning of this idiotic venture they were free of pursuit, and he damn well meant to keep it that way. One thing was certain. There was no going back to Angers.

The so-called missing 'forbidden' ingredient? Ridiculous, a one in a million, though they hadn't been told 'forbidden.' 'Banned,' was the word, which narrowed things. Still, the bastards would be watching Angers, he knew that. That cooking school, and her apartment. And no going back to Lyon for her car. They'd be watching that, too. He'd have to convince her it was time to lick their wounds and get the hell home. If she refused — well, that was a question each would have to answer for themself...

"Mornin'."

163

He looked about. Tim had joined him at the railing. He was holding a steaming cup of coffee.

"Comin' up ter somethin' yur'll wan ter see. Seven locks i' a row, one afer da uver."

Scott followed Tim's nod. Directly ahead was just that, seven locks, one on top of the other, climbing seventy, eighty feet.

"Les Sept Ecluses," Tim was saying, his French more easily understood than his English. "Marvel uv engineerin'. If' yew was t'ask me, way's ashore, climbin' da steps longside, meet da barge at da top."

With that, Tim pushed away. Scott hadn't got all of it, but he'd gotten enough. The on-shore climb would provide what he craved, *always* craved when confronted with emotions that left him exposed. Retreat.

Fifteen minutes later as the Escargot tied up alongside the concrete embankment, waiting in line for two smaller canal boats slipping together into the first lock just ahead, Scott was ashore. The pathway, alternating with stone steps every twenty yards or so leading up alongside the locks, was deserted. Which is what he wanted, to be alone. Time to put things together. He'd been pulled out of his comfort zone and he needed assessment.

When… *Shit!*

Coming up the steps to the pathway was, of all things, in short dark-velvet ill-fitting coat with narrow white collar and mitre cap, a French padre, an abbe, indefinable features, overweight.

"Bonjour, monsieur," the abbe said, reaching Scott, puffing from the climb.

"Bonjour," Scott muttered, hoping his lack of enthusiasm would send the abbe on his way. No such luck.

"You are wiz Escargot?"

The man knew his barges. Scott nodded, a perfunctory yes.

"One uf zee most luxueux on zee canal. You are English?"

"American."

"Ah. I ave cousin in Detroit. His name is Marcel. You know him?"

Scott shook his head, no. He hadn't the pleasure.

"I come from the orphelinat in zee morning for pratique, what you say, exercise."

"Orphelinat?"

"Orphanage."

Oh, Christ. So *that's* what this was. Get some poor sap off one of the barges, climbing the locks, no place to hide, hit him up for a donation. Scott looked hopefully down for the Escargot. No way back. The barge had entered the lower lock.

"Come, vee climb," the abbe said.

In the cabin, Tally had feigned sleep while Scott rose from the bed, disappeared into the bathroom. She'd had a sleepless night with one thought running through her brain: *What have I done?* She was a woman who seldom questioned her behavior, but this time she did. What would he read into it? What did *she?* She'd closed her eyes tightly as he'd come from the bathroom, tried to control her shallow breathing as he'd dressed, till he left the cabin and she could return to her — *analysis?* She'd had five sexual encounters in her life — well six now, two long lasting. None had been casual. It was important to her that she have affection, empathy at least, for any partner she was with, she always had. Then what was *this?* She hadn't been seduced. In fact she'd invited it. *Why?* He was everything she didn't want in a man. Cocky, self-possessed, presumptive, unprincipled, lacking a core. *Where was the suffering?* She shook her head, a quick violent little shake, hoping it would rearrange her thoughts into logical order. It didn't happen. She forced all introspection to Angers. When they got to Angers they'd have a talk. Not yet, she reasoned. "No, Goddammit, *now!*"

Rising, Tally went into the bathroom, brushed her teeth, showered, found her underwear mostly if not completely dry. She'd live with it. Her outer clothes, she realized, were borderline rank. She'd have to do something about that, though what or how she'd no idea. Maybe when they got to Beziers that night, which is where she and Scott were to disembark by agreement, the end of Tim and Lynn's largesse. Dressing, she left the cabin, entered the salon, prepared for encounter. The Houghs were there, seated at the dining table over Danish and coffee. So were the Finnegans. There was no sign of the Frenchmen. Nor Scott. She forced a smile, muttered shared greetings, turned to the stairway leading up out of the salon.

Reaching the sun deck, she looked about, pronouncement prepared. "Look," she was ready to say, "This is not going anywhere," when she saw Scott. He was ashore, climbing the pathway to the top of the locks, in conversation with…a *priest?* She could see, she couldn't hear. She had to smile. She knew how these things worked. He was trapped.

"Zee climate, fortunately," the abbe was saying to Scott as they climbed in preamble to his solicitation, "is suitable for any sort uf luxuriating. Is never too hot, too cold. Alzo some of zee orphelins find it trying vin I escort zem to zee caves, especially Chauvet-Pont-d'Arc in Ardeche. Around fifty meters from zee present entrance in zee Brunel Chambre zere are two ensembles uf painted red dots. Zey are in fact prints made from zee palm uf a right hand millenniums ago. Certain anatomical details are identifiable…"

"Yes, well," Scott tried to curtail the lecture.

"But I bore you," the abbe said as they reached the midpoint in their climb. "What else can I tell you uf interest," he said, looking at the slowly rising barge below before adding, "M'sieur Fitzgerald."

The shock that went through Scott's body was electric.

"What did you say?"

"Nussing uf importance," the man said. "But now I shall." He turned, was leaning back against the railing, looking squarely up at Scott with small dangerous eyes. "Zee Escargot vill reach Portiragnes in four hours, for déjeuner, for lunch. Two men vill meet you, wiv orders to escort you and M'amselle Garner to zee airport at Beziers. Zey are primitive men, you ave met zem. You have embarrassed zem once vis your escape outside Beaune. Perhaps zey vill acknowledge orders," he shrugged, "perhaps not, I cannot guarantee, to join you on a flight to Paris, and zen to see you on anozer to New York, vere, bestowed wiz excellent judgment, you and Miss Garner vill remain, if blessed by fortune, all toughts uf your quest abandoned. If I ave not made myself clear, be assured, M'sieur Fitzgerald, zay vill."

With that he turned and headed back the way he came.

It was an hour before the Escargot cleared the final lock, the barge tying up alongside the upper quai, dropping its gangway.

"Lor luv a duck," Tim was saying to the gathered guests in the salon. "Be 'alf an 'aahr. Chance ter stretch yaahr legs ashawer if yew like. If yew fancy yew can ride da bicycles up ter Portiragnes, meet up wif us in a couple."

With that he bounded ashore to settle charges with the lock keeper, the others, including the emerging two Frenchmen, though at a distance from each other, following Tim off the barge.

Remaining behind with Lynn who was cleaning up breakfast dishes, Tally waited for Scott. It was several minutes before he appeared down the gangway, looking shaken, walked up to Tally, paused.

"You don't have to tell me," she chided, grinning. "You're not the first to get ambushed. What was it this time, a home for novitiates?"

The look on his face dissolved the look on her own.

"What?" she asked.

He seemed about to answer, stopped at the sight of Lynn, turned instead, disappeared down the companionway and into their cabin, which is where she found him, perched on the edge of the bed, bent over, elbows on knees, staring off into space.

"They know we're here," he said at length.

"Don't make stupid jokes."

"They'll be waiting for us at the next stop."

"Waiting for us," she repeated.

"Portagnes."

"Portiragnes," she corrected.

"They've been told to get us out of the country." He paused.

"And?"

"These guys aren't great at taking orders."

Tally's legs deserted her. She dropped beside him on the edge of the bed.

Scott shook off a shiver, rose abruptly and began to swear. He looked at his hand and moved his fingers, which were cramping. By tomorrow morning, the thought ran through his mind as it had too often before, 'The Remains Of David 'Scott' Fitzgerald...'

"I *told* you we shouldn't have gotten involved in this! I *told* you about these guys!" he berated. "Did you *listen?*"

"Big help, Scott."

"You and your fucking restaurant! I mean, Jesus!"

"Mistake."

"No shit!"

"I wasn't talking about the restaurant."

"Hey! Who turned up naked in that bed last night?"

"Mistake."

"Well, I'm sure it wasn't your first one."

"What exactly did he tell you?" she asked, ignoring the cut.

"What I said. That's it."

"Portiragnes."

"Fuck!" he said, turning away with a defeated shake of his head, looked back, his mouth still filled with words yet to say. The look on her face aborted them. Something, he saw, was rattling through her brain. She rose, slowly from the edge of the bed, thoughts crystalizing, grabbed her purse, then turned to the door, pulled it open, went through, slamming it closed behind here.

"Hey," he called after her. "*Hey!*"

She was crazy! Nuts! What'd she think she was she *doing?* You don't go out in the open! Stay in the cabin, have their meals here, keep the door locked! If they came? Yeah, well, let 'em! Maybe one of the others aboard had a gun. Maybe Tim. He'd buy it from him. With what? He didn't have a dime. *She* had the money. Besides, what did he know about shooting a gun? Once when he was out in the country a friend gave him his to shoot at a target, a .22 automatic, that gouged a rip on the side of his hand with its slide recoil. He looked around. The closest thing to a weapon he could find in the cabin was a toothbrush. The longer he thought it over…He turned, grasped the handle of the door, eased it open three inches. The companionway, he saw, was empty. He pushed away, trying to come to decision, turned back to the door, pulled it wide, left the cabin for the salon, found no one there, when he heard Lynn's voice. He couldn't make out what she was saying, but it wasn't conversational. It was filled with good cheer and salutation!

Climbing to the sun deck, Scott found Lynn beaming.

"I told her there's a bistro a kilometer up with a good local red."

Scott looked off. Tally was astride a bicycle, pedaling up the tow path away from the barge.

Twenty-Three

By the time Scott had secured a bike from Lynn and hit the tow path himself, Tally, he could see, was well ahead and gaining. Pumping for all he was worth, he quickly found he was not in the shape he thought he was. He was not in shape at all, despite his weekly Saturday morning visits to Elissa's Personal Best Luxury Gym on East Seventy-Ninth, which in fact was little more than a gab fest decrying the President's reelection with other Fifth Avenue denizens also pretending they were there to work out, the machine getting the most action being the vending machine. Chest heaving, lungs searing, he looked back at the barge, then ahead again, nearly fell off his bike as it hit the exposed root of a tree. Recovering, he looked forward again, and brought his bike to a sliding halt. Tally was gone, no sign of her, disappeared from sight.

For a long moment Scott could do nothing but stare, ogling the empty pathway before him. Setting off again, standing astride the bike, pumping in a frenzy, he drove himself along, scattering a family of ducks crossing before him, past a pair of lovers ignoring a laid out picnic for more corporal pleasures, past a side road…

Side road! He swung his bike about, returned to it, and looked. Less than the traditional D Route, the lowest designation of the French road system, it was basically a surfaced lane running north from the canal into and through woods. Nothing in sight, he took it, legs screaming, cramping, found Tally a kilometer up, seated at the side of the road by her bike. She was leaning forward, knees drawn up, hair falling across her face, barely out of breath, unlike Scott, who felt his next would be his last.

Tumbling from his bike, he dropped beside her, sweating, lungs exploding, neither saying a word. He felt suddenly very tired. His body was aching, so was his ego. He half-expected her to turn him, lips parted in contempt. Instead she sat there staring across the road as though he didn't exist. As his breathing receded, one thought came to him. He'd made a fool of himself, a whining, wailing fool, which seemed to have become a pattern. Before another day was passed, he would be for her, he was certain, nothing but a pathetic memory. The realization was lacerating and painful.

"Look. You just don't know...," he started to say.

"I know more than you think," she answered and was up with her bike and astride it, purse dangling from her handlebars, heading up the road.

Well, so long as *that's* understood, he thought with a silent sarcastic oath as he rose himself, nothing else to do but follow. She wasn't racing away, so it was clear she was inviting him to keep pace. The road, vacant of structures and traffic, proved to be a circuitous one, coursing past colorful wild late summer dahlias and shrubs, past umbrella shaped pine trees, none of which Scott noticed or cared to. He'd had one encounter with French woods, 'bois' they called them, with its threat of wild beasts, adders and raptors and that was enough. He wiped his forehead with the back of one hand, trying to fathom what in fact she had meant. "I know more than you think," she'd said. But his brain seemed to have left his body. All he knew was there she was, keeping to that measured pace in front of him, moving steadily on.

A half hour later, calves and quads howling, Scott followed Tally from the woods, found her stopped, straddling her bike, looking about. The road, he saw, drawing up beside her, split a sprawl of tents and campers and caravans. Off to the right was a bleached wooden one room structure. A placard affixed above the door read "Bureau de Camping," along with two stars.

Unlike most campgrounds Scott had experienced during his sentence to Indian Guides by his mother as a preteen for stealing from her purse, this one was different. Aside from the usual tents and campers, a tamarisk tree supported an array of arrow-shaped wooden signs pointing in various directions: Magasin, Toilettes, Laverie, Douches, and Restaurant. Some he could see through trees, the toilets and concrete shower stalls. The restaurant, Laundromat and store he couldn't, but he could smell cooking. There was also a bus, Scott noticed, a canteen trailer hitched behind it. About fifteen youths, boys and girls, sixteen to eighteen years, Americans from what he could make out, clustered in some distress about two adults.

"Croque-Monsieur, s'il vous plait," Tally said. "Avec une Orangina."

"La même chose pour moi," Scott followed.

Orders given, the youthful serveur withdrew.

French campgrounds are rated much as their hotels, one star having the least facilities and accommodations, four the most. This one was designated a two. But like some throughout the country its rating was in danger of losing a star should inspectors revisit.

The campground restaurant was little more than a shack, three unmatching tables and a counter, a faded limited menu displayed above it. Aside from Tally and Scott, the place was empty other than a weary French mother bent over a salad, her hyper ten-year-old son munching a French excuse for a hamburger two tables away.

Tally had bought herself and Scott the cheapest sweat suits available at the campground store, which they now wore, Scott's, to his dismay, an ill-fitting pea-green with cuffs ending half way up his forearms and calves. Twenty minutes more to kill before the Laundromat was done with their clothes, they'd settled in the restaurant to wait it out. Staring out at the grounds, something was clearly on Tally's mind as Scott leaned back in his chair with a wheeze of uncertain relief.

"Let 'em chew on *that!*"

Tally's head came about.

"That?"

"Finished. Done. We beat the bastards."

Reaching down, Tally brought her purse off the floor, plopped it on the table, dug inside it, pulled out a multi-folded map, handed it to Scott.

"What's that?"

"A map. From the barge."

"What about it?

"Open it."

"Why?"

"Open it."

He opened it, shrugged in confoundment.

"What?"

"Look at it."

He did as told.

"What am I looking at?"

"Find the Canal du Midi. It's that blue line running from Sete to Toulouse."

"So?"

"Les Sept Ecluses. The Seven Locks. That's where we got off the barge." She pointed to it.

"'Kay."

"You were told they were going to pick us up at Portiragnes."

"Yeah."

"They'll be there, waiting to take us off."

"Their bad. We won't be there," Scott said.

"They'll find out we took off on bicycles heading up the canal."

"Let 'em choke on it."

"Look at the map."

He did so again, no idea what she was telling him.

"How many roads cut off that path between the locks and Portiragnes?"

A chill ran through Scott as he saw it.

"Shit."

"One. If we were not on the path, where else could we have gone?"

Scott looked up. Tally's jaw was locked.

"What're we going to do?" Scott moaned.

"We've got about two hours to come up with that," she said.

"Jesus!"

He tried to rescind the whine in his voice, too late, broke off as their sandwiches arrived.

"Orangina?" the waiter asked.

"Oui," Tally replied. "Pour deux."

"Et ketchup," Scott added.

"Ketchup?" the waiter asked, in shock and disdain.

"Ketchup!" Scott repeated. It came out in a hostile scold covering Scott's mounting alarm at what he'd been told, and he didn't much care who got the brunt of it. "*Ketchup!*"

When a howl of protest from the boy at the adjoining table drew their attention.

"Maman?"

"Non!" his mother replied.

"Il obtient!" the boy said, pointing at Scott.

"Il est Américain qui est pourquoi son interdit à votre école, et interdit par moi."

"Maman!"

"*Aucun ketchup!*" the mother answered harshly, terminating the conversation.

"What was that about?" Scott asked as the woman went back to her salad, the boy to his burger.

"Ketchup," Tally answered as their drinks and a bottle of ketchup were plunked down on their table. "It's been banned in schools here in France. Too American."

"Well, fuck them," Scott said, pouring ketchup on his sandwich. "Demeaning, self-centered…"

"…hegemonic, elitist," she interjected, "superior, hypocritical…"

"You got it."

"…arrogant, ethnocentric, self-absorbed, loud, brash…"

"Right on!"

"I wasn't talking about the French," she answered, a flash of anger in her eyes, then added, "So much for my editor's training, all those adjectives."

"Hegemonic?"

"Dominating."

"Listen…" he started in face reddening.

"To what? More of your Francophobic blather?"

Scott flushed.

"Who awarded you the judgment wand? Like I belong in some fucking, well you haven't a clue!" he raged. "I'm out there between the lines, Goddamnit, I don't need your assessments…"

When he was aware. She wasn't listening. She was staring, a sudden deep frown across her face.

"Look," he said, banking his temper. "What are we running from? They just want to get us out of the Goddamn country before we come up with something we're never going to anyway…"

"What was it we were told?" she asked.

"I said…"

"I don't mean that?"

"You're not listening!"

"That chef," she said.

"What chef?"

"In Moldova."

"We're up against the Union Corse, the fucking French Mafia, he said."

"Something else. As we were leaving."

Scott shook his head, no memory.

"The missing ingredient to the recipe. What'd he say about it?"

Scott's stare was blank, trying to flush the cobwebs.

"He said," she said, answering her own question, "it's been banned."

"Yeah?" he said, still puzzled where this was going.

She reached down, picked up the bottle of ketchup, looked up at him. He waited for her to continue, to explain. She didn't. She held her gaze, waiting for him to put it all together when the realization struck him.

"That's idiotic!"

"Something banned, he said."

"Ketchup?"

"That day I was at that restaurant. I couldn't put together what was missing. A tomato flavor, subtle, with a hint of vinegar."

"Ketchup's subtle?"

"Lightly used."

"I think you're nuts."

"The judgment wand?"

"They don't go around using ketchup in gourmet recipes!"

"Maybe they just don't admit it."

"*Ketchup?*"

When the door was pushed open, into the room came a woman, utter frustration on her face. Scott recognized her, had seen her when they arrived, at the bus with the canteen trailer, surrounded by that group of late teen American kids. In her forties, tall, reed thin, she wore short-sleeved khakis.

"Excusez-moi. Est qu'il quelqu'un ici qui parle Anglais?"

She was more than frustrated. She was frazzled. Tally turned to her.

"I speak English," Tally said.

"I'm in a mess and I thought someone here…"

"What is it?"

"I've got fifteen kids on tour from Midland, Michigan, and our French cook, he just ran off with one of them."

"How old was she?" Tally asked.

"It wasn't a she."

"You need the police."

"I've called the police."

"I'm sorry," Tally said, not understanding the problem.

"We've got to be in Bordeaux the day after tomorrow to catch our flight home. Carcassonne, Toulouse, then Bordeaux. I need a cook!"

"Excuse me, we're having a conversation here…" Scott said with no little acrimony.

"I'm a cook," Tally cut in.

A look crossed the woman's face as though she'd just found the Holy Grail. Scott opened his mouth to protest when it struck him what Tally was after.

"Our rental car broke down outside Agde," Tally lied.

"Broke down," Scott jumped in quickly.

"We've been trying to make our way to Bordeaux, too."

"You really cook?" the woman asked.

"Cordon Bleu," Scott offered. His breath was hurried, almost beyond control.

The woman looked him over.

"Who's he?"

"Him?" Tally took measure of Scott. "You ought to see him peel potatoes."

"Who does dishes?" the woman asked, making clear that went with the job.

"Oh, that's the guy that cooks," Scott said.

Twenty-Four

It had gone that smoothly, a meager verbal contract quickly agreed to and thirty minutes later, clothes retrieved from the Laundromat, which both changed into, Tally and Scott were aboard the students' charter bus traveling west on AutoRoute 61.

The woman's name was Butterfield, Tally thought she'd heard her say, Ms. Butterfield when they'd given their names. She'd spoken with such desperate urgency it was hard to tell. A twelfth grade teacher of Romanesque History in Southern France, the woman had organized a two week academic excursion throughout the area now ending a week before commencement of fall classes. Whatever inspiring lectures she'd prepared were quickly superseded by keeping her teenage charges from exploring their favorite new French word, *copulation*. In this she was accompanied by the school's eagle-eyed gym teacher, Mr. Galliday, who wandered their campsites till well past midnight with a riding crop. A foot shorter than Ms. Butterfield, he was muscular, body seemingly as wide as it was tall. Speculation among the students about the two was rampant.

"When they're nose to nose his toes are in it. When they're toes to toes his nose is in it," Scott overheard, ear cocked to their whisperings. Jesus, he thought to himself, that tired old wheeze. Kids think today they invented the wheel. Ask them who was the first to discover the world was round, half would tell you John Glenn.

Seated next to Tally, directly behind the driver, Scott dropped his head against the headrest. For the first time since Angers he felt legitimate relief. They were two days from Bordeaux. Carcassonne, Toulouse, then Bordeaux. They could get a flight from Bordeaux to New York, he was certain of that. Maybe even out of Toulouse. In three fucking days, maybe two, he'd be home. Tally had been right. Memories were short. He'd hit the watering holes on Madison and Fifth and with the story he had to tell, who the hell needed Medlock. They had nothing to show him anyway. Ketchup? Talk about desperate. There'd be no bull shit about the

177

homeless this time, but taking on the fucking *Union Corse*? Christ, the bidding for that!

He glanced across at Tally. She was staring out the window at the passing landscape. Lagoons and salt pans and vineyards, olive groves and cemeteries, most small with plastic flowers laid next to tombstones, Pyrenean peaks in the distance. What of her, he found himself wondering with a sudden unaccustomed pang of concern. She was in this as deeply as he was. The imperative thing was to get out of the country. Both of them. Now. That was what the Corsicans wanted, that's what *he* wanted. Okay, there was her car, her apartment and things. But these guys weren't something you messed around with. Neither he nor she had what he'd come for, there was safety in that. So they were in limited danger, but no good pushing these guys. He tried to stop thinking about it, he couldn't. There was a look on her face, a longing as she stared out at the passing landscape. She loved this country, though for the life of him he couldn't see why. They'd had an argument about it on the flight back from Moldova.

"Why?" he'd challenged. "What do you *see* in this fucking place?"

"Why waste my time," she'd answered, which had cut off a war of words that he was smarting for.

So what was that grinding in his stomach all about? And the more he studied her, the worse it got. His mind went back to the night they'd spent together on the barge. Was it just last night? The way she'd clung to him. The way he'd clung to *her*. She was everything he didn't want in a woman. Bright, intelligent, independent. The imperceptive, obtuse, subordinate, that was the woman for him. And yet...

Screw 'and yet.' And yet...

When Ms. Butterfield was at their shoulders.

"We'll be in Carcassonne for the night. The farmer's market's only a ten minute walk." She handed Tally 250 euros. "We're on a tight budget. Work wonders."

Turning south off Route N112, the black Mercedes entered the campground at the edge of the woods from the north, slowed to a stop. It was one-thirty in the afternoon. In the front of the car sat the two men who'd trailed and escorted Scott from Beaune. In the back sat the 'Abbe' Scott had encountered at the Seven Locks.

In fact no Abbe at all, though still dressed as one, his name was Nacer. Well-placed among the notorious Union Corse, his roots were Corsica. Although politically a part of France since the days of Napoleon, the Mediterranean island, a hundred miles off the French coast, with long ties to Italy, spawned a culture of violence and vendettas, more secretive and tightly knit than the Mafia itself, with one commanding caveat. You do not challenge its primacy in matters supreme or trivial. Not once. Not ever.

Emerging from the car, the three men looked about. The grounds, as before, seemed serene enough. The bark of a dog, the cry of a child, a burst of drunken laughter from one of the caravans. With a gesture akin to a queen's wave, Nacer sent his cohorts off. Patting the side of his stomach, which could have been from indigestion or verifying a concealed weapon beneath his tunic, Nacer, holding his hand against his side, began a scrutinizing wander past tents and groups of campers — more than one doffing his cap in passing with 'Mon Père' at the apparent cleric — when one of his two companions came running.

"Patron!"

Turning, Nacer followed him quickly, past tents, through trees, came at length to the restaurant where the third of their group stood by two bicycles leaning against the building. Metal plates dangled from their center bars. Clearly emblazoned on each was 'Propriété d'Escargot.'

Nacer stared at the entrance, jaw set. The place, they saw upon entering, was empty, other than the youthful waiter who approached, drying his hands on a half-soiled dish rag.

"Peux-je vous aide, mon père?" he said with deferential respect at sight of the collar.

"Je recherche deux Américains, mon fils," Nacer replied with an aura of benevolence, "Assez jeunes, un home et une fille."

"Ah, les Croques Monsieurs," the waiter said, pointing to the table occupied by Tally and Scott.

"Ou sont-ils?" Nacer asked, looking about, seeing no one.

"Parti, il y a une heure."

"Une heure?" Nacer said, seeking certain verification.

"Oui, mon père. Avec un groupe de tourisme."

Nacer seemed to think that through, turned, stared at the indicated table.

"Ils y assit?" Nacer said, more a statement than a question.

"Oui, mon père. Cette table la," said the waiter, once again pointing out the table occupied by Scott and Tally.

Nacer slowly crossed to it, stared. Reaching down he picked up the bottle of ketchup still there, turned it over in his hands. His face, till now under control, turned dark as he lifted his head, stared out the window, over tents, through trees as his two compatriots stood by, awaiting instructions.

"Se sont-ils mentionner," Nacer's voice was gravelly, "où ils allaient?"

"Oui, mon père," the waiter replied. "Carcassonne."

Arriving in Carcassonne, reservation confirmed, the bus was directed to its site, the campground three stars, well-earned. Shady sites, swimming pool, manicured hedges and trees, good restaurant, store, showers and toilet facilities, its famous fifth century castle with its thirty-two turrets brooding over all. A portable stage was being erected for a 'boom' that night, the French version of an electric rave.

Tents, the first order of business, Scott noticed, were being pitched under the watchful eye of Mr. Galliday, riding crop in hand, making certain there was distance separating "vaginas from penises," Scott heard him say. From Mr. Galliday's perspective, the trip had been a disaster, and he didn't mind saying so, no one paying attention to Ms. Butterfield's lectures, smirks behind his and her backs. When breaking camp outside Narbonne he'd found a condom on the ground where a tent had stood. Discarded after use, or left there to bait him? He whacked his crop into the palm of his hand and went about policing layouts, leaving Scott to privately exult, "Tough shit, your problems. Mine are history."

Opening the canteen kitchen trailer, Tally found it clean and well-appointed. There was a six burner butane stove, pots, pans, utensils, condiments, along with a minimally stocked refrigerator and freezer, operating off a generator. Securing two large canvas bags with handles, she handed one to Scott.

"Where..?" he started to ask.

"Follow your nose," she answered.

300 feet from the campground, he learned what she'd meant. The scent of strawberries. Aromatic, pungent. And the closer they got, the more so it became, till turning a corner they came upon it. A multi-tiered open-air market, jammed with shoppers, locals and tourists, the mid-afternoon sun high, its rays unleashing a collision of intoxicating aromas. There were meat and fish merchants. And fruit and cheese and honey and vegetable vendors, all calling out the latest bargains in singsong tunes, coaxing you to come sample.

"Venez, prélevez une cale de mandarine!"

"Tomates de jardin!"

"Le fromage de chèvre a appareille avec de votre vin, expertise!"

Scott did the math. 250 euros for twenty people? Some slices of ham, some cheese and bread, perhaps, Croque Monsieurs the best to be had out of it. Except the list Tally withdrew from her purse, scribbled on the back of a receipt, was long and extensive. And the first thing on it he saw was...*venison?*

She caught his expression, brow furrowed, astonished.

"What are you doing..?" he started to ask.

"With you or without you," she said.

"On 250 euros?"

"I've got my own."

"Why?"

"Look for ketchup and rosemary."

He grabbed her arm.

"That hurts!" she cried.

"We're out of this, on our way."

"Let go of my arm!"

"I'm not going to let you do it!"

"You're not going to *let* me?"

"All these guys want is us out of the country!"

"Suppose we've got the recipe, suppose this is it!"

"Do it when we're home."

"I can't!"

"*Why?*"

"I can't!"

"Tally...!"

"We're that close!" she railed.

"Who do you think you are, Indiana Jones?"

"Let go of my arm...!"

The next moment, Scott almost fainted. The shock of realization brought him to his senses.

"Don't look up! Look at the tangerines."

"They're tangelos!"

"*Look* at them!"

"Why...?"

"They're here!"

"Who's here, what are you talking...?

A glance over his shoulder she saw them. Nacer and his two accomplices. As yet they hadn't seen Scott and Tally, but they soon would, searching the crowded aisles.

"How...?"

Words chocked off in her throat, she was barely aware Scott was clutching her wrist, almost dragging her through the crowd, past stalls of iron mongers, produce, clothes, crafts, flowers, baked goods, butchers, garden plants, out of the market, into Place St Gimer before the castle swarming with tourists. Across the Place, Scott saw, was a line of parked taxis. Still holding to their canvas bags, Scott dragged Tally toward it, shoved her into the first taxi they reached, followed her inside, drew closed the door.

"Toulouse," Scott ordered, breath searing his lungs.

"Je ne quitte pas la ville, Monsieur."

"What'd he say?"

"He said he can't leave the city," Tally answered, her own breath coming in short painful gasps as she rubbed her wrist where Scott had grabbed it.

"Ask him how we get there?"

"Comment pouvons-nous y arriver?" Tally asked.

"Autobus, train, aeroport," the driver answered.

"Il y a un aeroport ici?" Scott asked, in reality more implored.

"Oui."

"Aeroport!"

The drive was short, the Aeroport de Carcassonne three kilometers west of the city, road signs as they approached making clear Ryanair was the airline servicing the city. But there was an airline. Where it went, Scott didn't care. Just out of there! The taxi started to pull out of traffic before the terminal entrance, a single story, low-lying building, active with tourists, when Scott's eyes widened.

"Not here, tell him!"

"What?"

"*Tell him!*"

When she saw them. The two men from the restaurant in Sete, watching passengers moving in and out of the terminal.

"Where?" Tally cried.

"Side entrance!" Scott shot back.

"N'arrêtez pas ici!" she told the driver. "Portez nous a l'entrée latérale!"

"Il y a aucune entrée latérale," the driver said, and there was growing tension in his voice as he began to sense there was more to his fares than first assumed.

"No side entrance," Tally translated as the taxi rolled on in low gear, then abruptly stopped.

"Tell him to get the hell out of here!"

"He can't! We're jammed!"

An eighteen wheeler had been crossing before them and was stopped, backing up traffic.

"Jesus fucking French!" Scott raved.

"Great time for a tantrum," Tally countered.

"Yeah, well you come up with something!"

"Like what?"

"What's that?" he was suddenly staring.

"What?"

"That!"

"A hangar."

"No, *that!*"

"*What?*"

"*That!*" he pointed.

To their right, on the tarmac, stood an ancient bi-wing, six passenger tail dragger, smoke billowing from its radial engine, the single four-bladed prop turning over at idle, sounding for all the world like a barrel of grinding nails. It was a time-worn Russian-built Antonov crop duster. The pilot, a dark, preoccupied man in workman's clothing with a churlish face, was bent over assessing one of the wheels that seemed low on air.

"Tournez juste ici!" Scott yelled at the driver, who did so, through a line of tied-down private planes. "Arrêt! Ici!"

The driver, now thoroughly frazzled, slammed on his brakes, pitching Scott and Tally forward against the front seat.

"Pay the son of a bitch!" Scott said and was out the door.

Fumbling for her wallet inside her purse, Tally checked the fare on the meter, handed the driver six euros, quickly exited herself, cloth sacks abandoned, saw Scott was in urgent conversation with the Androv's pilot. Reaching them Scott turned to her.

"He'll fly us to Toulouse for 400 euros."

"Wait a minute…" she started to say.

"Pay it!"

"You said they just want us out of the country…"

"Pay it, Tally!"

"They're not going to do anything, they just want us gone!"

"*Pay it and get in the goddamn plane!*"

The pilot opened the side door, Scott literally boosting Tally inside the passenger compartment, following her in himself, the two of them finding two of the six seats cleared of open boxes, tools, and unopened sacks of crop dust atrazine. Entering himself, the pilot pulled closed the door, took his seat on the left side of the pilot's compartment, looked back at them.

"Vous êtes en voyage de noce?" he asked.

"He wants to know if we're on our honeymoon."

"*Pay him!*"

"This is ridiculous…"

Her hand, he saw, was shaking as she went for her wallet. Grabbing it from her purse Scott hauled out 400 euros, slapped them into the pilot's waiting hand. Shoving the money into his shirt pocket, the pilot turned to his controls, dropped his hand to the throttle, clutched the steering yoke. The rattling turned to a high-pitched moan as the throttle was advanced. The plane groaned forward, a reluctant beast of burden, accepted increased power and broke into a bone rattling taxi toward the head of the runway. The two minutes to reach it were the longest in Scott's life, made more so as the pilot turned the plane facing down runway, held it, brakes full on, checking flaps, rudder, disengaged the carburetor heat, accelerated the throttle quarter full, monitoring magnetos.

"Get this fucker up, get it *up!*" Scott muttered.

Pre-flight check completed, the pilot pulled back on the steering yoke, advanced full throttle, and the plane began its slow lunge down the runway.

"Up, *get it up!*"

Three quarters down the runway, the Antonov's wheels left the tarmac, Scott throwing his hands in the air in relief.

"God," Tally shook her head. "If you could hear yourself…"

When there was a splintering of window glass, followed instantly by the same on the other side of the cabin as the bullet passed through! A quick glance out the window told why. The black Mercedes was running parallel to the plane on the taxi way, muzzle sparks from a handgun, revealing someone inside the car was firing! At the plane!

Scott's future passed before him in a flash. He would go to church, give to charity, honor his mother, never seduce another married woman. He looked at Tally. She was frozen. Green-black oil was splattering against the cockpit window; the oil line severed by a random shot.

With an audible "Merde!" the pilot activated the windshield wipers and pulled back on the throttle as the engine began to overheat. The plane staggered toward a stall, setting off the stall horn. Eyes wide as saucers as the pilot dropped the nose, Scott looked down. Ahead was a vineyard, a dirt service road cutting through parallel rows of vines. The pilot made for it, dropped flaps, pulled back further on the throttle, the Antonov turned into a glider, its principal attribute just that, able to stay aloft at less than forty miles an hour as he closed down the throttle, switched off engine, hydraulic power and gas valve. An explosion from the engine as overheated cylinders popped. The stall horn blaring, the plane settled over the road, pancaked in with a jarring jolt, its lower wings clipping off the tops of vines till the wings themselves were sheared from the plane as it came to a stop.

Dead silence, broken by a stream of French invective impossible to translate as the pilot plowed his way out the cabin door, Scott and Tally looking at each other, trying to arrange thoughts. Exiting the plane themselves, they saw the pilot fiercely assessing damage, when suddenly both their hearts were in their throats. The dirt service road, they saw, terminated at a highway fifty yards ahead. Approaching along that highway was the black Mercedes.

Instinctively, with a move so foreign to him he probably wouldn't have done it had he had time to think, Scott stepped protectively in front of Tally, shielding her as the Mercedes reached the service road, slowed, seemed about to turn onto it when, seemingly without reason, it accelerated, off down the highway and away. It took five seconds to realize why. Close behind and slowing, turning off the highway, onto the service road, approaching was the greatest sight Scott had ever seen in his life. A police car, blue and white, dome lights flashing.

Expressions of ecstasy take many forms. Endless reverie, heaven, divine revision, the hood ornament on a Rolls-Royce. For Scott and Tally it was instinctive and the same, arms thrown around each other, holding each other, breaking apart only to face each other with uncontrollable grins. Hand in hand they turned toward the heaven-sent two officers emerging from their car. One was lean, business-like, a sergeant from the stripes on his sleeve. The other was younger, once athletic, turned somewhat bilious.

"M'sieur, M'amselle?" the sergeant inquired.

"Oui," they both answered enthusiastically.

"Iss my position to inform," his English was terrible, "zee are uner arrest."

Twenty-Five

The Carcassonne police station, two story concrete, with the French flag flying above a second story balcony, was located in the heart of town on Rue Courtefaire. Narrow slit windows gave testimony to the difficulty of escape from within.

Sequestered in a plain, unadorned white walled room, no more than ten by ten, Tally and Scott sat next to each other at a plain wooden table facing a single door that opened, revealing Ms. Butterfield.

"That's them," she said, pointing an accusing finger at the two. "I knew the moment I laid eyes on them. You could tell. Con artists, thieves if ever…"

The police sergeant, close behind her, held up a hand that he understood the charges, nodded to his partner to escort Ms. Butterfield to a proper location, entered the room, closed the door, took a seat at the table across from Scott and Tally. He wore a well-cut uniform, shiny boots, slick-back hair, and a pallor that seemed to suggest he spent more time in an office with paper work than on the streets. The name on the I.D. name plate attached to his tunic read 'Sgt Ariege'.

"I think this is what she's looking for, Sergeant." Tally said, producing the 250 euros, laying them on the table.

Opening a drawer, Sgt. Ariege took out the stub of a pencil and an official form.

"Quand êtes-vous arrivés en Carcassonne?" he began.

"Nous sommes venu…" Scott started to explain, broke off with a muffled yelp as Tally drove the heel of her shoe into his instep.

"I'm sorry," she explained, "we speak little French."

"Noms?" the officer said.

"Noms," Tally looked at Scott in deliberate confusion.

"Vos noms."

"Noms," Tally repeated. "What's that mean? Noms."

"Passports," the officer said with some irritation.

"Ah," Scott answered, getting with the program. "Noms means passports."

"I'd like to explain, if I may…" Tally turned to the officer.

"Passports!"

Handed over, Sgt. Ariege opened them, stared at their name pages as though trying to figure what to do next.

"You must realize," Tally started in, "that an attempt was made to kill us…"

"I vill ask zee questions," the officer interrupted.

"Of course."

He thought for a moment, trying to formulate a question in response to what he'd just been told. But what he'd been told took him off course.

"Someone tries to kill vous?"

"Shooting at us in that plane," Scott confirmed.

"Vy do vous not report ziss to zee police?" the officer asked.

"We *are*. You are the police," Tally said.

"And vy vould someone vant to do ziss?" His eyes were rather wide. This was not a normal interview.

Tally and Scott stared at each other.

"I'm afraid…" she started to answer, looking to Scott for confirmation.

"You know our orders," Scott warned her.

"Yes, but given the circumstances…"

"That's something we can only confide to…"

"I know, but this good man…"

"Do you want to be brought up on charges before the committee?"

"Of course, not."

"Well?"

"No."

"*Do* you?

"No!"

"The administration won't protect you."

She seemed to think that over, to inwardly shudder at the thought, nodded, turned back to the Sergeant.

"You understand."

Sgt. Ariege, for the first time, sensed he just might be in over his head. Stolen property, pickpockets, drive-by purse snatchers, that was his expertise. Still, there was the complaint.

"Zen vy ziss?" he asked, pointing at the euros.

"Did it occur to you Ms. Butterfield just might not be who she claims she is..?" Scott offered.

"Scott!" Tally stopped him.

"Of course," Scott answered, seemingly remorseful by what he'd revealed.

"Remember our directive!" Tally admonished.

"Vous êtes..?"

"Let's just say," she interrupted, "we are two tourists on holiday."

Sgt. Ariege hesitated, sat back slowly in his chair.

"My suggestion? Do not attach any importance to what you've just heard, Sergeant — Arage?" Tally said, pronouncing the name incorrectly.

"Ariege," he corrected, feeling the day slipping away from him. Still, there was a professional face to save, his own, if he could. "Zees killers…"

"Have you studied abnormal psychology?" Tally asked, her voice turned husky.

"Répétez?"

"That raises an awkward problem," Scott threw in.

"I want you to cast your mind back to the time you arrived at the plane," she instructed the increasingly apprehensive officer.

"Caution," Scott warned.

"There was a black Mercedes just ahead of you…"

"The less we reveal, I think," Scott severely counseled.

She seemed reluctant to give up the interrogation, but did so, turned to the Sergeant.

"Return this money to the woman, Sergeant," her voice assuming commanding authority. "That way she will not suspect she is under suspicion. As for you, sir, let us suppose for the moment their shooting had been more accurate. You would be dealing with something more complicated than this euro business. So now. If you would have your officers escort my colleague and me under protection to the airport at Toulouse where we can catch a flight to the UK — I have no doubt they will try again if given the chance — I feel without question you will be receiving in due course a commendation from our government for your service."

Twenty-Six

Dammit it! *Damn!*

The alarm had gone off as Scott had set it. 9:45 a.m. He hadn't really slept since returning home to New York two days ago, despite still occupying the opulent Eastside condo Medlock had provided, the five hour change in time zones upsetting, so what the hell, he'd try to get in at least a half hour more, and now he saw it was, Christ, 11:15 and he was supposed to be at that restaurant at *noon?* He threw himself into the shower, speed shaved, jumped into his clothes and loafers, going sockless, took the emergency stairs two at a time, came out onto Park just north of Seventy-Second Street, muggy, overcast, found every taxi he hailed was going uptown or to lunch, finally, in desperation, flagged a bicycle cab.

"Forty-Eight West Fifty-Fifth!" he shouted to the cyclist, a twenty-year-old college student in sweatshirt with NYU superimposed on an evil-looking bobcat, the university mascot. "Double if you make it by noon!"

It was a challenge Scott instantly regretted. Splitting car lanes, the young grimalkin took off down Park, cutting off traffic at will, powered through stop lights, spun his trailing cab semi-upright on one wheel as he pumped west on Fifty-Fifth, crossed Madison and Fifth, again against traffic, pulled to a stop before La Bonne Soupe. Shoving more bills than intended into the cyclist's hand, Scott bolted for the entrance.

Inside, the luncheon crowd was just beginning to arrive as Scott found Tally seated at one of the wooden tables, back to the wall, facing the room, a glass of Arnold Palmer, menu, note pad and pen before her. She wore a long-sleeved shirt and jeans, her hair pulled back. The place was her choice, which Scott applauded, price being of current consideration as he glanced about the room. Not finding who he was looking for, he dropped onto a chair across from her. He'd gone to his bank the day before, withdrawn half of his earlier five hundred dollar deposit, reluctantly had called Medlock's office at Tally's insistence, gotten a call back to meet, now, today. Too soon. Too soon. They needed time to test what they had. *If* they had. Try the recipe first on Barry, see what he thought. Like what'd *he* know?

"He's late!"

"Everyone's late in New York," Tally answered.

"Twelve o'clock sharp, he said!"

"Scott..?"

"The fucking..!"

"Scott!"

"I'm going to give him shit!"

When the door opened and Elihu Sykes, late of Scott's meeting at Aquavit, entered with his ever-present briefcase, spotted Scott who rose, thrusting out his hand with an ear-splitting grin.

"Mr. Sykes!" Scott greeted the arrival with outright geniality who accepted Scott's hand limply, glancing off as he did so, the sort of grip that said, 'I've really no interest in you.' "Good to see you again," Scott chimed on. "Let me introduce you. Tally Garner…"

"And she is?" Sykes interrupted.

"We met in France," Scott answered, circling to the bench seat next to Tally. "An expert chef. Her assistance has been invaluable in discovering…"

"The agreement was with you, Fitzgerald."

"The agreement was for a recipe," Tally corrected with a disarming smile.

"I beg your pardon?"

"The agreement was for a recipe."

Sykes turned crimson. He was not a man used to dealing with contradiction, least of all the unexpected. His instructions were to deliver instructions to one-person, that person only. He was a Company Man, the sort that religiously took orders, whatever, however they might be, never questioning nor putting himself in a position of making a decision himself, thereby never having to fail. The corporate towers of Manhattan were full of them. And Sykes was a disciple.

Blood receding from his face, Sykes lowered to a chair as though there'd been no crisis at all, placed his brief case atop the table, sprung the latches, opened it, took out a glassine covered single page document, handed it to Scott.

"What's this?" Scott asked, flipping it open. He was nervous, and he knew it showed.

"Instructions."

"About?"

"Delivery. Time, address."

"What's it say?"

"The date will be this Thursday."

"Thursday! That's the day after *tomorrow!*"

Tally held up a calming hand as she jotted a note on her pad.

"Thursday," she said in affirmation. "And?"

"Further, it reads, you will contact Mr. Medlock's kitchen staff today. That folder contains the direct number…"

"Today," Tally verified, jotting that down too.

"…during which you'll notify them of ingredients called for in the recipe. Staff will purchase what's required, you understand. The kitchen will be available to you Thursday throughout the day, Mr. Medlock's chef and sous chefs in assistance 'til delivery to Mr. Medlock's private dining room for presentation at eleven-thirty that night."

"Eleven-*thirty?*" Scott was stunned.

"Did I not make myself clear?"

"That's midnight!"

"Mr. Medlock arises at seven-forty in the evening. Breakfasts at eight, lunches promptly just before the end of the day, you understand. When you arrive, call the kitchen. They'll send down an escort."

With that, Sykes closed his briefcase, rose as though there was nothing to be gained by explaining anything further, when Tally stopped him.

"If I may review, Mr. Sykes."

Eyebrows arched, Sykes looked back at her as she turned to her notes.

"Contact Mr. Medlock's kitchen staff, notify them of ingredients for recipe. Staff to purchase what's requested. Kitchen available Thursday, throughout day, Mr. Medlock's chef and sous chefs in assistance 'til delivery."

"Precisely," Sykes nodded, again started to withdraw, again was brought up short.

"We will not be calling staff, Mr. Sykes," Tally ventured in a most genial tone. Sykes's mouth snapped open but Tally cut him short. "We will purchase all ingredients ourselves. Mr. Medlock's chef and sous chefs will not be in attendance. Only Mr. Fitzgerald and I will occupy the kitchen. Please notify security we will arrive at 9:45 p.m. Thursday for presentation at the hour requested." She smiled. "You understand."

For a moment, Sykes stood his ground, Tally waiting for his response with a half- cocked eye and a smile. Turning on his heel he stalked from the place, Scott on his feet, half reaching after Sykes. Whipping about, he glared at Tally who'd picked up the menu.

"What the hell are you doing?"

"Ordering lunch."

"Fucking suicide!"

"They make a great fondue," she offered.

"That was *Medlock* you were talking to!" Scott all but brayed, dropping, arms extended, palms gripping the edge of the table.

"Onion soup, too."

"You think he'll admit to anything you come up with now, even if you've got it right? Which you don't. You're bluffing."

Tally sat back slowly, taking full measure of him,

"Scott, level with me. You wimping out?"

Scott's upper lip curled as though trying to find a witty counter. He couldn't. He pushed back from the table. Pivoting with such force he almost sprained an ankle, he was through the door and gone.

At $2,595 a month, Tally's seventh floor contemporary Murray Hill one bedroom with its East River view had long been considered a bargain. While working at *New York In Review* Publications it was. Now it would have to be reconsidered given she was no longer with the company, her prospects for the future, though not limited given her reputation, certainly promising lesser income and insuring a downsized rental. But what to do with her treasured Modern Library collection. For decades young collegians had cut their intellectual teeth on Modern Library books. The series, offering literally all the world's classics, shaped their tastes, educated them, provided them a window to the world with their run in the forties and fifties, selling, at the time, for $1.25 to $2.50 a volume. Further, frugal, albeit not to a fault, Tally'd always had a nest egg stashed away guaranteeing at least six month's survival, though France had eroded its core. As for her apartment in Angers and rented car left in the airport in Lyons, well, get through this first.

The kitchen was small, a narrow corridor between cupboards, sink and refrigerator-freezer on one side, a four burner gas stove, oven, more cupboards, pots, pans and utility closet on the other. And there on the counter to be sequestered away till early Wednesday, the following morning, was the result of her afternoon's acquisitions.

She'd made four stops, starting off in subways, ending up with cabs as the bulk of her purchases became prodigious. Five pounds venison bones with marrow, along with three pounds of highest quality prime loin venison cut from the ribs from Ottomanelli & Sons on Bleecker Street. Onions, carrots, celery, parsley, fresh herbs, juniper berries, pomegranate, lemon, rosemary, shallots from Union Square West Green Market. Tellicherry pepper, fleur de sel, and, on a hunch, Aceta Balsamico Tradizionale vinegar from Dean and Deluca. Safflower oil, olive oil, brown sugar, crème fraiche, ketchup, and a half dozen nesting plastic quart and pint and half pint containers from her local Whole Foods. And a bottle of Old RAJ Gin from the Park Avenue Liquor Shop along with a bottle of dry vermouth. The gin had cost $52, the vinegar more, extravagantly expensive, but Madame Morille had made it clear. A recipe, no matter how well intended, should never contain any ingredient other than the finest.

Did she have everything? She went over the recipe she'd formulated in her mind three times. Tomorrow would be dedicated to making the stock. A nearly all-day process. What had she forgotten? Dinner! She'd forgotten about that. She'd gone to the corner convenience store the day before, the day after her arrival home, bought coffee, milk, butter, bread, raisin bran, and bananas, had joined a couple of old friends from the magazine for a quick supper that night, but had forgotten about the next day. She looked through what she had on hand, found a can of Progresso split pea soup, settled on that, found further she was suddenly exhausted, too bone weary to eat, body aching from lugging groceries all over town. And tension. And along with tension, or because of it, the doubts. Creeping in at the edges. Was this really, after all, just a goose chase? She had only Scott's word for it, this pot of gold awaiting. Had he in fact just made it up? Or heard it wrong? Had Medlock just led him on for the jollies of it? Was the pot at the end of this rainbow filled with lead?

Turning the burner off under the simmering soup, she ignored it, went into her living room, dropped to her couch, turned on the TV, barely aware that McDreamy was fuming over the loss of a ping pong match to an intern as he performed a delicate ventriculogram on a rerun of *Grey's Anatomy*. And there, at six the following morning, sunlight playing in on her face, she awoke, clothes still on from the night before, TV still on, Elizabeth Hasselbeck trashing Obamacare on *The View*.

Shower. She needed a shower. Moving into her bathroom, she looked in the mirror. Her hair was a mess. But first there was something that had to be done. Entering the kitchen, she turned the oven on to 375 degrees, removed the venison bones from the refrigerator, placed them on a chopping board, cracked them open with a wooden mallet exposing the marrow. Depositing them in a shallow roasting pan, she inserted the pan in the oven when it reached temperature, there to roast for forty-five minutes.

Brushing teeth, showering, Tally slipped on a pair of workout pants, T-shirt and jogging shoes, phoned for an appointment at two the next afternoon at the Drybar Hair Salon on East Thirty-Fourth, bolted down a breakfast of banana and dry cereal with milk and set to work.

Bringing out an eight quart cast iron Belgian cooking pot, she set it on the stove. There was history to the pot. Red and orange enameled, it was more than a half century old, had been willed to Tally by her grandmother, Mimsey. For good reason. Not only was Mimsey a brilliant cook, she was the author of a half dozen cookbooks, proofing every recipe twice in her kitchen with Tally at her side, daily after school, chopping, scrubbing, measuring, peeling, learning. When her grandmother was chided for her first book being something only wealthy and accomplished chefs could achieve — a lot of ribbing for left-over pheasant under glass — she followed with a second, filled with recipes new brides could perform and afford. A paragraph always attended each, how it was imagined, how it was developed. It was Tally who wrote the text.

Removing the roasting pan from the oven, Tally let the now caramelized bones cool and placed them into the cook pot. Deglazing the pan with vermouth, she deposited the scrapings into the pot, added two of the three pounds of venison cut into cubes, two onions chopped in half, two medium carrots and two large celery ribs both diced, juniper berries, two bay leaves, five sprigs of fresh parsley, ten whole peppercorns from her cupboard, and the fresh bought herbs. Covering all with an inch of water, she turned on the burner. When brought to a gentle boil she reduced the heat to the lowest simmer possible, partially covered the pot where it would sit for the next three hours. In a half hour she would have to begin skimming every fifteen minutes or so. It was, she knew, the easy part, the basics. The rest would come later. The rest was everything.

Returning to her living room, she opened the *Times*, which she'd renewed upon her return. Turning to the editorial section, she was just about to read Thomas Friedman's article on "A Decade Of Despair," when the phone rang.

Twenty-Seven

The walk up Lexington to the Affina Shelbourne Hotel at Thirty-Seventh was relatively short. Reaching it, Tally hesitated, as though having second thoughts. It had turned dark, seven-thirty. Dressed simply, slacks, shirt, cardigan, flats, hair in a ponytail, she turned, facing the direction she'd come from. Theatre traffic was heading uptown, some spirited souls even walking it. She looked back at the hotel, drew in a metaphoric breath and entered.

The lobby was relatively small but muted elegance. Burnt orange couches, black leather chairs, a large Afghan rug on the floor. Crossing to the elevators past the check-in desk, the attendant giving her what she thought was a knowing smirk reserved for assumed call girls, Tally summoned the elevator, waited out its arrival, stepped aside as two couples made their exit, entered herself, and pressed the button to the sixteenth floor rooftop Rare View Bar.

It was not the first time Tally had been there, offering by well-earned reputation one of the city's finest views. This night, perhaps because of the early hour, or the economy, the room was lightly populated as Tally stepped from the lift, found Scott seated in a booth looking out on the Empire State Building, fully illuminated, three blocks away.

Rising at her approach — when did *that* start? — she saw he was dressed for a more upscale occasion: doe-skin trousers, silk shirt, coat, and loafers.

"Hey," he greeted her with expansive cheer.

"Hey," she responded with a sense of caution.

Sliding into the booth opposite him, Tally noticed the half empty bourbon and soda before him.

"You get back into it yet? I'm going nuts with the change."

"They say it takes a day per time zone," she said.

"Worse coming home than going over."

"Heard that."

"Go figure."

The small talk was aborted by the arrival of a waiter. He was handsome, clearly a devotee of a bronzing salon, and, by guess, an out-of-work actor.

"The hamburgers are the best in town," Scott offered. "It's on me."

"Hamburger's fine. Medium. Ice tea."

"Make mine rare," Scott said. "And another one of these suckers," he said, pointing to his glass. "Wild Turkey."

The waiter withdrew with his order, leaving a void that neither, for the moment, filled. But it was clear to Tally that Scott was bracing himself for something. Whatever it was, he wasn't yet fortified enough to address it.

"Hell of a view," he said at length, looking out on the Empire tower.

"Reminds me of that movie," she said, looking out on it too.

"You liked that movie?"

"One of my favorites."

"Me too!" Scott enthused.

"You're kidding. You?"

"How often do you find a love story like that?"

"Was it ever," Tally matched his fervor.

"That final scene atop the building."

"What an ending."

"Never thought she'd make it up."

"*Boy*, did they milk that," Tally fell back against the back of the booth, collapsing from the memory.

"The way they looked at each other."

"Find me someone like that!"

"To each his own," Scott said, throwing up his hands as though holding her at bay.

"If it hadn't been for his son," she said.

Scott stared. "What son?"

"He got them together."

"His *son?*"

"In the movie."

"There wasn't a kid in the movie."

"Of course there was?"

"No kid. I've seen the damn thing three times."

"Well, so have I. And there was a kid!" she insisted.

"Just…"

"What?"

"What picture are you talking about?"

"*Sleepless in Seattle.*"

"*Sleepless In Seattle?*"

"What're you?"

"*King Kong!*"

For a moment, they sat stupefied, then broke into laughter, which soon subsided, leaving them where they'd been.

"So," Tally said at length.

"So?"

"You called the meeting, Scott."

"Right. Look. I been thinking."

"That's why you got the big bucks."

"What?"

"Go on."

"I think we should postpone."

"Postpone what?"

"This thing with Medlock."

Tally sat back slowly. Her voice lowered, gathered like a fist.

"Quit."

"I didn't say that. Is that what I said?"

"I think it is."

"We get one shot at this," he said.

"If a cat sits on a hot stove, Scott, he'll never sit on a hot stove again. For that matter, he'll never sit on a cold stove either."

"Whatever the hell *that* means."

"It means this *is* our shot."

"I just think we need time."

"For what?"

"To work this out, make sure we've got it, that's all."

"Let me try another scenario."

"Scenario."

"What's really going on."

"Another fucking analysis?"

"You drop your transparency all over the floor. An assault course on the sensibilities." Then with a shake of her head, "You don't want to hear this."

"Don't let *that* stop you," he answered, acid in his voice.

"This is your ticket back into the game. Isn't it?" As his mouth dropped open to refute, "I know it, you know it. As long as this thing's open you've got a story. *New York In Review* — those guys'd buy from *Eichman* if it's something they can sell — they'll grab it, forget everything you did ripping off that homeless. They're no different from you. You think they are? Look in the mirror, you'll see them. But fail with Medlock, you've got nothing, just a ridiculous run through France." He's staring at her. "How'm I doing?"

"If you think for one minute…" He was beginning to rock.

"You know what you are, Scott?"

"I'm not going to listen to this..!"

"One word."

He was out of the booth.

"Run, Scott. See Scott run."

"I'm going to the bathroom."

"It's off the lobby. On your way out."

"What word?"

"Poltroonish."

He stared at her, no idea what she was talking about.

"Look it up."

It was then that the waiter arrived with their drinks, staring in confusion after Scott, who was heading toward the elevator.

"Take back the ice tea," Tally said, a dispirited tone to her voice as she reached for the bourbon.

Twenty-Eight

Thursday morning.

The headache wasn't terminal, but Scott went with the hypothesis that whatever pain he had was the worst in the history of man. He'd awakened with it, downed two Tylenol with his coffee and only now, forty minutes later, was beginning to feel human again. It had been, quite simply, a horrible night. He needed reaffirmation and he knew where to get it. His model the night of the Ellies. He'd gone to his phone book. He'd forgotten the name, but he remembered it began with an S. It wasn't that hard to find. Sjostrand. He dialed.

"Hej," her voice came on the line in Swedish. "Hej?" the voice repeated when Scott said nothing.

He hung up without a word. *Damn* her! And he wasn't talking about the model. It was Tally. You'd think this indigestible mess she'd gotten them into would stir some kind of regret. Caution, at least. Nada. Nothing. Well, let her make a fool of herself, fall on her face. He thought about calling her. About what? There was nothing to talk about, she'd made up her mind, stupid, stubborn. By midnight tonight she'd be crawling into her shell, humiliated and beaten, face rubbed in the mud. It was not an image he reveled in. But she'd brought it on herself, dabbling in nonsense way over her head! He'd tried to warn her, tried to stop her, hadn't he? Hadn't he? On impulse he picked up the phone, dialed.

"Hey. It's me," he said when the phone was answered. "Can you meet me for lunch at the Carnegie Deli? How's one?"

Located on Seventh Avenue and Fifty-Fifth, The Carnegie, considered the Granddaddy of New York Delis, offered sandwiches that could feed a battalion, and cheesecake considered the standard by which all other cheesecakes should be judged. There in a booth Scott sat waiting, nursing a beer, food, for the moment, the last thing on his mind. He'd gotten there early, rehearsing what he wanted to say, which seemed to change every time he went through it. At one o'clock, promptly, as he knew it would, the door was pushed open and Barry entered. Spotting Scott, he approached with a grin and outstretched hand.

"Jesus, Scott! Where the hell you been? You disappeared from the face. I been calling, calling!"

"Listen, cut to the chase?" He was edgy.

"Go."

"I need your help."

"Scott, I told you, you can live at my place 'til you get squared…"

"I don't mean that. I mean with Dan."

Barry sat back slowly. Dan Randall? Managing Editor of *New York In Review* Publications? He was Barry's boss, Scott's former one. He'd ordered Scott's firing.

"The thirty-third floor's pretty pissed, Scott. After that homeless business at the Ellies."

"They won't be when you tell them what I've got."

A waitress arrived. From the look of her one might fairly conclude she'd been with the deli since its opening in 1937.

"Half a pastrami to go," Barry said.

"I'm good," Scott said, acknowledging his beer, then realizing, "To go?"

"Sorry. I'm on a short leash, just got a few minutes," Barry explained.

The waitress withdrew, Barry looked to Scott, waiting.

"I've got something that'll knock Dan's fucking ears off, Barry. I'm not talking Ellies, I'm talking Pulitzer."

"Kay?" Barry said. It was one of those 'kays' filled with doubt and suspicion.

"That night in my apartment when I got that hit on my computer?"

"Yeah?"

"It was Medlock."

"Who?" Scott asked, not sure he'd heard correctly.

"Hugo Medlock."

"*Hugo* Medlock?"

"Six hours later I'm in his penthouse suite. You ought to see the fucking place, the guy's, well, anyway, he's got this assignment for me. France. There's this recipe he can't get in this fucking restaurant and I've run into Tally and we're going after it…"

"Scott…"

"…except the French Mafia, they own the place, chasing us over half the country till we end up in this fucking crop duster…"

"Scott!"

"And there were these guys in this black Mercedes…"

"It's all going to work out, buddy, don't panic," Barry said with genuine compassion.

"You're not hearing!"

"I told you, one door closes, another opens..."

"Wait a min, let me start again. You're pushing me to the wall here with this time thing!"

"But you got to back off the crap...!"

"No, listen. Call Tally!"

"I've been testing the waters. Look, there's an opening for a proof reader on the *Daily Recycler*..."

"No, *you* look! The guy gives me 50,000 down, and this condo on Park..."

"*50,000?*"

"Against God knows what when I come up with the thing."

"You got the check?"

"No."

"Where is it?"

"Well, shit, there were expenses."

"You go to Dan with that, without something to show him, the first thing you're going to hear is there's a meeting of Bullshit Anonymous on the third floor on Thursday nights."

Scott's face turned black.

"I thought you were my friend."

"I *am* your friend, Scott. Which is why I'm telling you. Don't try to bullshit your way back into the game. No more homeless, no more cons."

"Fuck you!"

"Scott..?"

"You heard *that*, all right! Fuck you! And that horse you rode in on!"

Out of the booth, Scott threw a ten on the table for his beer, headed for the door and was gone. Barry's chin dropped to his chest, his head rocking slowly back and forth in regret and dismay.

Tally had awakened that morning from a dreamless half sleep, needing clarity so desperately she was willing to sacrifice everything to avoid being an emotional mess. *Grandma? I don't know what's going to happen. All I know is I have a deep, loving need of you! Grandma?*

Pulling herself out of bed, she'd entered the bathroom, slipped on a light summer robe, and gone to the kitchen. Removing the cast iron pot from the refrigerator, she'd lifted the lid. A slight film of congealed fat covered the contents. Extracting it with a spatula, she'd set the pot on a low flame, made herself some toast and coffee, had run through the

Times, and returned to the kitchen to find the stock had reached room temperature. Setting a colander in a deep dish bowl, she'd drained the stock, separating out bones and vegetables, where she discarded all but the liquid, which she'd returned to the pot, set back on the stove, and over a medium low flame began the process of reducing the stock by half. By noon, completed, she'd left the condensed stock partially covered to cool, showered and dressed, and walked the one and a half blocks to the Drybar Hair Salon.

Her favorite operator was Jenny, China born, forty years old, looking thirty, five foot one, with a rosebud mouth, and a seventeen-year-old daughter headed for Brown University, full scholarship. Jenny was quick, yet a sculptress with comb and scissors, and gratefully, this day at least, not conversational. Tally had too many things to sort out. With Sinatra's "New York, New York" playing through background wall speakers, she tried to force her mind into reviewing, making certain all was in order for the coming night's preparation and delivery. But Scott invaded her thoughts, like a tune she couldn't get out of her head. God knows he had been an adventure. Arrogant, full of malice, a cheat, liar, bully, a monument of non-attachment with his own personal morality or lack of it. And yet, that night together. Was it only four nights ago, five? No. Don't go there. Go with the song. "If I can make it there, I'll make it anywhere…" And yet afterwards, the way he'd clung to her, naked, not just in body, but, she could feel it, the vulnerability coursing through him, heartbeat racing, holding onto her as though holding onto substance — was that what it was? Or imagination. She tried to shake it off. Did every lover have to have a need of her?

Jenny was finished, and a look in the mirror told Tally that Jenny had done it again.

Jenny's prices were insanely low. $35. For a trim? In New York? Paying her fifty, Tally praised her effusively, sent her best to her daughter, and stepped from the salon into what she knew would be the most intense night of her life.

By nine-fifteen, there was nothing more for Tally to do at home. She had transferred items separately into the plastic containers, depositing all, along with her bottled purchases, into her large-size L.L. Bean canvas tote bag, added an apron, then dressed — how to dress? — no jewelry, light lipstick, white blouse, dark slacks, flats, and a cardigan. The taxi she'd called for was on time and waiting. Verifying the address on the single page document received from Sykes, she glanced about her apartment one final time, took the elevator to the street, entered the waiting cab. The ride she knew would be short across lower Manhattan, then south to the financial district.

She sat back in the cab, eyes closed, her canvas bag at her side, realized suddenly she had every right to feel Scott was right. Maybe she *didn't* have the recipe. Maybe there was no getting it at *all*. The realization was sharp and frightening. So much so that when the cab braked before the black glass-faced high rise it took three confirmations from the cabbie to alert her that they'd arrived. Paying her fare, Tally left the cab, tote bag in hand, looked up at the gold block lettering on the face of the building: Medlock Towers.

Climbing the steps to the entrance, tote bag in hand, she rang the after-hours bell, saw through the glass entrance doors one of two dark-suited night guards rise from behind the highly computerized reception desk, cross to the doors, unlock them, admitting her, having been notified of her pending arrival. Otherwise deserted, the lobby, she noticed on entering, was Spartan but elegant, with floor and walls in polished Italian black marble, and two separate waiting areas furnished in plush deep-set leather chairs — when her eyebrows raised in surprise at the sight of Scott rising from one of them.

Twenty-Nine

The initial shock at seeing Scott, turned to wariness as Tally watched him emerge from near-darkness into light when her caution dissolved. There was something about him she'd never seen before. He looked vanquished. His body language projected it. Collapse, defeat. For a moment more they stared at each other. Turning to the guard who'd admitted her, Tally nodded.

Off reception was a bank of six elevators, three on one side facing three on the other. Leading Tally and Scott past them, the guard took a turn into a semi-lit corridor, then down it, past operations, security, maintenance, coming, at length, to a locked door. Punching in numbers on a wall key pad, the door opened to a vestibule housing a single elevator. Running a key card across a metal plate, the guard stood aside as the elevator door slid open. Gesturing Tally and Scott were to enter, he reached inside, ran the card across an inner plate, and stood back as the door closed.

The elevator, Scott noticed, unlike the one that had brought him initially to Medlock's suite, was pedestrian, other than the camera eye looking down upon them, turning, both noticed, from Scott to Tally and back again as they made the rapid ascent in silence. Easing to a stop, the elevator door opened, admitting them to what was clearly a large pantry, illuminated by a fluorescent light, white walls, floor to ceiling cupboards as well as trash and garbage chutes leading, presumably, to receptacles in the basement. Ahead, they could see, glass topped swinging doors opened to a brightly lit inner room. Leading the way, Tally pushed through the doors, introducing them to a kitchen wonderland, and face to face with an Irish leprechaun.

Five foot five, thick glasses, hair slicked back, black pants, white serving coat, he came forward in greeting literally in a jig.

"Jimmy here," he said with a grin and thick Irish brogue, hand outstretched in greeting. "Whatever yis after findin' — not ere to pest, what would yis be tinkin' — if yis anyting wantin', jus' push tha button, give a shout. Oterwise, eleven tirty, I'll be ere enough."

With that he was gone, leaving Tally and Scott alone, for the moment immobilized, then looking around.

The kitchen was immense, uncluttered with rich warm tones. English yew wood cabinets were covered in smoky red glass. Iroko chopping blocks on the granite covered island richly balanced the Andre Rothblatt architecture. There were two sinks, a six burner gas range, multiple ovens, two dishwashers, a huge refrigerator, a floor to ceiling wine cooler and a warming drawer. Le Creuset Signature copper pots and pans hung from hooks above the range. A Wusthof Classic Ikon Knife Block Set stood on a counter, housing a dozen various-purpose cutlery. A wall clock told the hour: 9:55.

Never had Tally seen anything like it. Never had she *imagined* anything like it. Setting down the tote bag, she began removing its contents, no acknowledgement of Scott who'd dropped onto a chair, sat hunched forward. For a long moment he watched her setting out bottles and plastic containers on the island.

"Poltroonish," he said at length. "I looked it up."

"If you want to be of help..."

"Lily-livered, cowardly?"

"You can start in on the shallots."

"Gutless..?

"Peel and mince."

Turning to cupboards and drawers, Tally found what she was looking for. Stainless-steel measuring spoons. A measuring cup set. Mixing bowls. Setting them out, she addressed the process of preparation, separating out each ingredient to be used. Shallots, olive oil, stock, butter, rosemary, gin, brown sugar, lemon, crème fraiche, the Aceta Balsamic vinegar, salt, pepper, venison, pomegranate seeds. And ketchup. A twenty-ounce bottle of Heinz 57 Varieties Tomato Ketchup. Soaping, rinsing her hands, she dried them on paper towels. Selecting a knife, she placed it along with the shallots on a cutting board, glanced over at Scott. Her expression saying, well?

"Do you know what I think?" Scott said. "I think you think I don't go where the fire is burning. Don't look for the battles."

"What are you doing here, Scott?"

"I'm here because I should be. Because I'd feel bad if I wasn't. I want to feel better and I want you to feel better, and..."

"And what?"

"Tell me what you think of us? Let's see if I'm even close."

"I'm through judging you."

"That's not what I'm talking about. That night on that barge."

"Don't go there."

"We never saw the moon come up. Which is the only thing that didn't."

"Scott!" A warning shot fired across his bow.

"Now that's very…it's a key question."

"I'm sorry, I'm not getting through," she said. "I know how honesty always upsets you…"

"Listen…"

"No!"

"Yeah, well I'm not begging for crumbs," he said, rounding into petulance. Turning to the shallots, he picked up the knife.

"Wash your hands," she told him. "There're towels on that rack."

"Shit!" he said, dropping the knife with a clatter, crossed to a sink, washed his hands with a peevish thoroughness of a surgeon. Securing a large frying pan from above the range, Tally set it on a burner as Scott returned to the shallots.

"How do you do this?" he asked.

Crossing back to the cutting board, Tally peeled the shallots, minced them with expert quickness, returned to the range, turned the fire on beneath the pan, poured in a couple of tablespoons of olive oil to warm, added an equal amount of butter, carried the pan to the shallots when the butter was melted, scooped them into the pan, returned the pan to the flame, setting it on low. With Scott watching, his brow creased in doubt and concern, Tally pulled a wooden spoon from a collection of spoons from what seemed to be a narrow-throated Venetian flower vase, began slowly stirring. Turning, Scott looked over the laid-out ingredients, found the stock, stuck his finger in to taste.

"What's this?"

"Get your finger out of it!" Tally flared at the sight.

"That's what my mother used to tell my dad," Scott answered, swept back into bitter recall. "My Dad. You know," he said, turning reflective, "from just about the first day he went to work he knew where he'd be the day he died. All he wanted was to do good work. And when he couldn't anymore, there wasn't anything for him anymore. That's one thing he always told me. If there's anything I remember. Keep your options open. And you know what? He couldn't live with it. I wanted to believe he was afraid of nothing. That he was absolutely fearless. I wanted to believe there wasn't a man, or woman, on earth that he feared."

It had come out in a stream, an unconscious revelation of sorts. Watching her shallots begin to soften, Tally added a sprig of fresh rosemary to her stirring.

"If that's the worst thing that ever happened to you," she said, not unaffected by what she'd heard him say.

"Not the worst."

"Really?"

"You want to hear this?" He was on recovery, escaping the past.

"Sure," she said.

"I took this river trip once. With these three guys. In Georgia. The Appalachians. There was this kid in a tree with a banjo…"

"Sorry," she said. "I saw that movie."

"Maybe I'm being a little too subtle."

"First time for everything."

Grabbing the bottle of gin, Tally poured in what approximated an eighth of a cup, tipped the pan flaming it. Scott watched for a moment in reflection.

"We got off on the wrong start, didn't we?" he said at length.

"You mean three months ago or yesterday," Tally replied, shaking the pan.

"You really hold grudges, don't you?"

"Maybe not against the one you think," she said as she stirred, the shallots slowly beginning to turn golden. "Did I suspect you were going in with somebody else's work and presenting it as your own? And I did nothing to stop it? I've asked myself that a thousand times."

"So this was about getting even, that night at the Ellies…"

"You don't even know your good parts, you know that, Scott? Maybe that's what I was holding out for."

"Fine," Scott said. "Hurrah, hurrah." His face had tightened. "The guy got any Scotch around here?"

"He's got everything else."

She glanced at the clock. Scott saw the look, glanced too. 10:20. A tense silence permeated the room as reality engaged. Turning the flame to a low simmer, Tally picked up the stock, ladled it into the pan, spoonful at time, stirring, stirring as Scott ran through cupboards looking for liquor.

"You were *right* in telling me don't come," he said at length. "What *am* I doing here. It's not too late. I can make some calls."

"There's always that model," Tally offered.

"Which model?"

"The one at the Ellies."

"They ought to build a monument to that one," he said, deliberately punishing. "I mean we tore the room apart."

"Product management."

"You asked."

Silence. The last of the stock whisked in, Tally went for the lemon, cut it in half. Holding it upright so no seeds would get in, she squeezed it, sending lemon juice into the mixture. Removing the rosemary, she scooped in a tablespoon of brown sugar. Then, and only then, she reached for the ketchup.

"Jesus!" Scott said at the sight of it.

"No time for rehearsal," she answered as she added a teaspoon of ketchup, stirred, then tasted.

"Too sweet."

"I want to throw up," Scott said.

Ignoring him, Tally added another slight squeeze of lemon juice, tasted again. Stirred again, tasted again, alternately stirring and balancing. Ketchup, brown sugar, lemon, Aceta Balsamico vinegar, now, thick, dark, sweet, syrupy, pepper, salt, rebalancing, tasting, Scott returned to his chair, head rocking back and forth in hands.

11:15.

It had gone by quickly, too quickly.

"You want to taste this?" she asked.

"What do I know."

She tasted it herself.

"You got it?"

"I'm not sure," she said with sudden doubt.

"Well, if you're not who the hell is?" It was a berating whine as he looked up at the clock.

Securing a dinner plate from a cupboard, she put it in the warming drawer already on. Turning to the venison, she put it on the cutting board, sliced it into three three-quarter-inch thick slices. Taking down a second pan, she set it on the range, turned the fire on to medium low, poured in two tablespoons of olive oil, added an equal amount of butter, laid the venison slices in the pan to sauté when the butter and oil were hot, the butter melted. Five minutes, the venison was turned. Five minutes more it was done.

Securing the dinner plate from the warmer, Tally removed the venison from the pan, centered it on the warmed plate, carefully folded a quarter pint of crème fraiche into the stock, warming it, stirring, tasting — hesitated — reached for the ketchup. With Scott looking on, wagging his finger in protest, *no, no,* on impulse Tally stirred another tablespoon of ketchup into the stock, spooned it over the venison, sprinkled it with pomegranate seeds as a door was pushed open by Jimmy who stood by the door, holding it wide.

Tally glanced at Scott, rising, white as a sheet as he stared at the ketchup bottle, everything, all they'd gone through, had fought for, tried to discover, coming down to *this?* Wiping a smudge of stock off the edge of the plate, Tally drew in a breath, lifted it, carried it, Scott starting to trail behind her, when Jimmy intercepted them both, took the plate from Tally.

"Meanin' no cheek, yis jus' be a jammers."

With that Jimmy and the plate were gone.

For a moment, Scott stood, shoulders bunched, riveted on the closed door, opened his mouth to say something, stopped. Tally had dropped into a chair. She'd held up through the ordeal, 'til now. Exhausted, drained, she sat, collapsed, her head shaking side to side. Unable to handle a sudden feeling of compassion, Scott turned from her, slammed the palm of his hand against the door, supported his weight on it, back to the room.

"What're you going to do if this doesn't happen?" he asked.

"You?"

"Unskilled labor," he answered, and he wasn't kidding.

"Do I weep for the artist?"

"What about you?"

"Hooking."

"If you can't make it at that?"

"Probably a lawyer."

Scott stared at the door. He had nothing more to offer, no assessments, no more quips.

"You never said that about me before," he said, voice hesitant, confounded.

"What?"

"Artist."

Tally didn't answer. Rising, she crossed to the range, carried the frying pans to the sink, scrubbed them down with soapy hot water and a brush, rinsed and dried them, returned them to their hooks. Repackaging her condiments, she placed them back along with the vinegar and gin in her tote bag, set it aside. Finding an all-purpose cleaner, she sprayed down counter top and chopping block, wiped both clean, deposited the used paper towels in a bin beneath the sink, when Jimmy was standing in the doorway.

"I tink," he said, his face inscrutable, "yis best come in."

Thirty

It was the following Wednesday morning before Barry could pull it off.

In reception, on the thirty-third floor of *New York In Review* Publications, Barry paced, glanced nervously at the clock above the reception desk, saw the hour, 9:56, when the elevator door gasped open disgorging Scott. He was dressed to the nines, suit, tie, button-down shirt, McAfee shoes. Grabbing Scott by the arm without greeting, Barry hauled him off to a corner.

"I got him to give you ten minutes. He didn't want to give you anything, but I promised to write his kid's term paper if he would. He'll piss you off, I guarantee it, but I swore you were here to apologize, so take it. The guy's a sucker for a confession. Maybe he'll hear of something for you, so play it cool, tail between the legs. Hear me?"

Scott nodded that he did.

"'Kay, let's go," Barry said.

The walk down the corridor past bays to Dan Randall's corner office brought startled glances from assistants, who quickly gathered in knots, whispering to each other, startled to see Scott, wondering what the disgraced former employee was doing there. Reaching Dan's outer office, his personal assistant, Thelma, told them to wait, Mr. Randall was on the phone. Thelma had been with Dan six years. Like many executive assistants she had come to assume the personality and characteristics of her employer. Color her snarly. Eight minutes later, a flashing green light on her console notified her to send them in.

It was the second time Scott had been in Dan's office, the first being the day he'd been introduced to Tally, the day he'd been hired. He'd never really noticed before, now he did. The room was done in dark woods. There was a mahogany wrap-around desk, its surface nearly bare. There were two oak glass-topped cabinets filled with bound editions of the magazine and a small stained-ash conference table with six black leather-backed chairs about it. A framed photograph was prominently displayed, not to be missed as one entered, of Dan's wife with Hilary Clinton, suggesting Dan didn't have time to have the picture taken with her himself.

Behind the desk sat Dan, on a head phone.

"I'm delighted you can get that kind of money for him, Fred, bully for you. Sell him to *Harpers*. Change your mind, you have my offer, I'm here 'til six or I'm going with Turow." The call disconnected, he scowled toward Barry and Scott. "So what is this?"

"I think," Barry said, waving Scott to a chair, "there're a few things Scott would like to say to you, Dan." Dropping into a chair himself, he indicated Scott had the floor.

"How are you, Dan?" Scott said, attempting a disarming smile.

Dan didn't answer, sat stoic, leaning back in his chair, awaiting Scott's mea culpa. Taking the cue, Scott plunged in.

"That was a helluva night at the Ellies. Guess you know that, Dan, you were there." Scott waited for a response, got none. "Well, anyway, for days I tried everything I could think of, mail, Monster dot com, e-mails, name it, all and anything to find work. The town was closed down, no takers, letters returned unopened, no one answering my calls. Never been so low in my life, furniture repossessed, virtually down to cat food, no way to pay the rent."

Barry nodded. Scott was doing exactly what he had to, crawling, figuratively on his knees, when it all blew up in Barry's face.

"When I got a hit on my computer," Scott was saying. "It was Hugo Medlock."

"I think…" Barry tried to cut him off, but Scott was going on.

"We met. He had this assignment for me — something he couldn't procure for himself that he desperately wanted, in France — a recipe, from this restaurant in Vezalay, if you can believe. Seeded me with $50,000, with more than I could imagine after that if I got it for him. I ran into Tally in Paris and we partnered. Turned out the restaurant was owned by the French Mafia who chased our asses over half the country. It's the story of the decade, Dan…"

"Journalism has always been a competitive profession," Dan cut in. "But today one is seeing a different journalist. We call them brokers of deceit. Actually, they have no purpose or principles but think they can spoil the image of those of us that do. Because they are not bothered by honor, they fabricate, plagiarize, totally lack integrity as they shamelessly abandon credibility…"

When he stopped. Scott had risen, was approaching. In his outstretched hand was a piece of paper, which he held out to Dan, who hesitated, then took it, looked to see what it was. His eyebrows rose in such astonishment they almost reached his hair line. It was a check, made out to David S. Fitzgerald, for $225,000, signed by Hugo Medlock.

The attendees in Dan's office had swollen to six, and it was a zoo.

"The invasion of privacy laws…"

"Public figures like Medlock…"

"…allows an aggrieved party to bring suit…"

"Did you sign a non-disclosure form, Scott?" Dan asked.

"Let me finish…"

"Scott?"

"No," Scott answered.

"Let me *finish*..!"

"Newsworthy events…"

"He didn't sign a non-disclosure form."

Aside from Scott, Barry and Dan, there were Senior Editors Jack Frenz, Morgan Sidler and Charles Von Platen, resident counsel.

"The Fourteenth Amendment, due process right to privacy…" Von Platen was trying to explain.

"The Fourteenth covers family, marriage, motherhood," Frenz interrupted.

"Public figures have less privacy…" Sidler added.

"Warren and Brandeis wrote…"

"Celebrities like Hugo Medlock are *not protected*!"

"But Warren and Brandeis…"

"All right everybody shut up!" Dan shouted.

The shout did it. Silence.

"I want that check superimposed under the text, page one of the article. Scott, how long'll it take you to write this fucking thing?" And before Scott could answer, "Give me four thousand words. Five. Barry can edit it. And a heading. This one's got Ellies all over it."

"What about Tally?" Scott asked.

"She walked out on me, keep her out of the story."

"But…"

"You're back on staff, kid," Dan said with a grin and a clap on Scott's shoulder. "Don't fuck me again."

The phone rang. It was the following Tuesday and Scott, back in his old office on the thirty-second floor, picked up the receiver.

"Yeah."

"Dan here."

"Oh, hey!"

"How's the article coming?"

"Great!"

"What page you on?"

"Lemme see," Scott said, scanning his computer. "About half. Page eight."

"On my desk by Friday. Want to take it home for the weekend."

"Got it."

"And don't forget that heading."

A click on the end of the line and Dan was gone. Slowly lowering the receiver, Scott slumped in his chair. For five days he'd struggled with the article. How to begin it, that he had, first couple of pages, but after that? Nothing. Not quite nothing actually. He'd opened a file, what he liked to call a "sludge pile," random free associated thoughts and notes of what might or might not be in the article. A character, a setting, a conversation, an argument, a recall, an event, a scene. Except all, as he reviewed, all that galvanized, gripped him, was Tally. Their meeting in Paris, her taking him in in Angers. Their trip to Moldova, then Sete, the canal barge, that night together. God, that night! Her discovery of the recipe, the ketchup, and yes, that ridiculous crop duster fiasco. All Tally. Keep her out of the story? She *was* the story. That meal she conceived, analyzing and perfecting the recipe that brought Medlock out of his throne-like dining room chair with such savage gratification one would have thought he'd just bested Gates and Trump. Further, though Scott had anticipated a munificent pay-out if he'd read Medlock right, nothing prepared him for what they received. And all of it, every dime of it, Tally!

Still, he was back in the game. Defy Dan on this, he wouldn't be relegated to the bench, he'd be out on the street with Dan's vindictive streak shadowing him wherever he went, as he knew it had before. And how long would that $225,000 last with his tastes? He'd gone through $50,000 in what, ten days? Medlock had already made clear he was to vacate the condominium on Seventy-Second and Park by the end of the month, so where did *that* leave him. No, the article as ordered was his salvation. Except. With a realization that fought for existence like a hair ball surging to be regurgitated, he'd come to acknowledge there *was* no story without Tally.

It had been almost two weeks since they'd spoken. He opened his iPhone, found her number, sat back for a full sixty seconds, then dialed. Two rings and a recorded voice came on the line.

"The number you have dialed is no longer in service."

Forty minutes later, two-thirty in the afternoon, Scott arrived by cab at Tally's Murray Hill apartment building. A sign was tastefully posted off the entrance designating an apartment was newly available for lease. Ringing the bell brought a middle-aged, well-tailored woman to the door.

"May I help you?" she asked.

"Yes," Scott said, "I'm a friend of Tally Garner's, we were class mates together at Penn. She said if I was ever in town…I called, but was told her phone was disconnected. I wonder if you could tell me where she's gone?"

The woman was not suspicious, but she was professional and therefore bound by decree.

"I'm sorry," she said. "I can't divulge that information without permission."

"Did she happen to mention anything?" Scott asked.

"I'm really not at liberty…"

"France?"

The woman's expression told him he'd hit the nail on the head.

"I'm sorry," she said.

"Of course," Scott answered. "I understand."

The sun was low, backlighting New York's towers, looking for all the world like cardboard cutouts against a fading day as Scott stood staring west through a window of his soon to be vacated Park Avenue condo.

It had been one of those days, filled with conflicting directives: Dan, tossing him a lifeline, yet Tally crowding everything out. Tally. What did she mean to him? She meant the end of his career, that's what she meant! Be smart, he told himself. He always had been with women. Stay with the money! He'd never let a woman control his destiny and he wasn't about to start now. No, not true. Tally had, with that fucking speech in front of 2,000 people. He could never forgive her for that. Cling to that memory, goddammit! Pull out the laptop and get to work on the essay. Be creative, do it! You've got the nose for this stuff, he told himself. Come *up* with something! But what? But Tally. Why did she surge through his mind so. He shook his head, violently, to rid himself of her. Tally, lithe and sensuous, her aura, the sensation of her that night lingering, refusing to dissipate.

On impulse, he reached for his cell phone, checked out a number, sat for what seemed forever, then dialed. A recorded voice came on the line.

"Air France, reservations. Your call is very important to us. Due to an unexpected high volume of calls, an operator will be with you in…twelve minutes." Music followed. Something with an accordion.

For minutes Scott hung on, assessing where Tally might be. The total Medlock had paid them for delivering not only the dinner but the recipe as well was not $225,000. It was twice that. $450,000, split between them. For finding a fucking *recipe? $450,000?* It wasn't the recipe, of course,

Scott knew. It was the winning. And winning to Medlock was all, insane as it sounded. $450,000 to keep his record intact of never, ever being denied a pursuit. Yeah, well, how was it different from someone laying out $30 million for some fucking tossed-off painting? The higher the price the more valued the conquest. When a light went on in his head. *That* was a story he could write! That was his way *into* this thing! He hung up on Air France, began to make mental notes. Dan, you son of a bitch, did you pick a warrior or what?

Thirty-One

The following Monday morning, Scott answered the call to come up to Dan's office. He knew what for. A notes session. As every writer born, he dreaded the thought of it. He'd turned his essay in on Friday as requested, all eighteen pages of it, and now it was in editorial's hands, every page dog-eared, he knew, who would tear his work apart as they had to, otherwise who needed them.

Getting to Dan meant going through Thelma. Greeting Scott with all the regard reserved for fermenting yeast, she nodded he was to go on in. With Barry, Jack Frenz, and Morgan Sidler spread about the room, it was instantly apparent to Scott as he entered that Dan was holding court.

"15,000 I told his agent," Dan was saying. "25,000 or no deal the guy says. So I get up out of my chair and tell him, 'Come on, let's take a walk.' He thinks it's out in the hall. It's down Fifth Avenue, July, hot and humid as hell. He's hanging onto twenty-five for his client, but pretty soon he's starting to sweat through his silk suit. We're at Forty-Third Street and I'm prepared to go on down to the Battery when that fifteen's looking better and better to him if we'd just turn back."

Barry, Frenz and Sidler, who'd heard this story twenty times, broke into laughter. Having never heard it himself, Scott laughed too. Dan shifted gears, gestured everyone to the conference table where copies of Scott's essay were laid out for each.

"Coffee?" Dan asked Scott. "Barry, get him coffee while you're resting."

Dan took a chair at the table, the others following suit.

"Who wants to start?" Dan asked.

"I'll take a crack at it," Jack Frenz led off, picking up his pages, stacking them against the surface of the table, laying them back down as Scott drew in his breath. "First of all, we're all of one mind."

Terrific, you son of a bitch, Scott said to himself. *Fucking writer sits up all night trying to twist this thing into plausible fiction, then boil him in oil.* Then Scott noticed: every copy of his essay — no dog-eared pages!

"Absolutely arresting, salient, pungent," Scott heard Frenz saying.

"I'm sorry, what?"

"Incisive, absorbing," Morgan Sidler cut in.

"Working this into a solo act…"

"Love the part where you come up with the ketchup."

"Threaded the needle, balls and creativity."

"And kept the bitch out of the thing," Dan stepped in.

"Yeah, well, that…" Scott offered limply, glancing off at Barry who wouldn't meet Scott's eyes.

"I thought we thought the same about things," Dan was reflecting on Tally, and it wasn't going to be pretty. "Let's pretend we're all human beings in here. You invest treasure and time on a fledgling talent, build her career, and she walks out the *door*? Well, what're you going to do, you tell me! Some people just don't give a shit what you've done for them, just don't care. No loyalties, no convictions. Who was it said..? Well, you wouldn't know anyway." He turned to Frenz. "Recipe For Disaster," Dan read the heading off the title page. "Great title. Can we get this into our November issue?"

"November's locked."

"December. And call accounting. Tell them to issue a $10,000 advance to Scott. And get a head shot of him for release. Who owes us?"

"Ryan Wofford. He's been on a shoot in the Caribbean. I'll ask him what he thinks?"

"We'll *tell* him what he thinks." He turned to Scott. "Where they got you?"

"My old office."

"Tally's is still empty. So's her position." As Scott stared, incredulous, "Think about it."

The enthusiasm of the thirty-third floor had somehow gotten to the thirty-second as Scott returned. Editors, staff and assistants who'd turned against him, ignored him since his firing, were suddenly fully on board again.

"Great fucking article!"

"Pulitzer, man!"

"When we going for a drink?"

Reaching his office, Scott entered, closed the door, locked it, dropped into the chair at his desk, tried to control his shaking. He couldn't. Elbows on the arm rests of the chair, hands clasped tightly before him, the fingernail of his right thumb jammed between two upper front teeth, he tried to constrain his rage and self-loathing.

"You fucking ass hole," he murmured half aloud, "You miserable son of a bitch." And he wasn't talking about Dan.

It wasn't even ten o'clock. Scott didn't care. Leaving his office, he took the elevator to the ground floor lobby and started walking the city. It was a bright clear fall day that could have been rain for all he noticed as he shambled up Fifth Avenue toward the park. His shoes, he became quickly aware, his beloved McAfee's, were not made for this. Neither were his high-end ultra-thin luxury socks. He'd always ridiculed Barry's thick cottons from Land's End as beneath comment, common, wondering why Barry wasted money on them. Now he knew why as he felt the onset of blisters. He didn't care. He *wanted* pain. In pain was absolution. And absolution is what he craved. Only absolution wouldn't come.

God, what was he, he thought to himself as he dropped to a bench. *Who* was he? Who on this bloody earth ("*bloody!*" a *synonym!*) would care if he disappeared from its surface. What legacy would he leave? A plagiarizing opportunist. Worse than that, he was for sale, always had been. How you want it, principled, unprincipled, pro-Tally, anti-Tally? No cost to him with that one. Well, what about principal isn't principal *unless* it costs. Shit, he was rambling, and not even sure he knew what he was rambling about. Except — that word, *except*, always turning up with thoughts about Tally.

Taking out his iPhone, he dialed. A man's voice came on the line.

"Barry? Me," Scott said. "Listen, can I pack up some stuff and leave it with you for a bit? There's not much. Clothes mostly."

"Sure," Barry answered. "What's up?"

"Got to vacate the apartment."

"How's the weekend?"

"Any chance tomorrow?"

"Meet you there after work?"

"After work," Scott verified. "Thanks guy."

The call disconnected, Scott turned again to his iPhone, checked a number, and dialed.

"Air France reservations. Your call is very important to us. Due to an unexpected high volume of calls…"

This time he waited.

Thirty-Two

The single-class fifty seat CRJ700 turboprop from Paris brought Scott to Nantes's Atlantique Airport at 10:40 p.m., following a nine hour flight from New York, a three-hour layover going through passport control and customs in Paris de Gaulle, and the hour flight south. Exhausted, going on fumes, brain rattled, he waited for his bag to come off the carousel.

He'd left on impulse, hadn't called Tally or e-mailed her he was coming. To this moment he wasn't sure *why* he'd come and it left him in a terrible mood unable to escape contradictory self-deceptions of being selfish, unable to relate to another, while affection, love, compassion were all bullshit. And what would the reception be when they met? The last time he'd seen her was when they'd come from Medlock's building late that night, those incredible checks in hand, standing wordlessly at the curb till a taxi whisked her away.

Her dream of the restaurant in Sete, he knew, was out of the question. She barely had enough to buy the place, much less overhaul and restore it. Besides, the rules and regulations for a foreigner, for anyone outside the EU, trying to purchase a business in France, he'd learned, were prohibitive if not impossible. He *did* recall something about her being invited to join Madame Morille in Angers at her cooking school, so that was where she would be.

His bag coming into view, he waited till it was abreast of him, hauled it off the carousel, turned to cross to the car rental agencies on the opposite side of the hall, stopped dead in his tracks. Standing before him, blocking his way, were two dark-suited men.

"Monsieur Fitzgerald?"

"Yeah? Oui?" Scott answered, eyes wide and startled.

One, he saw, had close-cropped thinning hair, mid-forties. The other, younger, had a tough, blunt face, an over-tight expression around the corners of his mouth. Both were flashing badges. DST, Scott saw, Department de la Sureté/Sécurité Territorial.

"If you would come wiz us, Monsieur," the balding one said.

"Why? What is this?"

"Wiz us," the man repeated, picking up Scott's bag.

Neither laid a hand on Scott. They didn't have to. Neither was some-one you tried to resist as they led him in grim silence to the far end of the hall to an unmarked door, which opened into a five thousand square foot room, a core critical operations center, glass and precast panel systems, attended by a half dozen personnel, mirroring that of the Air Traffic Control Tower along with pilots' voices of incoming and departing flights.

Ushering Scott into an office off the center, the two men withdrew, closing the door behind them, leaving Scott standing alone. He looked about. There was a metal desk, a swivel chair behind it, two wooden chairs before it. A barred window looked out on the lights of the runway. Bare and featureless, with the odor of stale cigarette smoke, it was clearly a room for interrogation, not unlike what he and Tally had encountered at the police station in Carcassonne. But why, for what? He'd done nothing wrong, broken no rules, when it hit him. The bicycles! They'd taken them from the Escargot and left them, abandoned, in that campground. Clearly they had been reported stolen. He'd forgotten that. Jesus! He'd have to explain, agree to pay for them if they hadn't been found — he wasn't going to go to jail over a pair of *bicycles* that had probably been pulled out of some canal — when the door opened admitting a third dark-suited man with an official tag hanging from the lapel of his coat. Mid-forties, deceivingly muscular, with the long thin sinews of a runner, he carried a folder and an absolute no nonsense look on his face.

"M'sieur Fitzgerald?" the man inquired, closing the door behind him. "My name is Drouant. I am wiz zee 'Surete'. In your country, FBI, you would say."

"Look," Scott said, "I can explain all this. FBI?"

"If you would sit down, M'sieur."

It was an order not only to sit, but to remain silent 'til spoken to. Scott did both, watched as the man circled behind the desk, sat himself, laid open the folder, studied it. He lit a cigarette, offered one to Scott who shook his head no, the final courtesy to the condemned before giving the order to fire!

"Let us begin wiz what happened," Drouant finally opened. "You did not, I understand, report zee matter to zee police in Carcassonne?"

"Well, no, I mean," Scott stuttered into an explanation. "It was such a trivial thing…"

"An effort to kill you is trivial?"

Scott froze, not sure he'd heard correctly.

"What did you say?"

"A little drama clears zee sinuses, eh, M'sieur? According to zee pilot of zee avion de chiffon — how you say in English?" — he couldn't find the translation, so went on — "who made zee report, shots were fired from a black Mercedes upon take off at zee airport in Carcassonne. It is very apparent someone meant to kill you. Why would zis happen?"

Scott stared, incredulous. So *that's* what this was about.

"I...don't know."

"You do not know."

"No."

It was clear Drouant didn't believe him. It was clear, too, alarms were spinning through Scott's head with the speed of a digital slot machine. *'Stay out of it! Stay out of it! Stay out of it!'* came up like three bars in a row.

"Zat does not help a great deal. You noticed nossing?"

"No," Scott lied, aware of the slight croak in his voice.

"You kept your eyes open," the man said, irritated at Scott's lack of response.

"I suppose."

"Let us hope so. Let us hope you are capable of recall. I sinc you were unwise not to invoke zee police."

"The police were there, they came."

"But zat is of only partial interest to me."

"What do you mean of partial interest?"

"Zer was a companion wiz you."

"A person, yes."

"A M'amselle Garner."

How did he know their names? Oh, Scott remembered. Off their passports. That officer at Carcassonne.

"Tally Garner, yes," Scott said.

"I have a duty to perform, M'sieur Fitzgerald. That duty is to protect you. As you are not interested in my doing so for yourself, zer is still M'amselle Garner."

"I'll tell her what you've had to say."

"Then you know where she is," Druant said.

"You don't?" Scott said in surprise.

"She had an apartment in Angers, we understand."

"Then that's where she is."

"Regrettably not."

"I don't see…"

Druant drew in on his cigarette, expelled a cloud of smoke into the room. "The apartment has been vacated. She is no longer in Angers."

It was six o'clock in the morning, daylight breaking, as Scott drove his rented VW into Sete. It had been a nightmare six hour drive south from Nantes through the night, mostly N Routes past the outskirts of towns and villages he'd never heard of. Twice he'd been saved by blasting horns as he found himself nodding off into oncoming lanes. Buying a thermos at a rest stop filled with thick black coffee helped, leading him to do as he'd seen the French do, more than once stopping to irrigate trees at the side of the road.

The first thing Scott noticed upon arrival in the Mediterranean sea-side ville was he had no idea where he was. The city, composed of canals and islands, was a mystery to him. He had no memory of how and where Tally had driven them as he drove alongside one canal after another trying to find a familiar recall. He thought he'd know it when he saw it, but cognition was not his clearest avenue to attainment at the moment given no sleep since leaving New York. But then he saw it: the restaurant. Vieux Logis. Pulling his car to a stop before the place, he stared out at it. It was still the all but run down shack he remembered. A low wattage light was burning inside. It was then he saw something else. Tally's Renault Clio parked beside it. And the for sale sign, "*à vendre,*" was gone.

For several minutes, motor left running, Scott sat staring at the place, attacked by clawing doubt. What was he doing here? He was a creature of impulse. When had *that* served him well? Why *had* he come, and now that he *had*? Exhaust fumes beginning to engulf him, he shut down the motor, sat a while longer, looking for movement inside, saw none. Opening the driver side door, he stepped from the car. The early morning air was soft, a breeze coming in from the Mediterranean lapping water against the quai. He stood for a moment, then crossed to the building, came to the entrance, hesitated, tried the door, found it unlocked, eased inside.

The place was a mess. Seemingly illuminated by a single naked light bulb hanging from a wire attached to the ceiling where a fan had been, the first thing Scott noticed was all three fans had been removed, were stacked in a corner. So were the tables, bar stools and chairs. No work, he saw, had been done to refurbish the place other than a two by two foot section of the floor, which had been sanded smooth, three separate samplings of varnish painted side by side across it, liter cans of capped varnish, topped by cleaned brushes, to one side.

It was then he saw Tally. She'd come from around the island kitchen, hair tied back in a bandana, shirt and jeans soiled with varnish and dirt, wire scrub brush in hand, her face — he'd never seen her face like that — worn, exhausted. She looked at him, eyes squinting through the glare of the bulb, when he realized. He was not the picture of elegance himself, clothes rumpled, unshaven for nearly two days.

"Hey." It was all he could think to say.

"What are you doing here?" she said at length.

"What are you?" he asked.

She thought about what to say next, settled on, "Have you eaten?"

"What've you got?"

"Give me fifteen minutes."

Disappearing back around the kitchen island, Tally left Scott to himself. He looked after her, curious what was around the island, found it was another, though smaller, dining area, illuminated solely by a wall light. As with the front room, old tables and chairs and discarded kitchenware, blackened pots and pans, along with a box of no longer worthwhile utensils were piled in a corner. At the far end of the room, a door propped open by a bucket and mop revealed a toilet and wash basin. There were two other doors, one standing ajar. It was, Scott saw looking in, a store room, eight by ten, shelves empty. The other led to what Scott didn't know, but he thought he heard behind it the sound of a shower.

Moving to the kitchen, Scott found it on its last legs. One side open across the counter to the front dining area, it was about fifteen by eight. There was a grease-encrusted six-burner stove, its gas line disconnected and capped, hooks above it, empty save for a couple of dangling pans and pots, a tarnished, grease-encrusted hood above that. An old commercial refrigerator with side-loading freezer stood humming against the far wall. There was a deep metal sink for washing dishes, a brush and bottle of bleach inside it, effort clearly having been made to remove years of rust and stain. There was a chipped wooden prep table, a hotplate atop it, empty shelves beneath it. Cupboards too stood open, mostly empty other than several dishes, the rest having joined the corner pile to be discarded along with out-of-date condiments and cooking oils.

Returning to the front dining room, Scott shook his head in dismay. What the hell had she done?

Twenty minutes later Tally reemerged, showered and dressed in fresh jeans, short-sleeved shirt and flats, no make-up, hair still tied back. On instinct Scott looked to see if she was wearing a brassiere, couldn't tell. Glancing out the front window she saw his VW.

"Big step up," she nodded at it.

"Yeah, well…"

"Grab a stool," she said, entering the kitchen.

Another ten minutes and Scott, seated at the counter, had placed before him a fresh baguette, butter, soft scrambled eggs with herbs, and a glass of white wine, the best scrambled eggs he could remember ever having eaten. When he was finished, he watched her cleaning up through the opening over the counter. A mixture of complicated feelings engulfed him, mostly his groin. He hadn't expected that. Nor the silence, each waiting for the other to engage.

"How'd you do this?" he said finally.

She looked at him. "What do you mean?"

"You don't just walk in and buy a business in France."

"Sleight of hand."

"I Googled it," Scott said. "The paper work before and after. No sympathy if you get it wrong. Taxes, court costs, no protection with bankruptcy laws. Commercial lease contracts, articles of association — that's months!"

"I told you."

"Sleight of hand, I heard."

"French business thrives on influential contacts," she explained. "Rules get bent for people in high places."

"Where'd you find *that?*"

She held back the answer. The last thing she wanted was Scott amusing himself over what she was going through.

"Madame Morille," he guessed.

By the look on her face he was right. Scott took in the place with a despairing expression.

"So it's yours."

"Yep."

"A broken down restaurant. What'd you settle on?"

"Settle on?"

"Cost."

"Every penny I had."

"The Medlock money."

"Less four thousand."

Scott looked about.

"What are you going to *do* with it?"

"That's what the bank wants to know," she said.

"I'll bet. What'd you tell 'em?"

"I told them how much I thought it would take."

"What'd they say?"

"Said I'd hear."

"Jesus, Tally. Shoes are in, you couldn't have gone into shoes?"

She moved out of the kitchen, determining whether she should go further or not. He wasn't part of this, and she had every intention of seeing it remained that way.

"The building's a lot more structurally sound than it looks," she said. "The exterior's mostly repair and paint. Same with the roof. The inside? From scratch."

"Why am I reminded of *Birth Of A Nation?*" he said.

"You don't want to hear this."

"Go on."

"You first."

He pulled back, not having expected the question.

"You didn't come three thousand miles to tell me I'm making a fool of myself," she added.

"Can we go someplace," he said evasively, more and more depressed by the surroundings. "Where you staying, some hotel?"

Her eyebrows arched. She smiled a half ironic smile, nodded he was to follow her, led him into the back dining area to and through the closed door into a one room apartment with adjoining three-quarter bathroom. A lot of effort gone into scrubbing it clean. There was a pull out sofa bed, a cheap but serviceable desk with lamp and chair, a couple of open wood shelves stacked with clothes, and a closet. A window looked out onto the back of the restaurant. Taking the chair at the desk, leaving the couch to Scott, she awaited his accounting.

"Big step up," he said, looking about.

Tally said nothing, sat waiting. Scott crossed to the window, looked out. He could see the superstructure of a small cruise ship docked at the Gare Maritime in the Nouveau Bassin on the other side of the island.

"I went to see Dan," he said, his back to the room.

"Randall?"

"Yeah." He paused, turning to her. "I took him the story. Medlock, the recipe, Moldova, France, the Corsican Mafia. He bought it."

"Bought it?"

"Showed him the check from Medlock. Ten thousand dollar advance, goes in the December issue. My old job back, all forgiven, God is love."

"Dan? Well, the God thing."

"There was a condition."

"Why am I not surprised."

"He wanted you out of the story."

Tally sat back slowly in her chair, studied Scott a long thoughtful moment.

"How were you with that?" she asked at length.

"I put up a helluva squawk. I said that's bullshit. You should have seen me, Tally, I had a foot out the door."

It was a lie, she knew it, settled by asking, "But?"

"What do I do, where do I go?" There was a letting down in his voice, a pleading for understanding. "He blackballed me up and down the Avenue. He'd do it again. You're right, in everything you said. I haven't the balls. I'm not you. No beliefs, no convictions, it's true. I wish I could do what you're doing, I can't. If you've no world of your own, what do you wish for? Someone else to fail? That's horrible to think that's who I am! The only thing I know how to do is seek sanctuary in someone else's courage and work. The only thing I think I really care about," he turned to her, "is you. I've watched you do the same things every day, in spite of everything. Not a moment I wasn't watching — or wanting you. I can't stop it. I try — breaking out when I see you doing…just leaning over a stove, and I can't think I ever felt like this."

She waited for him to go on. He didn't. She rose, went to her bedroom door, stood beside it, looked back at him.

"Goodbye, Scott."

For a moment Scott stood, just stood, trying not to look startled. Putting the best face on it he could — there was no doubt it was an order to leave — he did just that, crossed the room, moved past her, hesitated, looked back. What was there to say? There was nothing.

The day was growing warm when he exited to the quay. Fishing boats, he saw, were reentering the harbor from their night at sea, sea gulls chasing them in hopes of a discarded morsel. Crossing to his car, he opened the door, looked across it at the restaurant, stupefied, dazed. He was walking out, pushed out of the first meaningful relevance — he broke off the thought. Shoulders sagging, he pulled out his car keys, turned to enter his car. The next moment there was a vice-like grip on his shoulder. He cried out in pain, whirled, came face to face with the brown-suited man of the black Mercedes.

Thirty-Three

The Mercedes was driving north from what Scott, seated in the rear seat, could see, flanked by the two men who'd been hunting him and Tally that night in Sete, the brown-suited man up front with his customary driver. They'd crossed an Auto Route, were on a two lane road, D2, he saw by a sign flashing by, when they took a sharp turn left, heading west.

Scott sat silent, heart thumping. He had not listened to Dourant at the airport at Nantes. When had he *ever* listened. He glanced at the brown-suited man's reflection in the rear view mirror. The man was sitting back with his eyes half closed, a half-smirk on his face as though his work for the day had only begun, when the car slowed, turned north again along a secondary road. The roadway was straight and lined with plane trees. Beyond the trees were mini-farms, Scott saw, some horses, cows. Soon, however, it began to rise and twist, the farms left behind. He knew one thing. If he surrendered to panic he would be lost. But that was a rationalization, a will. His shaking body countermanded it.

Still the car purred on. Sixty minutes out of Sete, it suddenly swung east onto a side road, began to crawl in low gear up a hill well-rutted from rains. There was a movement at his side. He turned quickly, blood rushing into his head, looked forward again, and met the brown-suited man's eyes who had turned to him and was nodding. It was a nod that said, "Oui, M'sieur Fitzgerald, this is just about as far as you are going."

The car was heading for the top of a rise and slowing, Scott pressing his feet against the floor, body rigid as the car crested the rise, when Scott saw before him a building, its substructure a long ago torn down dwelling, only its stone foundation remaining, supporting a recently constructed two story wood-sided house.

Pulling behind a Hummer, which blocked the narrow parking area, the brown-suited man was out of the Mercedes, the two in the back seat out with him, guiding Scott up steps to a pair of double doors. The brown-suited man pressed the doorbell. One of the doors was opened almost immediately by a swarthy, humorless guard, a Heckler and Koch semi-automatic clutched in his hand. Escorted into an entrance hallway, Scott saw it was bare, other than a stairway. With a nod, the guard indicated they were to go up. Emerging at the top of the stairs, Scott was led down a featureless corridor with the growing conviction that he was being led into a nightmare.

Reaching a door at the end of the corridor, the brown suited man stepped aside. It was clear Scott was to go through. Drawing in a shuddering breath Scott stood frozen. The brown suited man came to his assistance, opened the door for him, exposing Scott to a barren yet-to-be furnished room. Across it, back to the room, staring down at the barren landscape below, was a man dressed in what appeared to be hunting clothes. Turning, he came face to face with Scott. It was Nacer, the faux abbey he'd encountered at the seven locks on the canal.

"Come, M'sieur," Nacer said, "Vee valk"

The walk seemed endless across rock-strewn ground that appeared to grow nothing, Nacer two steps ahead of Scott, the guard with the riot gun close on his heels. In fact it was three hundred yards, terminating at what Scott saw was a gorge with a hundred foot drop to a stream bed below.

"Once," Nacer was talking, "it must be difficult to imagine, zis was a forest. After zee collapse of Rome zere vas une invasion of greedy tribes and much abuse uf zee land. It is difficult for animals today. Tragedy, no?"

Scott was only half listening. With a sense of dread, he was staring down at the gorge, at jagged, razor sharp boulders when a sound brought him up abruptly. Nacer had picked up a rock and had struck a match across it, was lighting a cigar. Quite deliberately Nacer tossed the stone out over the edge of the drop. It took several seconds for the sound of it crashing of the rocks below.

"So. You are a writer, M'sieur, Fitzgerald. An intellectual. Indispensable to reason. Excellent. Zen you vill understand vot I am about to say. Some veeks ago you ver captured out of Beaune by two of my agents, assigned to put you on un avion. Wezer zey meant to obey, to do as ordered," he shrugged, "so difficult to get good people today — zey stupidly let you escape. Clumsy and amateurish. I am not so." When, "A peregrine!"

A golden falcon swept down, captured a field mouse and flew away with it hanging from its beak. Nacer turned back to Scott, returned to his narrative.

"It should have been a warning, M'sieur. Instead you chose anozer course. You are following zis?"

Scott shook his head, no. In fact he followed it too well.

"Zen let me make it clear. You have stolen vot is mine."

The recipe. Scott stared at Nacer, not wanting to know where this was going. The fucking recipe. If Scott wasn't so terrified, he'd have to laugh. But there was that cliff.

"Let us suppose for zee moment my associates had been un petit more efficient. Vee would not be standing here haffing zis discussion. You would, quite possibly, be rotting in some field."

Scott turned white. His stomach was in knots.

"But I am prepared for reason, to pay you *twice* your share vot you haf invested in zis business wiz M'amselle Garner."

Invested? What was he talking about? He hadn't invested in the restaurant. So *that's* what this was about. Nacer was *assuming* he had.

"Wizout furzer financial support, yours or mine" Nacer was saying, "zee bank, I am assured, vill not give her zee money, zee restaurant fails. En ruine. Un eye for an eye. You understand?"

Of *course* he understood. He was a cipher to Nacer, no threat, willing to do whatever to survive, to betray, delude, forsake, and Nacer knew it.

"I haff your agreement, no?"

"No," Scott heard himself saying, so faintly it was almost inaudible. No? Where'd *that* come from you stupid son of a bitch? *No?* He was the tail of a donkey, about to be pinned to a board. Except the darts weren't darts, they were 9mm hollow nosed rounds. *No?*

"A shock, M'sieur?" Nacer seemed unmoved. "It is one thing to emerge from a trench, un deserter in full view uf zee brigade, quite anozer to slip off unseen in zee night. Tink of it. She is nossing to you. Tomorrow morning you are in London stretching your legs."

"No!" Scott said. And this time it was firm and out loud.

For a long moment, Nacer studied Scott, no tightening in his face, no clamping of lips.

"I'm afraid, M'sieur," Nacer said at length, "you must be very naive. Or you tink it uf me. But I haff a request to make. In zat you haff caused me so much — how does one say — chagrin, would it be too much to ask you to cause me no more. Would you step to zee edge of zee gorge, please."

Scott didn't step to the edge of the gorge. He turned — not toward the house, but across the field toward the road, exhausted, barely aware of where he was going, stubbing his toe on a rock, almost falling, recovering, stumbling on — when behind him he heard the sound of the slide on the Heckler and Koch, depositing a round into the chamber.

Thirty-Four

Tally sat at the counter of her restaurant over her second cup of coffee. She sat as she had sat for an hour, trying to make sense of things. It was a Saturday, so she wouldn't be hearing from the bank till Monday, if then. But even that, as pressing as it was, was overridden by the confusion of her feelings for what she'd heard from Scott. It was no surprise what he'd had to say, she knew that about him. Yet hearing him say it...

She forced herself to shrug it off. She'd tried, in her mind, to mold him into something he could never be. The clay was hardened, an unworkable mess. Besides, she had work to do.

Her project for the day was to remove the oyster trough attached to the kitchen side of the open counter. Made of corrugated metal of some sort it was an eye sore, battered and stained, to be replaced, when and if, by a new one of stainless steel.

She'd bought a few essential tools as needed, frugally watching her expenditures, one a crescent wrench. The trough was held by one-inch bolts running under the counter, one at each end, each capped by a rusting nut. Applying the wrench, Tally found it was frozen. Turning to a hack saw, she spent the better part of half an hour sawing through the nut, forming a blister in the process, till the bolt, cut through, dropped the near end of the trough to the floor, barely missing her foot.

She needed air. Circling to the front room, Tally pushed through the entrance onto the quay, stopped short. There in the parking area stood Scott's VW, driver's side door open. Anger flushed in her face. What little game was this? She'd thought she'd seen the last of him. Well, she damn well had! Returning to the restaurant, she slammed closed the door, locked it, went about finishing the removal of the oyster trough, sensibly supporting the end to be worked on with a stool, which took the drop of the trough and held it when the nut was cut through.

She was exhausted, no little of it caused by tension, and it was not even mid-day. Still, one thing left to do, to try to do, remove the trough from the kitchen to the pile to be discarded. She tried, could not even budge it, too heavy. She'd call the University in Montpellier in the morning and hire a student who could use the money to help. She'd make a list of things that need doing. She went into her bathroom, showered again, dressed, tied a scarf around her head, put antiseptic on her blister, now broken through and bandaged it, secured a mesh bag for groceries and left, locking the building.

She noticed Scott's VW was still where he'd left it — and so, in her mind, it would stay, 'til he came to his senses — when something caught her attention. On the ground by the driver's side door were a set of keys. She crossed to the car, picked them up. They were from the rental agency identifying the keys as belonging to the VW. A numbered, lettered tag matched its license plate.

She looked up slowly, stared about her. She didn't have to wonder at the chill that ran through her body.

The local commissariat de police was located in a one-story building on the Quai de Bosc. Entering, Tally found the reception area surprisingly filled. Crossing to the desk, she addressed the officer in charge.

"J'ai un rapport à faire, une personne a disparue," she said with urgency.

"Complétez cette forme, Madame," the officer said, handing her a clipboard and pen with two papers to fill.

"Il est urgent," Tally protested.

"Cette forme," the officer repeated.

The form was endless, and it was twenty minutes before Tally discovered why so many were present and waiting ahead of her. A seventy-two-year-old man had apparently committed suicide, and every officer at the station was involved. Two hours later, the form long since turned in, Tally was called to the desk.

"En bas du couloir," she was told, "troisième porte sur votre droite."

Down the corridor, third door on the right, Tally entered a small non-descript office with desk, chairs, and little more. Behind the desk, reading over her form, sat an officer. He was a short, thin man, mid-forties, with a placid face, the sort that said, 'I am here to suffer your complaint, but not you.' A name tag identified him as L. Mieussy.

"Good day, Madame," he said without looking up, in excellent English.

"M'amselle," Tally corrected, sliding into a chair. He wanted English it would be English.

"What is it you wish?" he asked.

"I need immediate attention paid to that," Tally answered as though it was obvious, nodding at the form in his hand.

"You are reporting the disappearance of a person of interest?"

"Yes."

"Seven hours ago?"

"I understand. The circumstances are exceptional."

"Reports of missing persons," he said, handing the paper back to Tally, "are taken after forty-eight hours."

"M'sieur, if I might..."

"Forty-eight hours."

"If you would allow me to see your chef de police."

"There was an argument?"

"That's not what this is."

"Une affaire du Coeur? A lovers' quarrel?"

"I've reason to believe the Corsican Mafia..."

"Ah, the Mafia," Mieussy replied with a touch of a smile.

"I'm not here to waste your time, M'sieur. I can assure you..."

"I do not question your assurances, Madame. M'amselle," he corrected himself.

"I was about to tell you," she tried with increasing frustration.

Mieussy held up a finger.

"One moment," he said.

Scratching out an address on a note pad, he tore off the top sheet, handed it to Tally.

"What's that?"

"The address of the American consulate in Marseille."

"I want to see your chef de police," she answered, no little irritation.

"Forty-eight hours."

Returning to her car, Tally sat gripping the wheel. She glanced at the paper she'd been given, with the consulate's address in Marseille, but knew what going there would entail. She would be turned over to what Tom Wolfe famously phrased, a *flak catcher*, someone who would listen to her in mock patience and remand her back to the French police. So what was it, forty-eight hours? That and that only? She slammed her fist in frustration against the wheel, winced. Dammit! That blister! She started the engine, drove down the quay, crossing the bridge to her own, wiping away tears. *Tears?*

Arriving at her restaurant, she parked, got out of her car, saw the VW was still there — where else would it be, she had the keys — started toward the entrance, stopped cold in her tracks. Seated on the doorstop was Scott!

Her immediate sense of relief gave way to rage as she crossed the parking area toward him, invectives she'd only heard, never used, ready to pour from her mouth, when she slowed. What she saw was not what she expected. He was filthy, covered with dust, clothes and face, his shoes, his McAfee shoes, torn and in ruins. He looked up at her, eyes bloodshot, beyond weariness. Reaching him she opened her mouth to ask the first of a thousand questions, stopped. In his hand was a piece of paper. He was holding it out to her. For the moment she didn't know what to make of it, reached out took it from him, stared at it. It was Medlock's check made out to Scott, for $225,000.

It was shortly after noon the following afternoon that Scott finally awoke. Rolling over in a daze, no idea for the moment where he was, he found himself in Tally's bedroom, in her bed, his suitcase brought in from his car, fresh clothes hung on the back of the door. Pushing up to a sitting position, he sat for a moment, in his underwear, arms extended, hands on the edge of the bed, trying to clear his head. The door to the restaurant was closed, but the bathroom door was open. Entering it he relieved himself, saw his toilet kit was on a shelf along with a wash cloth and towel. Scarcely recognizing himself in the mirror, he quickly shaved, showered, not so quickly, dried himself off and dressed.

He found her in the kitchen putting food away in the refrigerator from a trip to the market. There was something in a pot simmering on the hotplate stove. The moment between them when they saw each other was awkward till she nodded at the counter.

"Sit down."

He did so. In ten minutes he'd devoured a dish of Navarin de Mouton, stewed lamb with onions, garlic, herbs, white wine, stock, carrots, potatoes, turnips, washed down with a glass of red. Looking across the counter at him, she finally asked.

"What happened?"

He told her, told her slowly, as though trying to understand what had happened himself. When he got to the end, his walking away, reliving it with a sense of disbelief, he told of the moment expecting a rain of bullets that never came. He got to the village they'd passed on the way up, hired a farmer to bring him back to Sete. From the look on her face it was clear she didn't know whether to believe him or not.

"Why?" she asked. "Why'd you do it?"

"What am I going to do with a quarter million dollars?"

"Very funny," she said.

"Can't help wondering what this place could look like. How's that?"

There was a pause, which Scott couldn't decipher.

"Well for starters," she said, looking about, "there'll be an eight burner stove, double oven, with grill. Glass door reach-in refrigerator. Stainless steel two door freezer. An electric counter-top fryer. Prep table, ceiling swamp cooler, under counter dishwasher, fire suppression range hood. And the usual. Mixer, microwave, cookware, cutlery, pots and pans. That's just the kitchen."

She stopped. Expectation? Or something else. There was a hesitancy in the way she was speaking.

"I can send pictures," she said.

"What do you mean?" he asked.

She hesitated further, reached inside her pants pocket, pulled out the check he'd given her, held it out to him.

"You can turn the car in at the airport in Montpellier, get a flight to Paris. You've got that prepaid reservation to New York."

For a moment he stared, stunned, at her outstretched hand holding out the check for him to take.

"What are you talking about?"

"What are you?"

"We'd be in this together, I thought," he said.

"How would *that* work?" she asked.

"Well, hell…"

"Go on."

"No you."

"You haven't the vaguest idea what you'd be in for, Scott."

"I thought…"

"What?"

"You and me," he said.

"In six weeks you'd be bored to death. Not only with this place but with me. And when Scott Fitzgerald gets bored — all the *belles femmes* coming down from Paris, April in Sete…"

"That's what's blowing up your skirt?"

"That's exactly what's blowing up my skirt."

"Bull shit."

"What did you say?

"Bull *shit!*"

"I didn't hear that."

"Taureau merde! You heard *that* all right.

"I can't trust you, Scott."

"Christ, the smoke screens!" He was approaching anger, and seemed to have no impulse to put a governor on it. "Bling, out it comes, rummaging, ransacking, putting on the screws! We're alike in that, you know, except I was never good at it, though God knows I tried. Just because you got your head handed to you — I'm not that ass hole. I've changed, I want to, I'm trying and you can't face it."

"Have you finished?"

"So why aren't you raging, slashing, calling me a rotten bastard, how you hate my guts! I'm standing here hardly able to get my words out, all I get from you is sand in my face!"

She stands a moment, unable to find the words, the check still in her hand.

"I'm in love with you, Tally. If not, I want to be, I want to try. I'm tired of spending my life hearing ciao, goodbye."

"Some people fall in love for revenge," she said.

"More sand."

"Sorry, I'm committed," she said. But her eyes were flashing.

"Who's the guy?"

"No guy," she said.

"The bank loan."

"Just so you know."

"You're not going to get it."

She stares at him.

"You don't know that."

"The bastards have seen to it. They offered me twice what they thought I had in this place. They're out to wipe you out." Seeing her shocked expression, "I'll take the store room, clear out the junk, get a bed. You'll have to share the bathroom."

He turned, walked past her to the store room to take stock. Tally stood where he left her, check still in hand, trying to assess what had just happened. His story about walking away from the mafia? He was good at stories, if seldom his own. The business about quashing her loan application? She'd see. A phone call. Like a crack in an old seventy-eight record, one thought clicked over and over in her head. For the first time since her aborted wedding day, she was not in control.

Thirty-Five

In three months, unheard of by French standards, with help from students hired from the University at Montpellier, contacts from Madame Morille, along with badgering companies for deliveries, the Vieux Logis took shape. The outside of the restaurant was refinished and patched, the roof repaired and painted blue, the outside walls light yellow, window awnings matching the blue of the roof, the front door burgundy red. The parking area on the quay outside, once hard-packed dirt, was now white-washed stones, an idea Scott ripped off from his stay at L'Esperance in Vezalay. Parked in front was a newly purchased Mini Countryman.

The inside was a total transformation. A trash removal truck was rented, hauling away all that wasn't nailed down, the kitchen gutted. Ceiling, inner walls and floor were sanded to bare-grained wood, the ceiling and walls stained a walnut brown. So were the kitchen cabinets when replaced and installed. The floor was varnished. Day by week the restaurant began to take shape. The stove was delivered and connected. As was the refrigerator, freezer, fryer, dishwasher and range hood. A stainless steel oyster trough replaced the old. Tables and linen, soft leather-backed cushioned chairs, bar stools, pots, pans, cutlery, dishes, glass wear, wine rack, glass rack, brand new overhead fans, lighting, the counter embossed, as Tally had hoped it could be, with fifty to sixty-year-old menus discovered at a flea market, speakers playing softly classical music from a library of CDs. First rate photographs of local models recreating the artistry of Renoir, Manet, Gauguin adorned walls. Food and condiments were ordered, to be bought in just before the opening. A menu presentation Tally had always had in mind was created, each table with its own framed twelve by eighteen inch chalk board written in Tally's highly legible script, *Nos Viandes* at the top followed by a half dozen meat dishes, *Nos Poissons* listing an equal number of dishes from the sea. The restaurant's unisex bath room, too, had been totally remodeled. So had her bedroom and bath. Scott's? True to his dictates the store room had been gutted and cleaned, a bed and dresser brought in, the room doubling as an office.

Staff was hired: A professional sous chef to work under Tally; A local dishwasher-bus boy; Two University students, Adrianne and Marcel, as servers; Scott the Maître d', trained by Tally through moments of tension if not downright snapping irritation, their relationship tenuous, arm's length, bizarre, yet strangely held together by some invisible adhesive. He accidently caught her one day coming out of the shower when he thought she was in the kitchen. She caught him one day staring at her in a way that put a catch in her throat. But neither seemed willing to cross the line. They ate together, worked together, occasionally coming up with collective solutions, the principal one being how to get the word out there was a new restaurant about to open in town, how to get people intrigued? There were web sites and the local paper, and flyers to be left in local hotels. *Ouvrir pour le diner, 6:30 à 10:00. Sept jours par semaine.* But how to get their interest?

It was Scott who came up with the answer.

"I don't know," Tally said when she heard what he had in mind.

"It'll work!"

"It's a scam," she protested.

"A scam has a victim."

"Well…"

"It'll work!"

Work it did. Advertising the restaurant was open for business the first Tuesday in February, Scott took the initial calls for reservations, answering with deep apologies and regrets in his ever-improving French.

"Je suis désolé, Madame," he'd say, then go on to explain the restaurant was completely booked for the opening week.

Nothing travels faster than "no." Within four days, three before the restaurant was *planned* to open, requests for reservations were pouring in. The proof, of course, was in the results. The results were immediate and outstanding.

"Une expérience extraordinaire," glowed a locale reviewer. "Impeccable!" said another. "Stupéfiant! Particulièrement recommande? Les jambes de poulet et cuisses braisées."

It was two weeks after the opening that it happened.

The restaurant was closing, ten o'clock at night, several straggling diners full of effusive praise finally giving up their tables, Scott and Tally, apron about her waist, seeing them out with "Au revoir. A bientôt," closing, locking the door when they'd left. Sending the staff home for the night — she and Scott would finish up whatever remained to put away in the kitchen — Tally dropped into a chair at one of her tables, more than exhausted, Scott seating himself across from her, counting receipts as both finally got to their dinner. A muted Mozart symphony was playing over the speakers. He looked up, about to give her the figures, caught an expression on her face. She quickly diverted it, stared out at the walls.

"I keep thinking there's a color…"

"Now, that's a very, it's a key question," he said, trying to assess what her look had been all about.

"There's a color, I've seen it."

"Has a sort of…"

"Those barns we saw on the Canal du Midi," she said.

"They were brown."

"The sky behind. That apricot dawn."

"Dawn behind the barns on the Canal."

The chit-chat had been just that, chit-chat. He looked at her with a slight frown of concern. She seemed unusually wan.

"You okay?"

"I was thinking."

"What?"

"François or Francine."

"The restaurant's *got* a name, bad luck to change it."

When there was a rap on the door.

"Somebody left something," he said, rising to answer it.

Reaching the door, he unlocked it, the door pushed wide as five men moved through. Four were the ones who'd driven Scott to the hilltop house. The fifth was Nacer.

Gesturing, two were to take up positions by the counter, two by the door, Nacer looked about the restaurant, Tally watching from her table, Scott standing frozen. Taking his time, Nacer wandered, looking the place over, his face dark, preoccupied, his wanderings taking him to the back dining room, opening the door to Tally's apartment glancing in, returning to the restaurant proper, lastly to the kitchen. On the stove were three pots, gas turned off, contents still warm. He lifted the lid of one, lowered it, lifted another, looked in, sniffed the contents.

"Les jambes de poulet," he said.

Neither Tally nor Scott gave an answer.

"I vill partake," Nacer exclaimed.

"We're closed," Scott intervened.

Nacer circled the kitchen, past Scott as though he were not there, set himself up at a table.

"Wiz a good Bordeaux."

Tally looked up at Scott. It was a look that said we can get through this, whatever this is. She rose, Scott following her into the kitchen where she turned the gas on under the pot.

"Get him a setup and the wine," she said.

"You're kidding."

"Please."

He saw she was frightened. But he'd had enough of these people.

"Please," she pleaded.

He hesitated, then did as she asked, more so for her than for Nacer, who ignored Scott completely. Scott boiled inside, wished it was just the two of them, though what he would do if it were he'd no idea. It was minutes before the dish was rewarmed, on a plate and presented to Nacer by Tally along with the requested Bordeaux.

"Sit. Sit zere," Nacer ordered her to the chair across from him.

Tally slid onto the chair as told, watched Nacer tuck a napkin under his chin, take a sip of the wine and cut into the dish. Scott glanced back at the two at the bar, saw they were keeping him under close surveillance. He looked back at Nacer, knew that beneath the crumpled suit with his doughy features, the man wore a gun. Except a rapturous look was spreading the Corsican's face as he filled it with a mouthful.

"Browned," Nacer said, mouth still half full. "Wiv tomatoes and onion." He swallowed, smacked his lips together in assessment, Tally's eyebrows arching in surprise as, "Herbes, garlic, feuille de laurier, legumes."

Nacer waved a finger in the air as though the gesture would assist his diagnosis.

"Vy do I taste mint? Corsican mint! Crème de Menthe!" he said with childish glee at his discovery. But then a frown, "Trop doux, too sveet alone. Vot is missing? Vot?" he said, eyes boring into Tally.

Tally stared back at him.

"M'amselle?"

"Classified," Scott replied before she could answer.

"Vot does he say?"

"Secret," Scott clarified. Then in French, "Un ingredient secret."

A dark cloud seemed to pass over Nacer.

"Not a good answer, M'sieur," he said.

"That offends you?"

"Au noyau."

"Sorry," Scott shook his head, not understanding the word.

"To the core," Tally translated.

"That gorge still awaits you, mon ami," Nacer answered, a not so subtle threat.

"There's always a gorge," Scott said.

Tally's heart dropped to the pit of her stomach as she saw Nacer's eyes lock on Scott's.

"A stupid zing to say," Nacer said.

"It's easy to explain," Scott said, "I don't suppose you'll understand. There really isn't a great deal to it. I've always thought people like you must be quite clever. I know, I've wanted that for myself. *That* was what was stupid. Maybe it's a little late to admit it, I don't know."

Nacer's mouth came open, as though to pounce.

"Do you know I haff always reveled in zee passion uff destruction vin I desired it."

"You think I should be overcome with awe because of that?" Scott asked.

"Zee writer," Nacer said with a touch of reluctant admiration at the line. "I vish I could say I sought of zat."

"You will." And then, "Dehors! Sortez!"

Nacer didn't move. And then he did. Reaching into his pocket he pulled out a hundred euro note, threw it onto the table.

"For ziss indigestible mess."

With that he rose and was gone, his entourage in tow.

In the kitchen, Scott and Tally cleaned up in silence. Mozart was still playing over the speakers. A jar of kosher pickles was the last to return to the refrigerator, Scott pulling one, munching.

"What *is* the ingredient?"

"You're eating it."

"You're kidding?"

But that wasn't the elephant in the room.

"You haven't said anything," Tally finally said.

"He's bluffing."

"I wasn't talking about that."

"I'm lost."

"François or Francine."

For a moment Scott didn't get it. And then he did.

"Jesus!"

"If you like that name better."

"How long?"

"Do the math."

"How'd you find out?"

"Three lost periods and the local gynecologist."

"Jesus."

"I think you said that."

"The first thing I created I didn't steal," he said.

"Work in progress," she said.

"When I was a kid…"

"I heard that."

"In school…"

"Heard that too."

A pause.

"Where's it go from here?" he asked.

"Where do you want it to go?"

"Where do you?"

She looked at him.

"You're sure about this." It was a statement, seeking confirmation.

"Working on it. You?" he asked.

"Terrified."

"Did anyone ever tell you how beautiful that makes you look?"

His face was in her hands, her lips on his. It was the longest, most sensuous, heartfelt moment in his life.

Thirty-Six

Two months later.

The wedding was performed at the town hall by the Mayor, a constant visitor to Vieux Logis, who had his own table on request. At the reception following at the restaurant, all who attended the wedding were invited. There was the restaurant staff, the Mayor and his wife. Madame Morille came by train from Angers. Her lesbian lover, Mme Angouleme, drove in from Nice. A dozen patrons, who'd become friends with Tally and Scott, attended, too. It was Madame Morille's hors d'oeuvres that were the hit of the party. Garlic roasted prawns with a six ingredient sauce. Sweet and spicy roasted nuts. Potato skin curls with fresh herbs. Ham, gruyère and honey-mustard palmiers. Figs with ricotta and pistachios in honey. Endive spears with sweet potato, bacon and chives. And, of course, oysters and mussels and champagne.

The Mayor rose to give the toast. He was a small man, with considerable girth, pink cheeks, and a personality that would easily win him reelection. He asked that a cup of champagne be handed Tally and Scott as they were called beside him, Tally six months pregnant and showing. In the Mayor's hand was a piece of toast, along with a glass of champagne for himself.

"At a wedding reception," he began in excellent English, "the couple customarily uses a toasting cup called une coupe de mariage. The origin of giving this toast began in France when a small piece of toast was literally dropped into the couple's wine to ensure a long and healthy life."

He turned to the pair, dropped the piece of toast into the glass Tally was holding. Cheers went up as both took a sip from the glass. Acknowledging the gathering for their friendship and perseverance as best he could in French, Scott got to what they were all waiting to hear.

"I don't think I can do this in your language," he said.

"I'll translate," Tally cut in.

"Okay," Scott said, and pulled a sealed envelope from his pocket. "We went to the gynecologist..."

"Nous sommes allés au gynecologue…"

"…to learn if it was a boy or girl."

"Si c'était un garçon ou une fille."

"He put the answer in this envelope."

"Il a mis la réponse dans cette enveloppe."

"We decided not to open it until today, in front of you."

"Nous avons décidé de ne pas découvrir nous-mêmes jusqu'ici."

"So here it is."

He handed the envelope to Tally. A beam on her face she tore it open, stared, incredulous, her face lighting up to a thousand watts as she handed it to Scott who shrieked at what he saw.

"We need a bigger car!" she said.

THE END

CPSIA information can be obtained at www.ICGtesting.com
Printed in the USA
LVOW13s1443261213

366911LV00001B/12/P